MARVEL
A NOVEL OF THE MARVEL UNIVERSE
Fantastic Four
THE COMING OF GALACTUS

T0407921

NOVELS OF THE MARVEL UNIVERSE BY TITAN BOOKS

Ant-Man: Natural Enemy by Jason Starr

Avengers: Everybody Wants to Rule the World by Dan Abnett

Avengers: Infinity by James A. Moore

Black Panther: Panther's Rage by Sheree Renée Thomas

Black Panther: Tales of Wakanda by Jesse J. Holland

Black Panther: Who is the Black Panther? by Jesse J. Holland

Captain America: Dark Designs by Stefan Petrucha

Captain Marvel: Liberation Run by Tess Sharpe

Captain Marvel: Shadow Code by Gilly Segal

Civil War by Stuart Moore

Deadpool: Paws by Stefan Petrucha

Doctor Strange: Dimension War by James Lovegrove

Guardians of the Galaxy: Annihilation by Brendan Deneen

Loki: Journey into Mystery by Katherine Locke

Morbius: The Living Vampire – Blood Ties by Brendan Deneen

Secret Invasion by Paul Cornell

Spider-Man: Forever Young by Stefan Petrucha

Spider-Man: Kraven's Last Hunt by Neil Kleid

Spider-Man: The Darkest Hours Omnibus by Jim Butcher, Keith R.A. DeCandido, and Christopher L. Bennett

Spider-Man: The Venom Factor Omnibus by Diane Duane

Thanos: Death Sentence by Stuart Moore

Venom: Lethal Protector by James R. Tuck

Wolverine: Weapon X Omnibus by Marc Cerasini, David Alan Mack, and Hugh Matthews

X-Men: Days of Future Past by Alex Irvine

X-Men: The Dark Phoenix Saga by Stuart Moore

X-Men: The Mutant Empire Omnibus by Christopher Golden

X-Men & The Avengers: The Gamma Quest Omnibus by Greg Cox

ALSO FROM TITAN AND TITAN BOOKS

Marvel Contest of Champions: The Art of the Battlerealm by Paul Davies

Marvel's Guardians of the Galaxy: No Guts, No Glory by M.K. England

Marvel's Midnight Suns: Infernal Rising by S.D. Perry

Marvel's Spider-Man: The Art of the Game by Paul Davies

Obsessed with Marvel by Peter Sanderson and Marc Sumerak

Spider-Man: Into the Spider-Verse – The Art of the Movie by Ramin Zahed

Spider-Man: Hostile Takeover by David Liss

Spider-Man: Miles Morales – Wings of Fury by Brittney Morris

The Art of Iron Man (10th Anniversary Edition) by John Rhett Thomas

The Marvel Vault by Matthew K. Manning, Peter Sanderson, and Roy Thomas

Ant-Man and the Wasp: The Official Movie Special

Avengers: Endgame – The Official Movie Special

Avengers: Infinity War – The Official Movie Special

Black Panther: The Official Movie Companion

Black Panther: The Official Movie Special

Captain Marvel: The Official Movie Special

Marvel Studios: The First 10 Years

Marvel's Avengers – Script to Page

Marvel's Black Panther – Script to Page

Marvel's Black Widow: The Official Movie Special

Marvel's Spider-Man – Script to Page

Spider-Man: Far From Home: The Official Movie Special

Spider-Man: Into the Spider-Verse: Movie Special

Thor: Ragnarok: The Official Movie Special

MARVEL

A NOVEL OF THE MARVEL UNIVERSE

THE COMING OF GALACTUS

An original novel by

JAMES LOVEGROVE

TITAN BOOKS

FANTASTIC FOUR: THE COMING OF GALACTUS
Print edition ISBN: 9781803369044
E-book edition ISBN: 9781803369037
Published by Titan Books
A division of Titan Publishing Group Ltd
144 Southwark Street, London SE1 0UP
www.titanbooks.com

First edition: June 2025
10 9 8 7 6 5 4 3 2 1

MARVEL PUBLISHING
Jeff Youngquist, VP Production and Special Projects
Sarah Singer, Editor, Special Projects
Jeremy West, Manager, Licensed Publishing
Sven Larsen, VP, Licensed Publishing
David Gabriel, VP, Print and Digital Publishing
C.B. Cebulski, Editor in Chief

Cover art by Jack Kirby. Paints by Dean White.

A CIP catalogue record for this title is available from the British Library.

EU RP (for authorities only)
eucomply OÜ, Pärnu mnt. 139b-14, 11317 Tallinn, Estonia
hello@eucompliancepartner.com, +3375690241

Printed and bound by CPI Group (UK) Ltd, Croydon CR0 4YY.

This one's for

Paul Wilson

Silver Surfer super fan

IN THE BEGINNING...

...IT WAS the end of everything.

The universe was dying.

Its multibillion-year lifespan was coming to a close. As all things in nature must decay, the whole of creation was decaying. A rot had begun to spread from the center outwards, moving from solar system to solar system, world to world, bringing oblivion wherever it touched.

It was a plague of dark radiation which altered the very building blocks of existence. It broke the bonds within molecules. It dissolved atoms. It unentwined DNA strands. It dispersed matter into nothingness.

The dark radiation fed on destruction, and with every planet it reached and every species it extinguished, it grew stronger and proliferated faster.

It was an inexorable spaceborne cancer, and nothing could stop it.

THERE WAS a world at the universe's edge, and its name was Taa.

Taa was a veritable paradise, the most advanced civilization in existence. It was a place of scientific marvels, social harmony and everlasting peace. Its denizens spent their long lives pursuing the arts and the acquisition of knowledge.

In the tall, shining towers of their cities, Taa-ans devoted themselves to contemplation and recreation. In their civic spaces they raised vast statues in tribute to the noted forebears who had helped make Taa the beacon of progress and reason it had become. They toiled enthusiastically in fabulous laboratories and gazed at the night skies from ultra-sophisticated observatories.

They traveled across their world in transparent thought-spheres to further their studies. The thought-spheres could hover amid the lava spewed from the mouth of a volcano, and endure the pressures of the deepest ocean depths, with no danger or discomfort whatsoever to their passengers.

In the entire universe, there was nowhere else quite like Taa. It was the civilization other civilizations aspired to be.

And one of its foremost inhabitants, and perhaps its greatest mind, was the man called Galan.

FOR MONTHS, Galan had been absent from Taa. He had taken himself off into the farthest reaches of space aboard a quantum-drive starship capable of subspace travel. He had journeyed far and wide, making surveys, taking readings, gathering data.

He wished either to confirm or to disprove certain observations he had made from the surface of his homeworld.

His researches led him to one dire, inescapable conclusion.

When he returned to Taa, he broke the news to his race.

The universe was doomed.

At first, Galan—an impressive figure in his gleaming metallic-blue armor-like outerwear, with a high forehead and strips of close-cropped hair—had difficulty finding words to express himself. He was addressing a room full of his scientific peers, with the event being broadcast planetwide to the transceiver units implanted in the brain of every Taa-an at birth.

When great Galan made an announcement, all listened. When he had information to share, all paid attention.

"I can scarcely speak," he said at last. "Of what use is speech at a time like this? A time of dread catastrophe. It is as I feared. Taa—and, indeed, the universe itself—has not long to live."

There was rumbling consternation among the assembled scientists, and likewise across the whole of Taa.

"Our world," Galan continued, "is one of the last still in existence. A terrible radioactive plague is sweeping towards us, here at the fringes of the known cosmos. I have watched as countless races have fallen before the contagion. I have seen billions upon billions of lives snuffed out, planets reduced to dust, suns become little more than clouds of cinders. It is hopeless. There is no avoiding this plague, and no remedy for it that I know of."

"Can it truly not be defeated, Galan?" a member of his audience cried out. "There must be a cure, and surely we Taa-ans, with our knowledge and our technology, stand a better chance than anybody of finding one."

"I have applied my mind to the question," Galan replied. "My thoughts during my return journey were occupied by little else. I programmed my starship's computer to run a septillion scenarios. It calculated and recalculated, and every time the answer was the same, confirming my suppositions. Nothing can escape the plague. The dark radiation defies being repelled. There is no countermeasure, no antidote. Perhaps, if we had decades, we might collectively be able to devise such a thing. But we do not have decades. The plague's progress is accelerating, and it is nearing Taa."

"How soon?" asked another audience member. "How long do we have before it is upon us?"

Galan's already grim visage became ever more somber. "Days, my friends. We have only days left."

There was, then, an outpouring of grief and horror from the entire population. Whether through speech, or via their transceiver units, person communicated with person, sharing their shock, their sorrow, their dismay, their anguish. It was some while before all these voices quietened and Galan was able to sum up the situation.

"What must we do, my friends?" he asked rhetorically. "I can think of only one thing. It is all we *can* do. We must prepare for the inevitable. We must simply await the end of all that is."

He looked down for a moment, then raised his noble head. His eyes glistened. His jaw was set.

"Our race must die with dignity," Galan said, "in a manner befitting Taa."

o———o

AND YET, Galan thought later, it was not fitting that *all* must perish.

Evening had come, and Taa's threefold suns were setting, creating that remarkable interplay of deepening colors and multiple crisscrossing shadows which made its dusks so incomparably beautiful.

Galan stood on the balcony of his apartment, at the summit of a forty-story tower, beholding the dying embers of the day with the heaviest of hearts. He had carried the knowledge of the universe's impending demise all by himself during his time in space, and had thought that revealing it to everyone else on Taa would relieve him of the burden.

But, in fact, he now felt the weight of it even more.

It seemed extraordinary that Taa should die. All that erudition, all that genius, everything Taa-ans had accomplished over countless generations—shortly to be snuffed out, as though it had never been.

Inconceivable.

There had to be a way, surely, for the glory and grandeur that were Taa to live on.

Galan brooded on the matter, even as Elder Child, Taa's largest sun, sank below the horizon. Its two siblings, Middle Child and Youngest, followed in swift succession, and night fell.

The sky bristled brilliantly with stars. But there seemed to be fewer than usual, and as Galan watched, he could have sworn he saw one or two of them wink out of existence.

A plan, born of hope and desperation, began forming in his brain.

IN THE days that followed, Galan roved back and forth across Taa in a thought-sphere. He guided the vehicle with his mind, visiting several specific locations: the homes of Taa's preeminent chemists, physicists and biologists.

He could have contacted these scientists by transceiver, but he elected to visit them in person instead. So much more could be achieved through a one-to-one conversation than remotely.

His proposal to each was this. They would assemble every scrap of knowledge on Taa and commit it to databanks. Then, together, they would depart the planet in Galan's starship with those databanks on board and head for the very source of the dark radiation, at the universe's heart.

To call this mission hazardous was an understatement. It was suicide.

And yet there was a chance—a very remote chance—that where the radiation originated from, there they might be able to fathom its nature best, and thus perhaps find a way to combat it.

The starship's computer, loaded with the accumulated brainpower of an entire race, would be put to work, to aid them in coming up with a solution.

The dark radiation, Galan reasoned, did not just appear out of nowhere. It had emerged from something, and in that something might lie the key to salvation.

From each scientist he garnered agreement, and a date was set for them to assemble at Galan's home and launch into space.

During those days, as Galan mustered his scientific allies, the effects of the dark radiation began to be felt on Taa. Journeying across the continents, Galan saw death laying its dark hand, now here, now there, arbitrarily, capriciously, as though this was all just some childish game to it.

Cities were slowly becoming necropolises as the sinister, invisible plague crept over them. People collapsed and died in the streets. Thought-spheres crashed to earth as their occupants were suddenly struck down. Towers cracked and fell. Forests and jungles turned brown, then black. Seas dried and became turgid swamps. Great ocean beasts floundered in the shallows, gasping their last. Mountains literally crumbled.

Galan hardened his heart to these apocalyptic scenes. He focused on his mission. He could not afford to give in to despair. With him and his colleagues rested Taa's one slim hope of survival.

AT LAST the day came.

The scientists gathered at Galan's residence. Several of them did not make it; death had claimed them in the interim.

The handful who did boarded Galan's starship, and they lifted off and rose into the sky, escaping the moldering, death-riddled shell that was once Taa. They felt some guilt at abandoning their fellow Taa-ans, their friends and their loved ones; but more than that, they felt dread and trepidation. Ahead of them lay an uncertain destiny. The only thing they knew with any surety was that they were more than likely going to die.

They flew through the darkness of a hollowed-out universe, on a course for its very center. Galan had erected an antimatter field around his starship which he hoped would mitigate the dark radiation's effects. Eventually the field would succumb to the plague and become useless, but it ought to protect the vessel long enough for them to reach their destination.

The fearful voyage soon neared its end. The starship's long-range sensors detected an extraordinary phenomenon ahead: what appeared to be a seething, blazing cauldron of sheer cosmic energy, vast as a sun. Galan and his colleagues analyzed it and came to an inescapable conclusion.

The pulsating energy mass was the source of the dark radiation. As Galan had theorized, the plague had to have come from somewhere, and this was it.

But not only that.

The energy was *sentient.*

The starship decelerated on its approach to the energy mass. Its protective antimatter field was by now just the thinnest of skins, barely keeping the dark radiation at bay. The vessel's life could be measured in hours.

Nonetheless, the Taa-an scientists, led by Galan, set about studying the phenomenon, trying to comprehend what it was made of, why it lived, and how its malign influence on the universe might be counteracted.

It was an urgent race against time, the greatest intellects of the greatest ever civilization applying themselves to penetrating what was perhaps the ultimate mystery—and in doing so, saving themselves and everything that was.

They failed.

The antimatter field gave out. No longer were they shielded from the plague.

All at once, the starship was inundated by the dark radiation. Here, right at its point of origin, it was stronger than anywhere else.

It dismantled the starship like a wave crashing over a sandcastle.

It flooded the scientists' bodies, reducing them in a nanosecond to their component elements and scattering those elements into nonexistence.

All of them save one.

Galan.

GALAN FELT himself being swept up by immeasurably powerful tides.

He felt himself being drawn towards the energy mass.

He did not know why or how.

He was as helpless as a leaf in a hurricane.

He plunged into the heart of the energy mass, a vortex of swirling, elemental forces which tore at him this way and that. He opened his mouth to scream, but his cries were lost amid the churning maelstrom like the squeaking of a mouse amid a raging cataract.

He knew that the energy mass in which he was now enfolded was analyzing him, much as he and the other scientists had earlier analyzed it. It was examining him with curiosity, as Galan himself might have peered at an amoeba through a microscope. It was poring over him, picking him apart, probing, subjecting him to scrutiny of the most intense, most intimate kind.

He had no choice but to submit to the procedure. He did not doubt that once it was over, he would die—and how appropriate it was, in the most ironic of ways, that a scientist such as he should spend the last moments of his life as an object of scientific study.

Then the energy mass spoke. Its voice resounded inside Galan's head. He felt rather than heard its words.

"Galan, last son of Taa," it said, "hear me. I am the Sentience of the Universe. I am the living embodiment of all that is, was, and ever shall be."

On Taa it had long been theorized that the universe was not merely a random agglomeration of galaxies and nebulae, and that an intelligent entity permeated its essence. All of creation could not exist, surely, without there being some consciousness behind it, giving it purpose and function.

And *this* was that very entity, and it was conversing with him.

Galan's mind reeled. He did not know whether to laugh or howl.

"Like yourself, Galan of Taa, I am dying," the Sentience of the Universe said. "I have lived long, I have aged, and now eternal night beckons. A sickness has come upon me and has infected every corner of my being, eradicating me bit by bit. All that remains of me is this last vestige of self, which even now I struggle to maintain. Soon I will no longer be able to support my own mass and collapse beneath my abysmal weight."

Galan sensed the truth of this. He had the impression of those mighty forces all around him turning inward, seeking some focal zero point and rushing to it. The Sentience of the Universe would be scooped into this infinitesimal terminus, taking Galan with it. Thereafter, all would be only void.

"But though we both must die, you and I," the Sentience of the Universe continued, "we need not die without an heir. That is why I have drawn you into me. Come, Galan of Taa, surrender yourself to my embrace and let us become as one. You are an explorer, a discoverer. You have dedicated your life to learning. Your mind has ever been open to new experiences. You, more than anyone, would wish to know what lies beyond the end of all that is."

There was no denying this. To find out what lay beyond the

veil of existence? To pierce the greatest secret of them all and be enlightened? Galan, in spite of everything, felt a thrill of excitement at the proposition.

"I can gift you that opportunity," the Sentience of the Universe said. "Let our death throes serve as birth pangs for a new form of life. In a time beyond time shall be born a new universe, and into that universe I shall dispatch a being like no other—an organism who possesses a matchless power and a raging appetite. It will be you, Galan, born anew, suffused with the last of the energies which animate me. Do you consent?"

Galan did not need to reply. The Sentience of the Universe was aware what his answer must be.

There was an almighty rending.

A coalescing.

A condensing.

THEN, FOR a time, there was stillness.

That which had been Galan of Taa remained in a nascent state, even as around him a new universe exploded into life. From nothing, all at once there was everything. In a huge flash of light and a burst of incredible incandescent heat, atoms formed, particles gathered, and matter began distributing itself in all directions. An expansion began, boundless, endless, like a balloon inflating faster than the speed of light. Neutrons, protons and electrons flooded the emptiness, the raw stuff from which an entire cosmos would grow.

At the epicenter of it all, Galan hung suspended within the remnants of his starship, which had been reformed by the Sentience of the Universe into a life-sustaining cocoon.

Insensate, unaware, Galan waited. Snug inside the artificial cocoon, he was slowly transformed. As millennia passed and the newborn universe settled and cooled, his body changed and developed, much like a chrysalis on its way to becoming a butterfly.

Though he slept, Galan was conscious of two thoughts. They were lodged deep in his mind, at some primal, instinctual level.

One was that his name was no longer Galan. The Sentience of the Universe had given him a new one.

Galactus.

The other thought was simply this.

He hungered.

13.7 BILLION YEARS LATER

EARTH.

The Himalayas.

The Hidden Land.

The Great Refuge, home of the genetically altered race known as the Inhumans.

Outside which four costumed, super-powered adventurers currently stood in various states of dismay and despair.

The Great Refuge had nestled for centuries in a remote valley in this mountainous region, surrounded by a palisade of snowy peaks and, until today, undiscovered by humankind. It was a city of teetering baroque architecture, all spirals and spires, buttresses and balustrades, everything glossy and gleaming. Elevated walkways linked the buildings, while broad, leafy plazas sat between, adorned with soaring statuary and shimmering fountains.

All of that majesty and wonder, however, had just been confined within a huge dome, a hemisphere of dense, solid sound perhaps a mile in diameter and half a mile high. Its surface was like a bank of swirling fog, impossible to see through.

The dome had been erected by Maximus, the black sheep of the Inhuman royal family and a man who truly lived up to his nickname: Maximus the Mad. This twisted intellectual prodigy had activated a device of his own making, the Atmo-Gun, which had brought the opaque, impenetrable sonic barrier down around the city, decisively cutting it and its inhabitants off from the rest of the world.

His motive was simple. He coveted the throne presently occupied by his older brother Black Bolt. Since only he himself knew how to lift the dome, Maximus anticipated that the Inhuman citizenry would come to him on bended knee and beg him to deliver them from captivity. He would agree to their request, but only on condition that they deposed Black Bolt and made him king in his stead.

The super hero quartet—known the world over as the Fantastic Four—had been witness to these events, and had barely managed to escape the Great Refuge before the dome descended.

Now, one of their number resolved to pierce the barrier and get back inside.

His name was Johnny Storm, and he was gifted with the ability to generate and manipulate fire, and also to envelop his whole body in flames and fly. Hence he was commonly referred to as the Human Torch.

He leaned forward and unleashed a jet of flame from his right hand.

"I can do it," Johnny said, teeth clenched in determination. His breath emerged as puffs of pale vapor in the chilly high-altitude air. "I can cut through this thing. I can get back to her. I can free her."

He was talking about Crystal, another member of the Inhuman royal family. She and Johnny had met by chance a few days ago in New York, and had fallen hard for each other, only to find themselves separated almost immediately. It was one of the reasons why Johnny and his three teammates had flown halfway across the world, so the two young lovers could be reunited. Unfortunately, it was then that Maximus the Mad had chosen to hatch his villainous scheme, and Johnny and Crystal were now parted again. And this time, it looked permanent.

Unless, that was, Johnny could burn his way through the barrier, as he hoped.

His flame, however, scattered across the dome's murky surface ineffectually, not even so much as singeing it.

Johnny let out a cry of pure, agonized determination and ramped up the power. The jet of fire went from orange to white. Its brightness was blinding, the heat it gave off as fierce as a blast furnace.

Still it did not even leave a mark on the barrier, let alone burn a hole.

"Johnny," said one of his teammates. This was Reed Richards, also known as Mister Fantastic, and not only was he the leader of the Fantastic Four and possibly the smartest person on the planet, he was married to Johnny's older sister, Sue. He laid a gently restraining hand on his brother-in-law's upper arm. "Johnny, stop. It's not making any difference. Remember how Maximus said his Atmo-Gun was designed to create a wall of negative-polarity sound? I don't think anything known to science can breach *that*."

Reluctantly, ruefully, Johnny turned off the flame. His eyes were brimming with tears.

"I can't believe it," he murmured. "I'll never be with Crys again. There—there isn't even a chance." All at once, his expression brightened. A metaphorical lightbulb popped into life above his head. "Wait a minute. *Wait a damn minute.* What am I thinking? Lockjaw! Lockjaw can just teleport her out of there. He can teleport *all* of the Inhumans out of there."

Lockjaw, a gigantic, slobbery, but very intelligent bulldog, was Crystal's pet and constant companion. The size of a hippo, and sporting a pair of antennae that together formed a kind of curving Y-shape, he had the ability to teleport himself and others wherever required.

Reed shook his head sorrowfully. "I'm afraid not, Johnny."

"What do you mean? The big mutt just has to fire up that wacky tuning fork on his head, and *blammo*, the Inhumans are home free."

"I've already considered that," Reed said, adopting his customary air of scientific authority. "There are three reasons why it won't work. One: if it did, Lockjaw would already have teleported out by now, if for no other reason than to establish whether he could. Two: negative-polarity sound functions all the way down to the subatomic level. Its resonations interfere not just with solid matter but with any kind of transmission going in and out, and that includes teleportation. Chances are, if Lockjaw tried it, he and anyone he was taking with him would boomerang back, ending up right where they started. Or, worse, they'd be shredded apart, obliterated at a molecular level. Which leads me to three: that's precisely why Maximus chose to use negative-polarity sound for his barrier, because he knows even Lockjaw can't get through it. He may be a mad genius, but he's still a genius."

Johnny was crestfallen. "So it's impossible," he groaned.

"Aw, nothin's impossible, Johnny," said another of the Fantastic Four, Ben Grimm. He was the strongman of the team, with a broad, squat, squarish physique. His entire body was covered in a rock-like hide the color of rust, and his facial features were correspondingly rough-hewn and lumpen. To the world at large he was known as the Thing, and while it might not be a flattering name—like something belonging to a creature from a black-and-white B-movie—it fit. "We'll find a way. You just have to be patient."

"You're only saying that!" Johnny yelled at him. "There *isn't* a way. I've lost her forever. And it's *your* fault. If not for you, I'd still be in there with Crystal."

At Reed's urging, Ben had yanked Johnny away from his girlfriend's side just as the dome began to form, and had manhandled him out of the Great Refuge, oblivious to his protests. Reed had made the calculation that Johnny was better off sticking with his own people rather than remaining trapped with the Inhumans. Johnny was not so sure about that.

"Yeah, maybe so, kid," Ben said. "C'mon then, take a poke at me. It'll make you feel better."

Ben offered Johnny his jaw to hit.

The gesture was sincere, but both of them knew that punching the Thing would do nothing except leave Johnny with bruised knuckles if he was lucky, a broken hand if he wasn't.

The fourth member of the team, Sue Richards, née Storm, slipped an arm around Johnny. Her ability to turn herself invisible and project similarly transparent forcefields had earned her the title the Invisible Woman. It was an unpretentious name, barely hinting at what she was truly capable of. For instance, if Sue hadn't deployed one of her forcefields to create a temporary tunnel beneath the dome as it lowered, the Fantastic Four might never have made it out of the Great Refuge at all.

"Reed was right to tell Ben to grab you, Johnny," she said. She was the senior of the two siblings by several years and cared for her little brother deeply, even though she found his behavior juvenile and infuriating at times. "And Ben was right to do it. One day you'll thank them for it."

Johnny just glared at her despondently.

"Yeah," observed Ben. "Sure he will. Look at him. He's just a big happy bundle of gratitude."

Johnny turned his gaze to the barrier one more time. He thumped a fist against it. Then he swung round and walked slowly away, shoulders slumped.

His three teammates followed him, heading for their nearby Pogo Plane, the VTOL intercontinental aircraft that had brought them to the Himalayas and now stood ready to take them back home.

THE TEN-HOUR flight was a glum affair.

Every time someone tried to engage Johnny in conversation, he just grunted, or else blanked them.

In his mind's eye, visions of Crystal danced and swam. He recalled stumbling across the gorgeous young redhead while wandering through a Manhattan slum neighborhood that was due to be demolished and redeveloped. He'd been instantly captivated by her. She was sitting all alone and, in that derelict setting, with her filmy white dress and long flowing hair, she clearly did not belong. She seemed almost unreal, like something out of a fairy tale.

It should be noted that Johnny was, at that time, on the outs with his then-girlfriend Dorrie Evans. For some while, Dorrie had been giving him the runaround, and then, seemingly out of the blue, she had declared that it was over between them. Johnny was unreliable, she'd said. He was always off super-heroing, she'd said. He never seemed to have time for her, she'd said.

So Johnny did what almost any other teenaged boy, feeling jilted and lovelorn, might do when confronted with an unknown but incredibly attractive girl more or less his own age: he approached her. It couldn't hurt just to chat with her awhile, could it? Maybe ask her to join him for a soda or a milkshake…

The girl, catching sight of him, leapt to her feet, startled. She looked ready to bolt.

"Wait!" Johnny called out. "Don't go away. I'd just like to talk to you. Don't be alarmed."

"No!" she replied. "Stay back. You mustn't."

Next thing Johnny knew, a ferocious wind whipped up as though from nowhere. Debris whirled around him—scraps of timber, sheets of newspaper, even chunks of house brick. He was knocked off his feet and thrown to the ground, where he lay covering his head with his hands.

When the gale subsided, as abruptly as it had arrived, the girl was nowhere to be seen. Johnny wondered why she hadn't been sent sprawling by it too. The only explanation he could think of was that she herself had caused the wind. She had conjured it up in order to get away from him. She, as he did, had super-powers.

He searched the neighborhood thoroughly, but there was no sign of her.

Back at the Baxter Building, the uptown skyscraper Johnny called home, he moped around, thinking about the girl. He was obsessed. He could not get her out of his head.

Eventually, stumped for a better idea, he went back to the slum neighborhood to search for her again. Somewhat to his surprise, he found her. This time, she tried to repel him with a bolt of flame, but that held no fear for Johnny Storm, Human Torch. He burst into flame himself to counteract the danger, fighting fire with fire.

When the girl perceived that Johnny had super-powers too, she relaxed, and the two youngsters took the first tentative steps towards becoming friends, and more than friends.

Johnny learned that the girl's name was Crystal and that she could exert psionic control over earth, air, fire and water, the four classical elements. She was an Inhuman, a race whose every member had some form of special ability. They weren't born that way. Instead, each was exposed as an infant to a strange, transformative substance known as the Terrigen Mist, which changed their biology at a genetic level.

In next to no time, a passionate adolescent ardor sparked between the two of them. They were separated soon after, thanks to a series of adverse circumstances and misunderstandings, and it had been unbearable for Johnny.

The feeling, it so happened, was mutual, as was their joy upon reuniting.

Now, they were separated once again, perhaps forever.

Johnny heaved the deepest, most heartsick of sighs.

Sometimes life could be so *unfair*.

o———o

FORMER USAF pilot Ben Grimm, at the aircraft's controls, heard the sigh and glanced over his shoulder at Johnny.

He felt sorry for the youngster. He wasn't so old himself that he couldn't remember what it felt like to be in love at that age. The all-encompassing magnitude of it. The gut-wrenching torment of it. Teen love could be worse than any super villain, the way it toyed with you and dominated you, wore you down and sometimes even drove you nuts. Ben would rather go ten rounds with the Hulk or the Sub-Mariner than endure all that tsuris again.

He was glad he was in a settled, stable relationship these days. No dramas, no traumas. Just him and the best woman he'd ever known, someone he trusted and could count on, no matter what.

Alicia.

Keeping one eye on the plane's instruments and a steady grip on the yoke, Ben let his thoughts drift to his lady love, much as Johnny's had to his own.

Ben and Alicia had met perhaps a year and a half ago, when the Fantastic Four were attacked by her stepfather, Philip Masters, the villainous Puppet Master. His specialty was molding puppets from a certain rare type of radioactive clay, which granted him mental control over the person whose likeness the puppet was made in. He had tried to kidnap Sue, and also taken over Ben's mind and pitted him against his teammates. He'd even, for reasons best known to him, started a riot at a maximum security jail.

After that encounter, the Puppet Master had returned to plague the Fantastic Four on a couple of further occasions. He was an aggravating little pest, and odd-looking, too, with his large, egg-shaped bald head and weirdly doll-like facial features.

His stepdaughter, the adopted child of his late wife, was as unlike him as it was possible to be. Alicia was kind, forgiving-natured, and beautiful. Virtually the only thing they had in common was a talent for sculpture, and in particular recreating the human form. Though sightless since she was young—the result of a laboratory accident that also killed her birth father—Alicia needed only to run her fingers over a face or figure, and could then fashion an exact replica.

But her skill ran deeper than that. Her pieces managed to represent not just how the subject looked, but what kind of person they were inside, their character traits, their flaws and foibles, even their emotions.

Naturally, this meant Alicia's work was in demand at all the best galleries in New York, London, Paris and everywhere else. The wealthy queued up to commission from her.

From the moment they met, Alicia had sensed a nobility within Ben Grimm. She'd told him this on numerous occasions since. His physical appearance had no meaning for her. She did not see, as others did, a hulking, misshapen being with a craggy face and skin like a cracked, dried-up riverbed. She saw the man beneath the surface, the true Ben, and she had fallen in love with that.

When the Thing came walking down the street, folk tended to shy away. Some gasped. Others cried out in revulsion. Little children wailed and hid their faces. One elderly woman had even fainted at the sight of him. He was frequently treated like a monster.

Not by Alicia. Never by Alicia.

She didn't mind that Ben was gruffly spoken and sometimes bad-tempered, not to mention a habitual wisecracker who never seemed to take anything too seriously. She knew this was all just a defense mechanism, his way of coping with the cruel hand life had dealt him.

She knew what lay at the core of him, and whenever he was with her, Ben did his best to live up to her impression of him. She made him want to be a better person. She *did* make him a better person.

Being with Alicia was the best thing that had ever happened to Ben Grimm. It almost made life as an ugly, cumbersome mockery of a man bearable. Almost.

As he guided the Pogo Plane out across the coast of China and over the Pacific, Ben found he was smiling to himself.

He couldn't wait to get back home and see Alicia again.

SUE LOOKED across at Ben in the pilot's chair, sitting there with a happy, wistful look on his face, and had a pretty good idea what he was thinking about. Or rather *who*.

Ben deserved the love he had found with Alicia.

Just as Johnny didn't deserve the misery of being separated from Crystal.

Sometimes Sue couldn't help but marvel at the ups and downs of their lives as the Fantastic Four.

There were definite benefits to being who they were. They were global celebrities, lauded as the greatest super team of all. They had saved the world countless times, and while that was its own reward, it was nice to be feted and acclaimed for it.

They didn't even have secret identities, the way so many other super heroes did. They didn't go around masked: their names and faces were known to all, and this meant they were perhaps better trusted by the public than any of their peers.

But there were drawbacks too. They were always in danger. Threats loomed on all sides, whether from alien races who wished to conquer Earth, such as the sinister, shape-shifting Skrulls, or human enemies like the Mad Thinker, the Red Ghost, the alchemist Diablo, or, worst of all, the armored Latverian despot Victor Von Doom.

Having super-powers came at a cost. Ben knew that more than any of them. But all four paid a price for being who they were. They all had burdens and responsibilities they hadn't asked for. So often the world's safety depended on them, at the potential risk of their lives.

Sue frequently wondered what it would be like if the four of them had never gone into space aboard Reed's experimental rocket ship. The events of that momentous day, a couple of years back, were etched indelibly in her memory.

Reed cajoling Ben into piloting the ship, even though both of them were aware the design was untested and the risks considerable.

Ben agreeing, because he knew that with him at the helm, the mission stood the best chance of success.

Sue insisting she accompanied them, unwilling to let her then-fiancé face danger without her by his side.

Johnny tagging along too, mostly because he was an adrenaline junkie and this ride into space sounded like fun.

The authorities had kept refusing Reed clearance to launch his craft. An appropriations board in some Washington backroom wanted to cut funding for the project and reallocate it to the military instead; and as long as the board members argued and prevaricated, and Reed protested their intransigence and lodged objections, nothing could happen. The project remained stalled, in limbo.

The more Reed waited, the less likely it seemed that the inaugural test flight would ever happen. And so he eventually decided to take matters into his own hands.

He and his three allies stole inside the spaceport under cover of darkness, avoiding the guards posted at the perimeter fence.

Takeoff was perfect. The rocket ship performed beautifully all the way into the ionosphere and beyond. It seemed that nothing could go wrong.

Until the cosmic rays hit.

Reed had made a tiny miscalculation. The ship's radiation shielding was insufficient. The cosmic rays penetrated the four astronauts' bodies. The pain was intense. Sue remembered her head pounding, as though it was going to explode. She remembered the cosmic rays passing through her, unseen, intangible, yet feeling like a million icy needles. She remembered the terrifying *tac-tac-tac* sound of the onboard Geiger counter going crazy.

The cosmic rays interfered with the rocket ship's telemetry. The craft veered around wildly, resisting Ben's best efforts to keep it on course, and began plummeting back towards Earth.

At the last moment, Ben was able to regain some semblance of control, and they came down, if not smoothly, then at least in one piece.

The four of them emerged from the crashed ship, shaken and unnerved. They had landed in a patch of wilderness not far from the spaceport.

Sue was the first to learn that they had somehow been irrevocably changed. Her body began fading out of sight, and only by a huge effort of will did she turn herself visible again.

Then Ben began to metamorphose into a thickset, rocky, orange-hued version of himself, blessed with incredible strength. Unlike Sue, he could not revert to his original state.

Reed was next. His limbs became as pliant as rubber, and he found he could stretch and contort himself in all sorts of extraordinary ways.

Finally, Johnny. He burst into flames, and discovered that in this blazing form he was lighter than air and could fly.

The four of them understood that the cosmic rays had transformed them into something other than human, something more.

Sue recalled what Reed had said next.

"Listen to me, all of you. Together we have more power than any humans have ever possessed."

Ben had butted in. "You don't have to make a speech, big shot. We understand. We've got to use that power to help mankind, right?"

"Right, Ben. Right."

As a manifesto for the Fantastic Four, Ben's words could not be bettered, and the quartet had made a solemn vow there and then to do just as he said. They had tried to live up to it ever since.

It hadn't been easy.

For instance, Reed still carried guilt over the mistake that had nearly killed them. In particular, he felt bad about Ben, and he was unrelenting in his quest to find a cure for his best friend's condition.

And then there were times like this, when Johnny's personal life was thrown into upheaval, all because he was in the Fantastic Four.

None of them could ever again live like normal people.

Sue, however, was not the sort to feel sorry for herself. Not for long. She was much too level-headed for that.

Johnny would get over Crystal, in the fullness of time. And even if not, then judging by Reed's pensive expression, he was right that moment contemplating ways of dispelling the barrier around the Great Refuge and freeing the Inhumans. Sue was well aware that her husband's brain never rested. He was always seeking solutions to problems.

It was reassuring to think that in times of crisis, the Fantastic Four pulled together. They were a family. By marriage. By blood. Including Ben, since he and Reed—one-time college roommates, longtime friends—were as close as brothers.

And family looked after one another.

Family never gave up.

This, Sue believed, was the Fantastic Four's greatest asset. It, more than their super-powers, was what enabled them to overcome all challenges. The rock-solid bond of kinship they shared.

And there would always be challenges. That was just a fact of life for them.

Even now, she thought, their next trial awaited. Somewhere—be it on Earth, or in another dimension, or out in the farthest-flung reaches of space—something was brewing.

NOT ON EARTH,

NOT IN ANOTHER DIMENSION, BUT…

OUT IN the farthest-flung reaches of space.

Countless light-years from the home of humankind.

A solitary figure, hurtling through hard vacuum at unimaginable speeds.

o———o

HE RODE a silver surfboard. He himself was silver, humanoid, slimly built, as smooth as mercury. His skin glittered with the reflections of a million stars.

He shot across the universe with single-minded purpose. His quest was remorseless and unending.

Imbued with the Power Cosmic, he needed neither sleep nor conventional sustenance. He was untroubled by the airlessness of space and impervious to its pockets of searing radiation.

He traversed nebulae. He soared through the coronal mass ejections of suns. He negotiated labyrinthine asteroid clusters unerringly. He flew alongside comets, within touching distance of their icy tails. His shadow rippled over the cratered surfaces of moons.

He was the Silver Surfer, and he lived for just one thing.

To do the bidding of his master.

The Devourer of Worlds.

Galactus.

o———o

THE PLANET Skrullos, ancient throneworld of the Skrull Empire.

Where panic reigned.

Deep-space monitor probes on the Skrullian frontier had registered the approach of the Silver Surfer. The Surfer's trajectory looked to take him within two parsecs of Skrullos itself. Far too close for comfort.

The news was flashed to Skrullos and relayed to Emperor Dorrek VII, the race's supreme leader.

Dorrek ordered immediate implementation of the Krr'ilth Protocol.

The Krr'ilth Protocol, named after its foresighted scientist inventor, was an emergency system set up for just this sort of eventuality.

Thanks to an innate instability at a cellular level, Skrulls were capable of shifting their bodies into any shape, organic or inorganic. Their default form was essentially reptilian, with green skin, pointed ears, overlarge eyes and a chin lined with vertical grooves, but they could reconfigure themselves into practically anything—a human, for instance, a giant serpent, an insect, a desk lamp, even a cow.

The Krr'ilth Protocol was an artificial planetary equivalent. Through a network of low-orbit satellites equipped with broad-scope holographic projectors, the whole of Skrullos could be camouflaged to resemble a barren world, devoid of life. Unlike a Skrull mimicking something else, it was pure illusion, but an effective first line of defense against possible invasion.

Not that the Silver Surfer portended any mere invasion.

He portended something far worse.

Total annihilation.

o———o

AN ANXIOUS Skrullos awaited the Silver Surfer's arrival.

An imperial edict went out that nobody was permitted to leave the planet. What could be more likely to attract attention, and belie the deception of the Krr'ilth Protocol, than a host of spaceships departing from a supposedly uninhabited world?

The populace cowered in their homes and workplaces, constantly checking their information hubs for updates on the Surfer's whereabouts. Many gathered in the temples and prayed to their gods, begging the likes of Kly'bn and Sl'gur't to intercede and deliver them from destruction.

Even a battalion of Super-Skrulls, bionically enhanced military specialists, would be no match for the Surfer. The Krr'ilth Protocol was the Skrulls' last, best hope, but was still no guarantee of safety. It was generally understood that the Silver Surfer's senses were acute to a godlike degree. He could track a single grain of pollen across the breadth of the cosmos, so it was said. The chances that the Krr'ilth Protocol could fool the herald of Galactus were slim indeed.

The several billion Skrulls on Skrullos cowered and trembled and hoped.

In Skrullian culture, as in so many others across the universe, Galactus was a nightmare figure. His name was spoken in whispers. Parents frightened unruly children into obedience by threatening that Galactus would come for them if they didn't behave.

His existence was not in question, but he had nonetheless taken on an aspect of myth or legend. You half-believed in him, mostly because you didn't want to believe in him wholly. That was too fearsome a prospect.

The Skrulls had their own special name for him.

Ch'grarr'zkk.

Roughly translated, it meant "He Who Brings About the Death of All There Is".

This was the entity whom the Silver Surfer might lead to Skrullos.

Little wonder, then, that the planet was gripped by terror.

HALF A solar cycle elapsed.

Then the glad tidings broke.

The Silver Surfer, for reasons best known to himself, had diverted away from the throneworld. He was now headed off in a different direction, leaving Skrull Empire territory altogether.

Ch'grarr'zkk would pass them by.

Throughout Skrullos there was celebration and rejoicing. Several billion souls breathed a collective sigh of relief.

There was even better news to come.

The Surfer's new course was taking him into the region of space known to Terran astronomers as the Large Magellanic Cloud.

Therein lay the domain of the Skrulls' mortal enemies, the Kree.

Perhaps, just perhaps, the Silver Surfer would lead Galactus to Hala.

The Kree homeworld, obliterated?

That, for the Skrulls, was a prospect greatly to be desired.

WITH THE Pogo Plane lodged securely back in its launch silo at the Baxter Building, Ben Grimm put on a wide-brimmed hat, a trench coat, and a pair of sunglasses that covered almost half his face, and set off downtown to Alicia's apartment.

It was one of those glorious New York days that could not, you thought, be improved on. The sky was a field of pristine blue, and the sunshine seemed to sweep the streets clean. Trees in full leaf sparkled greenly. The buildings were practically aglow.

People were out and about, taking the air, ambling, enjoying ice cream, sitting in the park or on their stoops. They were even doing something very rare for Manhattanites: smiling at one another and engaging in polite conversation.

Ben drew a few puzzled frowns as he walked by, but that was mostly because he was overdressed for such pleasant weather. Otherwise, this unusually bulky pedestrian went unremarked.

He couldn't have been happier about it.

Halfway through his journey, he stopped at a sidewalk flower stall and bought a bouquet of gardenias. They were Alicia's favorite flowers, their scent strong but not cloying, their petals velvety soft to the touch.

"Hey," said the flower seller. "Ain't you him? From the FF?

The, whatchemacall… the Thing?"

"Nah," Ben said. "You've got the wrong guy."

"No, you're him. Sure you are."

"Ehhh, I get that a lot. I guess we do kind of look alike. I'm way better looking though."

The flower seller chuckled wryly. "Well now, if you do ever happen to bump into the Thing and his pals, you just tell them thank you from us, the folks whose lives they've saved over the years. We appreciate it."

Ben proffered a fistful of dollar bills.

"Nuh-uh," the flower seller said, shaking his head. "This is on me. Least I can do—for a Thing lookalike."

Moving on from the stall, Ben started to wonder whether someone had slipped something into the city's water supply. This outbreak of niceness—it couldn't just be the weather, could it? It was downright unnatural.

He decided to test whether or not the whole of New York had gone mad, by taking a diversion down Yancy Street.

Ben was leery of Yancy Street, with good reason. The neighborhood was run-down, untouched by gentrification, but that didn't bother him.

What bothered him was that it was home to a bunch of roughnecks called the Yancy Street Gang, who dedicated themselves to tormenting him whenever they could.

Ben had grown up not far from here, and had been something of a tearaway in his youth. He had got out of that life thanks to a football scholarship to Empire State University, which in turn had led to a distinguished career in the air force.

For this, the Yancy Streeters considered him a sellout, someone who'd forgotten his roots, and they took every opportunity to remind him of the fact. Ben couldn't go anywhere near their turf without having abuse hurled at him, or being pelted with cabbages, or getting paint poured on him, some such undignified treatment like that.

He took it in good spirit. The Yancy Street Gang weren't malicious. It was just how they showed pride in their blue-collar background, and it suggested, in a weird way, that they held him in respect and affection. They wouldn't go to so much trouble to harass just *anybody*.

He hadn't gone more than half a block before the catcalls started.

"Yo! Thing! What're you doing here? Ain't there an ugly pageant you should be winning somewhere?"

"Thing, you looked in a mirror lately… without it shattering?"

"I bet when your momma gave birth to you, the doctor slapped her, not you."

"Those flowers for someone you need to apologize to for being you? 'Cause there ain't enough flowers in the whole wide world for that."

The voices came from open windows and doorways, or out of side alleys. Damn Yancy Streeters were like snipers. They fired from cover, and never showed their faces.

"Joke's on you," Ben retorted, speaking to none of them in particular. "I'm on my way to see my girl, and she's prettier than all your mothers put together. And unlike them, she ain't got a mustache neither."

"The Thing has a girlfriend?" said a Yancy Streeter in incredulous tones. "Now I've heard everything. Next you'll be tellin' us the Hulk wears ballet pumps."

"He don't," said Ben, "but he's got better manners than any of you yahoos. His breath smells better too."

Ben carried on, satisfied that all was, in fact, normal with the world. If the Yancy Street Gang had been anything less than insulting towards him, then truly the End Times would have come.

There was construction work ahead on the next block. The front of a tenement was clad in scaffolding, and laborers in hard hats were replacing windows and shoring up the brickwork. Some slumlord must have been caught out on code violations and been legally forced by the housing department to make repairs.

"Thing!" yelled a voice from an unseen source. "Betcha too chicken to walk under that scaffolding."

Ben knew a trick when he heard one. It wasn't as if any effort was being made to be subtle here. The Yancy Street Gang were about to play some prank on him.

He studied the scaffolding, and spied a wheelbarrow poised at the edge of a decking level about twenty feet up. It was heaped with dry cement, and a rope was attached to one of its handles, leading up through a pulley and into a window. If he passed below, all it would take was one yank on the rope, and the wheelbarrow would tip and dump all that cement—there looked to be about a hundred pounds of it—onto his head.

This trap had been rigged up purely on the off chance that Ben Grimm might one day happen along.

You almost had to admire that level of preparedness.

"Yeah, ain't going to happen," Ben said to his anonymous taunter. "You don't get me that easily."

He stepped out into the road, keeping well away from the scaffolding.

That was when a huge gush of water hit him.

It came from a fire hydrant on the sidewalk opposite. Someone had unscrewed the outlet cap, and the water sprayed out directly at Ben.

The cement-filled wheelbarrow had been simply a decoy. The real trap was this.

And Ben had blundered straight into it.

He leapt out of the jet of water, barking curses and insults. He wasn't hurt. He hadn't even been staggered by the sudden blast of water pressure, as an ordinary man might.

But he was drenched now, from head to toe.

Worse, the bouquet of gardenias in his hand was sodden and damaged. Some of the stems were broken, and plenty of the petals had been blasted off.

He glimpsed a couple of people disappearing down a basement stairwell near the hydrant. One was carrying a large wrench. Both were snickering.

"Goldarn it!" Ben cried. "You lousy bums! You ruined my flowers."

All he got in response was mocking laughter from all around.

"I'll fix you," he growled.

He stomped off to the nearest street corner, leaving a damp trail behind him, his shoes squelching. At his back, the hydrant continued to spout spatteringly over the asphalt.

The signpost on the corner carried the names of both Yancy Street and the avenue it intersected with. Ben bent the post down and broke off the Yancy Street part of the sign. Then he proceeded to snap the rectangle of aluminum into sections, each containing one letter of the name.

He discarded the sections with the C and one of the Ys, and reassembled the remaining ones in a different order, crimping them together with thumb and forefinger. He jammed the remade sign back into its slot and straightened the post again.

Where once the sign had read YANCY STREET, now it read TEENY RATS.

"Yeah," Ben said, admiring his handiwork. "How d'you like that, huh?"

Sorry-looking flowers in hand, Ben Grimm continued on his way to Alicia's.

o———o

BY THE time he got there, his clothes had begun to dry but were still damp.

Alicia lived in the penthouse of her building. Ben had a key and let himself in. He went straight to her sculpture studio. The sound of music drew him there—a radio tuned to a classical station—but regardless, he'd have known that was where she was. When home alone, Alicia loved nothing more than to work.

The studio was spacious and airy, with large windows along one wall and a skylight as well. It was filled with the earthy smells of marble dust and modeling clay, and dotted around the floor, on plinths and pedestals, were various finished statues and a few works in progress.

There was a headless, armless male torso, based on Michelangelo's *David*. Alicia had visited the Galleria dell'Accademia in Florence a few months ago and been given special permission by the curators to touch the world-famous statue, memorizing its well-muscled contours so that she could reproduce them exactly for herself at a later date.

Beside it there was a bust of J. Jonah Jameson, editor and proprietor of the *Daily Bugle*. Alicia had caught Jameson's irascible, hardheaded nature perfectly.

There was another bust next to that one, the facial features only just taking shape, but Ben was pretty sure it was billionaire inventor Tony Stark.

A number of super heroes were represented, as well. Alicia, through her Fantastic Four connections, had met the Avengers and several others in the long-underwear community. Not one of them had refused the renowned sculptor when she'd asked permission to feel their faces and replicate them as artworks.

Out of these effigies, by far the most striking was one of Captain America. Ben could not help but feel a pang of jealousy. Even with half his face hidden by a cowl, old Winghead was too handsome for his own good—square-jawed, clean-cut, piercing-eyed. That and he was a Living Legend of World War II, *and* the embodiment of the spirit of a nation, the Sentinel of Liberty, draped in the Stars and Stripes…

Some fellas had it all.

The Yancy Street Gang would never ambush Cap with a fire hydrant. Heck, no. For him they'd throw a danged block party.

"Ben!" Alicia exclaimed in delight as he entered. She set down the loop tool she was using and hurried over to him.

"Hey, how'd you know it was me?" Ben said.

"Who else has a tread as heavy as yours?"

"And here I was thinkin' I was as light-footed as a fairy."

"I'd hug you," Alicia said, "but my hands are covered in clay."

"Go ahead anyways. I don't mind."

She wrapped her arms around him and sank her head against his chest. Ben slid his own arms carefully around her waist and held her as tightly as someone with his prodigious strength dared.

He was with his love, they were embracing, body against body, sharing warmth, and nothing else in the world mattered.

Alicia pulled back slightly. "Ben, you're wet. How did you manage to get rained on, on a beautiful day like this?"

"Ahhh, it's a long story, babe. I brought you some flowers, but they also got, ahem, rained on."

He held up the soggy, crumpled bouquet.

"Gardenias," Alicia said. "They smell lovely."

"Not as lovely as you. I mean, as you look. Not that you don't smell nice too. 'Cause you do. I mean..."

Ben felt like slapping his forehead. What a smooth-talking Casanova he was!

"Give them here," Alicia said, smiling. "I'll put them in a vase."

She strode out of the studio, flowers in hand.

By the time she returned, Ben had taken off his hat, coat and sunglasses, leaving just the blue trunks he habitually wore, his equivalent to the form-fitting bodysuits sported by the other members of the Fantastic Four.

He was studying the piece Alicia was currently working on.

It was none other than an image of himself. It stood a couple of feet high, and it showed him in a pose that few people would think of when they thought of the Thing: relaxed, contemplative, fists unclenched, shoulders low. He wasn't quite smiling, but there was a certain serenity about him.

"Y'know, sweetie, call me biased, but I think this one's your best yet. Never ceases to amaze me how you make 'em so lifelike. That's a *real* super-power, if you ask me."

"It's not nearly finished. When it's done, I'll make a plaster mold and get it cast in bronze. What do you reckon to that?"

"I reckon bronze'll look terrific. The right color and everything."

Alicia caressed the figurine delicately with her fingertips. "It helps when the subject is the kindest, handsomest man I know."

"Awww, c'mon. You're makin' me blush."

"I wish others saw you the way I see you, Ben," Alicia said. "I wish they knew how gentle you can be. I wish they understood how hard you fight too. Not against super villains and menaces from outer space. I'm not talking about that. Against all the adversity that's come your way. You refuse to let it get you down. That's the Ben Grimm in that statue. That's who I'm in love with."

"Is that so?"

"You know it, my darling."

"Come here." Ben took her chin in his hand and drew her close for a kiss.

As before, it was as though nothing else mattered in the world but the two of them. For a time, Ben could almost believe that life was good. That all would be well. That there wasn't some new, potentially earth-shattering event waiting round the next corner.

THE SILVER Surfer sat on a meteor, arrowing through space. His surfboard lay on the meteor's pitted surface beside him.

The Surfer seldom needed rest, but at times it was good either to relax and let inertia carry him through the frictionless void for a while, or else, as now, to step off his board and hitch a ride on some celestial object. It was a brief, pleasant respite from his unending task of searching.

He was startled when an armada of spaceships abruptly manifested around him, glimmering out of warp-space.

Each vessel bristled with armaments. These were warships, and from their design, the Surfer knew whom they belonged to.

The Kree.

Among the most belligerent races ever known, their aggression was rivaled only by that of the Badoon and the Shi'ar Imperium.

One of the Kree warships was larger than the rest, and he took this to be the armada's flagship. It signaled to him by flashing its hull lights, which the Surfer understood to indicate that someone aboard wanted to talk.

He leapt onto his surfboard and skimmed over to the flagship, leaving the meteor to carry on its way without its passenger. A huge hatch opened in the ship's bow, revealing a hangar crammed with small, sleek attack craft. The Surfer passed through an atmosphere retention field, going from vacuum to breathable air, and halted on the other side.

A welcoming committee awaited.

It consisted of rows of heavily armed soldiers, the majority of them drawn from the Kree's dominant blue-skinned racial group. All wore standard Kree militia uniform, with crested helmet and stylized planet motif on the chest. All, too, had their plasma rifles trained on him.

Behind them stood a handful of Sentries, the towering humanoid robots the Kree employed for both guard duties and battle.

At the front, and clearly the leader of this assemblage, was a representative of the Accuser Corps. Tall, massive-shouldered, and dressed in flowing green robes with a monastic hood, he bore a huge, long-handled warhammer which he leveled threateningly at the Surfer.

"I am Ronan the Accuser," he said, "and I have come to deliver a warning. Depart now, herald of Galactus, or face the full wrath of the Kree Empire."

The Surfer stepped off his board, leaving it hovering just above the floor, and walked calmly towards Ronan and his subordinates, with his hands held palms-out by his sides. "I am not afraid of you, Accuser Ronan, or of your troops and warships, or even of the much-vaunted Universal Weapon you hold."

"You should be," Ronan boomed. "Rest assured that we will fight you to our last breath. There is not a single Kree who is not willing to die in defense of the empire."

"Then," said the Surfer, "you are lucky I have no desire for battle with you."

Ronan's face, with its thick, symmetrical stripes of black warpaint, creased into a scowl. "You admit our combined power dwarfs yours? You cringe in terror?"

"No." The Surfer spoke with little inflection or emotion. His face, likewise, was inexpressive. "I mean merely that it is not my intention to engage in hostilities with the Kree. I have no vested interest in doing so."

"Because we will slay you!" Ronan declared.

"No. Because you need not fear me."

The Accuser blinked. "Need not…?"

"I am not here to lead Galactus to any of your planets. My master has a predilection for a certain type of world, and not a single one of yours suits his current appetite. Each and every planet the Kree claim as their own, from Hala outward, is grievously over-industrialized. Its mineral resources have been stripped clean for the purposes of manufacture, mainly to increase your already sizeable stocks of military hardware. Its wildlife is depleted to the point of extinction, its skies polluted, its greenery gone, and any indigenous people either enslaved or eradicated. It is a gray, riddled husk of its former self, with nearly every square acre of land built on and exploited. What would great Galactus want with such paltry, denatured fare?"

Ronan did not know whether to be pleased or insulted. "Then we are not in peril?"

"My master would not be pleased, were I to present him a Kree world to feed upon," said the Surfer. "Although I cannot promise that will not change. At present, his hunger is within normal bounds. Should it not be sated soon, however, he will become less choosy."

The herald of Galactus held up a hand.

"To me, my board," he said, and his surfboard sprang into action, sweeping towards him from behind. Without looking round, he jumped onto it at just the right moment.

Then, as one, Surfer and surfboard zoomed back towards the hangar hatch.

"Consider yourselves fortunate, people of the Kree," he called over his shoulder. "You have been spared. For now."

o———o

BACK ON Hala, Ronan reported to the Supreme Intelligence, the organic supercomputer construct that controlled every aspect of life in the Kree Empire.

The Supreme Intelligence took the form of a giant, bulbous green head floating in a huge holding tank. Its cable-thick strands of hair wafted in the nutrient fluid around it like the fronds of a sea anemone. Stored in its memory banks were the brain patterns of every great Kree politician, scientist, philosopher and military general down through the ages, giving it a collective intelligence so vast as to be all but incalculable.

Ronan was down on one knee before it, head bowed, holding his Universal Weapon upright beside him. He had just finished recounting the recent events aboard the flagship.

"Tell me straight, Accuser," the Supreme Intelligence said in its deep, slow, sonorous voice. "The Silver Surfer simply departed? With not a shot fired?"

"Not a single Kree weapon was discharged, Supremor. We stood ready to attack the Surfer, should he offer any clear threat. It was apparent, however, that he, and by extension Galactus, thinks the Kree Empire beneath his contempt. I viewed this as insulting, but then..."

"But then, since it means Galactus will pass us by, leaving us unmolested, we must be thankful."

"Indeed."

"You did not think to attempt to eliminate the Silver Surfer regardless?"

"It occurred to me. But had I and my troops made any hostile move towards the Surfer, he would doubtless have retaliated, and there would have been bloodshed. Hence, although it was un-Kree-like, I felt that allowing him to leave unhindered was the safest option. If that was wrong, I humbly beg your forgiveness and will accept whatever punishment you see fit."

"No, you did well, Accuser Ronan," said the Supreme Intelligence, its baggy, gargoyle-like mouth forming something akin to a smile. "I endorse your actions. What interests me is where the Silver Surfer will go next."

"Our navigators plotted the course he took after leaving us," Ronan said. "If followed true, without deviation, it would take him towards a large spiral galaxy some 200,000 light-years from here."

"Yes. I know the one." The Supreme Intelligence frowned as it consulted its own colossal system of cybernetic networks. "We have dormant Sentries seeded on worlds throughout that galaxy. Our scientists have conducted genetic experiments on lifeforms there. One world in particular yielded intriguing results. A primitive hominid race developed an array of extraordinary abilities, but the work was eventually abandoned."

"Abandoned, Supremor? Why?"

"The race—they have come to be known as Inhumans—were deemed a potential threat to the Kree. Thus it was decided that the experimentation should be confined to just that small sample, rather than extending it to the entirety of their species."

"Yet these Inhumans were allowed to survive. Dare I ask what for? They should have been eradicated altogether."

"In hindsight, perhaps so," said the Supreme Intelligence. "While they exist, they may yet imperil us. I have long predicted that this could happen. It might not be too much to hope, however, that the Silver Surfer's current vector leads him to that very same planet. It is a world abounding with life. Its biosphere has been damaged by the activities of its dominant species, *Homo sapiens*, but flourishes nonetheless. It would be a very attractive proposition to his master."

"Galactus, in short, would be doing us a great favor by destroying it," said Ronan.

The Supreme Intelligence's mouth now shaped itself into a grim grin.

"The Devourer of Worlds," he said, "is a force of nature. Sometimes forces of nature work against you, but sometimes they can work on your behalf. In this instance, I calculate, to a high degree of probability, that the latter will be the case. Galactus will rid us of a pest, and all Kree may breathe easier for him having done so."

JOHNNY STORM loved two things most of all: cars and girls.

When one caused him grief, he could always seek consolation in the other.

Which was why he was down in the Baxter Building's basement parking garage, tinkering with one of several hot rods he kept there.

It was a V8 Chevy sedan with a small-block engine, chrome trim and whitewall tires. Its paint job was a gorgeous cherry red, and when on the road, it normally purred like a tiger.

Something was wrong with the engine though. It had started to misfire slightly, and Johnny was under the hood, torque wrench in hand, toolbox at his feet, trying to identify the source of the problem.

He located a hairline crack on the carburetor intake manifold.

Bingo.

It wouldn't be too hard to fix. All it required was some precision welding, and he happened to know someone who could generate an oxyacetylene-torch-like flame from his fingertip and control it with pinpoint accuracy.

In no time, the repair was done. Johnny switched on the ignition, and the Chevy thrummed into life. The engine ran as smooth as silk. The sound of all eight cylinders working in harmony was music to his ears.

If only his love life could be mended so easily.

Johnny sat in the bucket seat, feeling the Chevy hum contentedly around him, and tried not to think about Crystal.

But he couldn't help it.

He'd dated plenty of girls in his young life so far, and he and Dorrie Evans had been going steady for several months before she'd decided unilaterally to call things off. He guessed he couldn't blame her. Often when they had been out together, some super villain emergency would end up dragging him away. Dorrie had got to thinking that he would rather go off and fight the Mole Man or the Molecule Man or the Hate-Monger or even, for crying out loud, Paste-Pot Pete, than spend time with her.

That wasn't true. Not entirely.

Dorrie was cute and funny, and Johnny enjoyed her company.

But he could never resist the lure of action.

And besides, as a super hero, you were obligated to answer the call of duty when it came.

He'd thought that, with Crystal, this wouldn't be so much of a problem. The Inhumans might not be super heroes but they belonged in a similar world. They had powers. They had enemies who hatched nefarious, world-endangering plans. They breathed the same rarefied air as the likes of the Fantastic Four. Crystal was no civilian, like Dorrie was.

Even though his time with Crystal had been only brief, Johnny felt they had forged a deep, intense connection. Here was someone he could truly relate to. In his head, he had mapped out a whole marvelous future for the two of them.

He'd foreseen himself showing Crystal the wider world. He would introduce her to the everyday miracles of human civilization, things she could have had no experience of in the Great Refuge. Movies, and Broadway shows, and rock music and, yes, cool cars. He would take her to see the sights, not just New York landmarks such as the Empire State Building and the Brooklyn Bridge, but America's natural wonders like Niagara Falls and the Grand Canyon, and the world's too, from Uluru to Kilimanjaro.

She, in turn, would teach him about her race, where everyone was different and unique, where people flew on wings like a bird's or a bat's, where a centaur trotted alongside a man who resembled an animated tree, where a golden-skinned cyclops could sit talking to a woman with quills all down her back like a porcupine's.

It would have been perfect. They could have learned so much from each other. Every day would have been a discovery.

And then it had all come crashing down around their ears.

Morosely, Johnny switched off the Chevy's engine. He'd been considering taking the car out for a spin, but he just wasn't in the mood.

He trudged up the service stairs to the Baxter Building's lobby.

WHO SHOULD he bump into there but the Fantastic Four's regular mailman, Willie Lumpkin.

"Young Mr. Storm!" said Willie. "How's it going, son?"

"Okay, I guess," Johnny replied.

Willie was small, old and wizened. He looked like he should have retired from the postal service a long time ago. His mailsack seemed almost too heavy for him to lift, and he moved so slowly on those spindly little legs of his that it must take him ages to complete his rounds.

Yet somehow he remained gainfully employed. Johnny wondered whether he had leverage over his bosses, compromising photos or some such, so they didn't dare fire him.

But then Willie wasn't the blackmailing type. He was too genial and innocent for that.

"You know I've got a new super-power, Mister Storm?" he said.

"No, really?"

"Yes indeedy! Remember that time Dr. Richards said wiggling my ears didn't qualify me for joining the Fantastic Four?"

Johnny did remember. He and Ben still joked about it to this day.

To be fair, though, Willie Lumpkin's ears were very large, and they stuck out at right angles from his head. It wasn't impossible he might flap them like wings and be able to fly, like Dumbo.

"Well," Willie continued, "I thought long and hard about it, and I figured if you didn't want me to join for that, you might for this."

He set down his mailsack, raised his head, and placed his hands just below his chin.

Then he began flicking his fingers rhythmically against the tautened underside of his jaw, while varying the shape of his mouth at the same time.

This way he was able to produce a series of hollow tapping noises that resembled notes, and even a melody.

"Did you recognize the tune?" he asked when he was finished.

Johnny shook his head.

"No? It's the *William Tell Overture*."

"Oh yeah. I see that now."

"I can do the theme from *Bonanza* as well. And *In the Hall of the Mountain King*, which is a tricky one because it just gets faster and faster."

"Amazing."

"So, how about it?" Willie said. "Is that enough to get me a place on the team?"

Johnny masked a smile. "Tell you what, Willie. If we ever decide to change our name to the Fantastic Five, you'll be the first person we call."

Willie beamed from ear to huge ear. "You will? Oh my

goodness, that'd be terrific! Now then, you just wait a moment, Mister Storm. I've got something for you." He rummaged in his sack. "Now, where is it, where is it? Here we are!"

He held out a letter for Johnny in a crisp white envelope.

It was marked METRO COLLEGE in large, formal script in one corner.

"Looks like a college admission decision letter to me," Willie said. "I've seen enough of them to know. Are you going to open it?"

Johnny stared at the envelope. He had almost forgotten filling out and sending off the application form to Metro, back in his senior year. There'd been plenty of FF-related excitement in the meantime, and it had pretty much slipped his mind.

"I said are you going to open it, Mister Storm?"

Johnny looked round at Willie. "Yeah, Willie, but if it's okay with you, I'm going to do it upstairs. On my own. You understand?"

"Sure I do, Mister Storm. Sure I do. Kind of a private moment. I get it. But do you know what?" He patted Johnny's arm. "You're going to get in. I have a good feeling about it. Bright kid like you? With your record of public service? You're a shoo-in!"

JOHNNY WISHED he could be as confident as Willie.

He wasn't actually all that bright, academically. His SAT scores were only a little above average. He definitely wasn't a big-brain like his brother-in-law. As a matter of fact, "big" was too small a word for Reed's intellect. It barely even began to cover it. There weren't any other brains that size. It was in a class all its own.

But maybe Willie was right when he spoke about Johnny's "public service". The Fantastic Four had done more for humankind than practically anybody, and the Human Torch had been instrumental in that. That surely had to count in his favor with the college admissions committee.

In his suite of private rooms at the Fantastic Four's headquarters, which occupied the Baxter Building's top five stories, Johnny gripped the Metro College letter tight. He was nerving himself to open it.

Ben was off seeing Alicia, and Reed and Sue were out having a meal. Johnny was all alone, and this was probably just as well. Whichever way the result went, he needed time to process before sharing it with anyone else.

College.

Johnny could easily see himself as a freshman, living in dorms, getting up to all sorts of high jinks around campus. And he'd be majoring in mechanical engineering, a subject he had an aptitude for and was keen to study.

Added to that, it might be good to move out of the Baxter Building and be away from the rest of the team for a while. He could stretch his wings, be more himself.

Sue wouldn't be there to scold him and boss him about the whole time. That would be a bonus.

It would be a shame not to have Ben around, he supposed. The two of them liked to spar, getting into arguments and playing practical jokes on each other. Pranking Ben—by giving him an exploding cigar, say, or slipping a whoopee cushion onto his favorite chair, or scrawling a beard on his face in indelible marker while he snoozed—was one of Johnny's great joys. But if the big old lug missed being made a fool of, he could always come visit.

And then there were the coeds.

That clinched it, for Johnny.

If he and Crystal were going to be separated for the foreseeable future, one way of easing the pain of her absence would be to meet other girls, and Metro College had those in abundance. His heart was firmly with Crystal and he wouldn't dream of being disloyal to her—but a little female attention never hurt. And he would get that for sure. A handsome, blond, young super hero with a string of fancy cars to drive? He would not be short of admirers.

Johnny ignited a flame at the tip of a forefinger and carefully burned open the envelope.

He fished out the letter inside and scanned it.

Dear Mr. Storm, it started. *Congratulations! On behalf of the Metro College admissions committee, I am delighted to say we have reviewed your application and would like to invite you to join the Class of…*

He didn't need to read any further.

He was in.

Metro College wanted him.

Johnny's feelings were mixed, much to his own surprise.

On the one hand, he'd got his wish. He had a place at college.

On the other hand, Metro was all the way over in New Jersey. It might be tricky to live there and still be a fully paid-up member of the Fantastic Four. And wasn't there a good chance his FF responsibilities would get in the way of his studies?

To go or not to go—that was the question.

As he pondered his dilemma, Johnny was vaguely aware of the sky outside the windows brightening. He assumed the sun was emerging from behind clouds.

Then he recalled that it was a cloudless day. The sun was already out.

He glanced outside.

What he saw shocked him.

No longer was there just one sun blazing away in the sky, like usual.

There were two.

REED AND Sue's favorite restaurant was a three-block stroll away from the Baxter Building.

Ferrante's was one of those cozy little basement Italian eateries with checked tablecloths, low lighting and candles stuck in the necks of raffia-wrapped Chianti bottles. The proprietor, Giorgio Ferrante, knew exactly who Reed and Sue were but pretended he didn't, treating them just as he did every other of his customers.

They liked that. It was nice, once in a while, to be able to go out in public like quote-unquote ordinary people. To be just themselves, not Mister Fantastic and the Invisible Woman.

They liked, too, that if someone at another table recognized them and got all excited, Giorgio would step in and politely but firmly suggest to this person that everybody at his restaurant had the right to privacy and a bit of peace and quiet. The implication being that if the customer did not calm down, he would throw them out. It always worked.

The clincher, as far as Reed and Sue were concerned, was that the food was delicious. Giorgio's Sicilian mother ran the kitchen, and every recipe was of her own making. The staff, most of whom were related to her in some way or another, feared and loved

Mamma Ferrante in equal measure. The restaurant was a proper family concern.

Now, over steaming bowlfuls of the best spaghetti vongole in all the five boroughs, the couple made small talk.

Or rather, Sue tried to.

It had been her idea they go out for lunch. She knew Reed. If she hadn't made the suggestion, he would have headed straight to his laboratory the moment they returned from the Himalayas and started trying to figure out a way of lifting the barrier around the Great Refuge, or else resumed one of his ongoing experiments, of which there seemed to be dozens.

He was a relentless workaholic and needed a break. Sue, for herself, needed quality time with her husband.

So, as soon as the Pogo Plane landed, she had presented Reed with a choice that was not really a choice.

"We are changing out of our uniforms and going to have a meal together, right now, or you won't see me again. I mean that literally."

Dr. Reed Richards was many things but he was not a fool. He knew she wasn't bluffing. The last time Sue had made this threat and he'd doubted she would go through with it, she had stayed invisible for an entire week. It had been torture for him. Not being able to look at her beautiful face, to know she was there in a room but out of sight…

Never again.

But at the restaurant table at Giorgio's, Reed was currently doing much the same thing to her. He was physically present, but his mind was elsewhere. Sue talked about Johnny, about Ben and Alicia, about mutual friends of theirs, about an evening gown she'd bought lately at Saks Fifth Avenue from their Janet Van Dyne designer range, about the possibility of the two of them getting away for a weekend up in Maine, maybe go fishing off the coast at Ogunquit again as they had last summer…

Reed just toyed with his food, supplying *hmmm* noises and a yes or a no as he felt appropriate. His eyes had an unfocused, faraway look. While he feigned listening, his brain was churning over some other unrelated matter.

Finally, Sue said, "Oh, by the way, Prince Namor and I are going to run off together."

"Really, dear?" said Reed uninterestedly.

"Yes. He's whisking me away to Atlantis and I'm going to rule his kingdom beside him. We've got it all worked out. The Atlanteans have a surgical process that can make me a water breather. I'm looking forward to being Mrs. Sub-Mariner and giving him lots of little mer-babies."

None of this was true, of course, but it had a basis in fact.

Namor the Sub-Mariner, ruler of the seven seas, though a frequent and implacable foe to the Fantastic Four, had a very soft spot for Sue. The first time they met, he had called her "the loveliest human I've ever seen," and on subsequent occasions he had flirted with her, even wined and dined her, and had once saved her life after she almost drowned.

Sue, for her part, couldn't deny feeling a strange fascination for him. He was a passionate man, physically beautiful, and carried himself with a regal bearing that she found very appealing. Those tiny wings on his ankles were kind of charming too.

"How does that sound to you?" Sue concluded.

"Fine, fine."

"*Reed*."

The sudden sharpness in her voice got his attention.

"What's that, Sue?" he said, blinking at her across the table.

"You haven't heard a word I just said!" she snapped.

"Of course I did. Something about... breathing water, was it? And Namor?"

"Oh my God. I told you Namor and I are going to run off together, and you didn't even bat an eyelid."

"You're going to…? But Sue, why would you do that? You're my wife."

Sue rolled her eyes. "Why would I choose Namor over you, Reed?" she asked rhetorically. "Oh, I don't know. Maybe because Namor would never ignore me when I'm sitting right in front of him. Namor wouldn't stare into the middle distance and grunt every so often when I'm talking with him. Namor would hang on my every word. He'd treat me like a queen—a literal queen."

"And would you want that?" Reed asked.

"What woman wouldn't?"

"I'm not so sure."

"You are on shaky ground here, Reed Richards. Be very careful what you say next."

"I'm only suggesting that, logically, while your assertion posits a desirable scenario, Sue, what you're proposing wouldn't, in fact, be the unalloyed utopia you seem to think. Studies have shown that a certain amount of friction between married partners is necessary if the marriage is to last. Constant agreement is unhealthy, as it indicates that each of the couple is surrendering their autonomy, and therefore their individuality, to the other. The best marriages are equal partnerships wherein both parties can feel free to assert their personhood, even at the cost of temporary antagonism."

"Reed…"

Reed went on, unchecked. "If, as you posit, Namor were to hang on your every word, then he would not be being true to himself. And if, likewise, you were to permit him to treat you like a queen, it would axiomatically confer inferior status on him."

"Reed…"

"I cannot see how such an unbalanced relationship would last beyond its initial stages. Infatuation persists for only so long, and while I don't deny Namor is a handsome physical specimen, and you, Sue, are undeniably gorgeous, once your immediate and understandable attraction to each other had run its course, the pair of you would be left in a sterile, futile predicament, neither of you able to be your authentic self with the other."

"Reed!" Sue raised her voice as loud as she dared in the restaurant's snug, subdued atmosphere. "Stop talking. With every word, you're just digging yourself deeper into a hole."

"I'm simply pointing out—"

"You're simply pointing out that you're an introverted, over-cerebral man who'd rather potter in his lab with his test tubes than enjoy a meal out with his wife."

"I don't tend to use test tubes all that much, not when sophisticated computer modeling allows me to—"

"You know what I mean. You're not here." She tapped the tabletop. "You're here." She tapped Reed's forehead. "And I understand why, really I do. You have the best of intentions. You always want to do the right thing, for the FF, for the world, for everyone. Just now, I imagine you've been puzzling over the Inhumans' situation."

"Correct. I was thinking that a tightly focused beam of infrasound might disrupt the barrier around the Great Refuge sufficiently so as to... But you don't want to hear about that, do you?"

"Not at this moment, no. The point I'm making is that with a brain like yours, you can achieve anything. That's your gift, and you use it wisely, and I love for you it, honestly I do. But sometimes I don't want Reed Richards, Mister Fantastic. Sometimes I want the real Reed, the man I fell in love with all those years ago and married, who I know can be sensitive and thoughtful and who cares for me deeply."

Reed held her gaze and said sincerely, "I do, Sue. I care for you very deeply."

"Same goes here," Sue said, adding, "although right now I'd happily pick up your bowl of barely touched spaghetti vongole with an invisible forcefield and tip it over your head."

"In front of all these other people? Make a scene like that? You wouldn't."

"Try me."

They both smiled then. Sue reached across with one hand and stroked Reed's temple, where his brown hair had gone white. She liked how this particular sign of aging looked on him. It gave him a distinguished, professorial air.

"Just for the record, darling," she said, "I'd never run away with Namor. You must know that. You're right, it would be thrilling with him for about a day, and then I'd get bored. I like a man I can depend on, and you are dependable. Dependably loving and sometimes dependably infuriating. Also, don't think I didn't notice you referring to me as 'undeniably gorgeous'."

"I did say that, didn't I?"

"That's the kind of compliment that goes a long way. Maybe when we get back home, I can show you just how far."

Reed arched an eyebrow. "I believe that's a demonstration I would enjoy."

"Oh, you most certainly—"

She was interrupted by a commotion at the front of the restaurant. Chairs scraped back, and customers were on their feet, peering up through the windows. From outside in the street, there was the sound of running footsteps and voices raised in alarm. Car horns honked.

"Judging by the clamor we're hearing," said Reed, "I fear our plans have been derailed."

He rose from his seat, and Sue followed suit. "I fear you're right," she sighed. "Giorgio? The check, please."

"No, no, signore, signora," said Giorgio, waving a hand. "I understand. You must go. We can settle up another time."

Reed and Sue raced outdoors.

IT WAS like something out of a disaster movie.

People were flocking this way and that, panic on their faces. Some were gathered in huddles, gesturing upward. Voices were raised in consternation.

Traffic in the vicinity had come to a standstill. The occupants of cars leaned out of their windows, staring at the sky. Cabbies and delivery drivers, more worried about the gridlock than anything else, fretted and cursed and banged their steering wheels.

"What is it, Reed?" Sue said. "What do you think is happening? Is it the Hulk on another rampage? Is the Mole Man back, with his monsters?"

"Not enough data yet to say," Reed replied. Agitated New Yorkers shoved past the pair of them, buffeting them with elbows. "Sue, would you create some breathing space for us?"

Sue, concentrating, enclosed herself and Reed in an invisible forcefield. It was like a lozenge-shaped wall with rounded edges, so that the two-way scurry of pedestrians on the sidewalk diverted smoothly either side of them, making accommodation for the obstacle while not knowing quite what it was.

"Now," said Reed, "let's see if I can get a better view."

He craned his neck, then craned it some more, and even more, until it was several times its usual length. Atop this slender, rubbery column of flesh, his head turned this way and that.

It was a bizarre sight, but the majority of the people around them were too concerned about themselves to notice.

"Ah. There," said Reed, pointing. "Look, Sue. Up there in the sky."

Sue followed the direction of his finger.

"Two suns?" she said, shading her eyes. "But that's just not possible."

"Of course it isn't possible." Reed contracted his neck to its normal size. "One of them is not a real sun."

"How do you know that?"

"The shadows, Sue. Look down at your feet. You're only casting one shadow, see? Dual suns would mean dual shadows. Then there's the fact that the ambient temperature hasn't risen. A second sun would increase it by a significant factor. No, one of those suns is some sort of optical effect. A projection, perhaps." He frowned. "But what is it for? And who's doing this?"

"Whoever it is, if their aim is to frighten, they're succeeding," Sue said.

Even as she spoke, an angry altercation broke out on the opposite side of the street, seemingly for no reason. Elsewhere, a couple of people had collided with some force. Both were now sitting on the ground, looking dazed and bleeding from their noses. Screams arose, near and far. A police officer clambered onto the roof of his car and began calling for calm through a bullhorn, but nobody was paying him any attention. There was a tinkle of breaking glass, a storefront window shattering.

"And it's only going to get worse," Reed said. "Look."

One of the suns was growing rapidly larger. In next to no time, it was double the size of the other, and it kept on expanding. Soon it occupied fully half the sky and had engulfed its lesser counterpart.

Still it grew, and if it continued like this, in no time the entire sky would look as though it was on fire.

o———o

THAT, CERTAINLY, was Johnny's thought.

The sky had caught alight, and soon enough the whole of it would be burning.

But not if he could help it.

Because if there was one thing the Human Torch knew about, it was fire.

Johnny flung the window wide open and let out his personal battle cry.

"Flame on!"

At the same time, his entire body burst ablaze.

Reed had once tried to explain to Johnny how his powers worked. It was something about being able to generate a plasma aura around himself and igniting a combustion process within it electrostatically. He could also alter his body density, making himself lighter than air, and possessed a natural immunity to flame.

To be honest, Johnny hadn't really taken much of this in. When Reed started using ten-cent words like "ultra-oxidation" and "thermokinesis", he tended to zone out.

All he needed to know was that the cosmic ray bombardment they'd all four been subjected to in Reed's rocket ship had left him with some pretty sweet fire powers.

Johnny leapt out through the open window and took to the air. Behind him, his rooms remained intact, nothing burnt or scorched. Everything in them, from the carpets to the furniture to the paintwork, was coated in a special fireproof film Reed had invented. It was derived from the fabric made of unstable molecules which the Fantastic Four used for their clothing and which could adapt to their powers. Thanks to this wonder material of Reed's, Johnny, for instance, could light himself up like a Roman candle without frazzling his outfit to a crisp and therefore having to go into action stark naked.

Soaring above the rooftops, Johnny took stock of the situation. Down below on the streets, crowds milled and thronged. In every building, windows were open and people leaned anxiously out. Alarms were going off. The wailing of emergency vehicle sirens echoed all over the city.

In the space of just a few minutes, New York had descended into chaos. Meanwhile, up above, the fire was still spreading across the sky.

Johnny rose higher, scanning the rippling flames far overhead. He estimated the fire must be taking place somewhere in the lower atmosphere, where the air was thin but there was still enough oxygen for it to burn. So far it seemed to be staying at that height, but what if it started to creep down into the troposphere, where the oxygen density was greater?

Could it end up consuming the whole of Earth's atmosphere?

Even as he entertained this apocalyptic thought, Johnny noticed something odd about the fire. The flames moved regularly, with a repetitive evenness, like waves on the ocean.

Fire was a wayward creature, as he knew better than most. It was consistent only in its inconsistency. It went where it liked, at whatever rate it liked, now here, now there.

What it did not do was pulse like a heartbeat, as the fire in the sky was now doing as it covered yet more of the firmament.

Not unless it was artificial in some way.

Johnny didn't know whether it was reassuring or not that the fire wasn't some naturally occurring phenomenon. Whatever its cause, it was still mushrooming inexorably outwards across the sky, and still sowing panic and terror below.

An explosion reached his ears.

He looked down and spotted a freight truck that had T-boned a car at a crosswalk. The crash had happened a few moments earlier, both vehicles had caught alight, and now the car's gas tank had just detonated.

It was only a matter of time before the freight truck's gas tank did the same. There were dozens of people close by, and the second, larger explosion would engulf them. None of these onlookers seemed aware of the danger. They stood and stared at the burning vehicles as though mesmerized.

Johnny went into a nosedive, leaving a fiery trail behind him as he plummeted five hundred feet in a matter of seconds.

He noted that the driver of the car had scrambled to safety just in time, before it went up. The man was squatting on the roadway, gazing shakenly at the burning wreck of his vehicle.

The driver of the truck, however, was still in his cab. He looked dazed and bewildered, probably having hit his head on the dashboard during the impact.

Hovering above the crash site, Johnny reached out mentally to the flames and drew them up towards himself. Their heat joined his heat, their fire becoming his. He absorbed them into him like a sponge soaking up water.

Within moments, the blaze was extinguished. Disaster had been averted.

Johnny looked around, expecting at least a few cheers from the people below, maybe somebody shouting "Go, Human Torch!" or words to that effect.

He didn't see the chunk of concrete coming.

It was a piece of broken sidewalk slab the size of a baseball, and it was hurled with some accuracy. Whoever threw it could have subbed as a pitcher for the Red Sox.

The concrete chunk struck him on the side of the head with stunning force, and Johnny fell to the ground in a heap, his flames fizzling out.

Instantly he was surrounded. He had a dim awareness of angry faces, yelling voices.

A mob.

"Blasted Human Torch!" someone cried. "He's the one doing this."

"It's his fault," another person snarled. "Got to be."

"Who else could set the whole darn sky on fire!?" said a third.

Johnny's head throbbed in agony. He could scarcely think straight.

All he knew was that there were irate New Yorkers all around him, and he had just saved a whole bunch of lives, but all they wanted to do was attack him.

He tried to flame on, so that he could get away, but someone came charging out of a corner bodega brandishing a fire extinguisher.

"This'll fix him," the guy said, and started to spray Johnny with firefighting foam.

The stuff not only put out his flames, it stung his eyes and made it hard to breathe. Choking, Johnny groped blindly for the fire extinguisher nozzle to push it aside, but the man just took a step back and kept spraying, covering him from head to toe.

Everyone else was laughing and jeering. The blazing sky shed a flickering, hellish orange light over the scene and made their faces look almost demonic.

Johnny had never felt so humiliated, or so scared. He could sort of understand why these people had turned on him. They were terrified. They were lashing out at what they thought was the source of their terror. It was a kind of madness.

But what would happen next? Once he was lying helpless, enveloped in the chemical foam, unable to resist, would they attack him physically? Perhaps tear him apart?

It was very possible.

And nobody was going to lift a finger to help him.

o————o

WELL, NOT quite nobody.

A grating voice boomed out.

"Hey!" it said in a thick Lower East Side accent. "*Hey!*"

Few in the mob paid any heed.

Ben Grimm came barging through the crowd.

"That's my pal Torchy you're messin' with there," he said. "You better move away from him, or you'll have my Aunt Petunia's favorite nephew to answer to."

He grabbed the man with the fire extinguisher and tossed him aside as though he weighed no more than a bundle of straw. He shoved a couple more people out of his way.

Everyone else backed off, wary of receiving the same rough

treatment. Space appeared around Ben and the stricken Johnny.

"Yeah, that's right," Ben growled. "You all leave him alone."

A man stepped forward, wielding a baseball bat. He wore a muscle shirt with a dumbbell logo on the front and looked as though he spent a great deal of his time at the gym. Each bicep was the size of a cantaloupe, and his neck was almost as thick as Ben's own.

"He's behind all of this," muscle-shirt guy said, gesticulating at Johnny, then at the sky. "You can't tell me he ain't."

"Think very carefully about what you're going to do next, buster," Ben warned.

"You people, you super folk," the man went on, "you're nothing but trouble. World was a safer place before you came along. Now look at it. Super villains everywhere, wanting to rule it. Aliens trying to conquer us all the time. And now the damn sky's on fire."

"You think Match-Head here did that? Why in heck would he?"

"I dunno, maybe 'cause he's out of control."

Ben nodded at Johnny, who was a sorry sight, lolling on the ground, clutching his head, swathed in chemical foam. "He look out of control to you?"

"Well, you *would* defend him, wouldn't you?" muscle-shirt guy said. "You and him are in cahoots."

Ben guffawed. "Cahoots, huh?"

"Yeah. And it's about time someone stood up to you." The words were punctuated with forward thrusts of the baseball bat. "Put you in your place."

"All right then, hot shot," said Ben. "You're so all fired up to take a pop at me, I'm going to let you. C'mon, swing away, Willie Mays. I swear I won't duck or nothin'."

"Okay. Okay. You asked for it."

Muscle-shirt guy took a run-up and whacked Ben round the side of the head.

The bat broke in half.

Ben just grinned. "That tickles," he said.

Muscle-shirt guy looked at the shattered stub of the bat in his hands, gaping in dismay.

"Now it's my turn," Ben said.

He flicked muscle-shirt guy beneath the chin with his forefinger.

The man flew head over heels. He was out cold before he even hit the ground.

"Anyone else want to have a go?" Ben said.

People shook their heads.

"No takers, huh? What a shame."

Ben bent down and helped Johnny to his feet.

"You okay, kid?" he asked.

"My head feels like Thor just used it for hammer practice," Johnny replied, "and this foam gunk stinks to high heaven. But yeah, I'm all right. Thanks for stepping in, Ben."

"Ah, it was nothin'. You'd do the same for me."

"I never thought I'd be so pleased to see your ugly kisser."

"What are you saying? You've always been jealous of my good looks."

Johnny laughed, then winced at the pain this caused him.

"Is he going to be okay?" he asked, indicating muscle-shirt guy, who lay sprawled on his back.

"Sure. It was only a little love tap. He'll come round with a sore head, maybe a loose tooth or two, that's all."

"Johnny!"

Sue's anxious cry was followed by Sue herself appearing from the crowd, with Reed not far behind.

"What's going on?" she asked her brother. "Why have you got that stuff all over you?"

"Long story, sis. Let's just say New Yorkers aren't too apprecia-tive of the Human Torch right now, what with all that weird fire burning away... up... there..."

The sentence trailed off.

Johnny was looking upward, scowling in confusion.

Other people were doing the same. There were gasps of surprise and relief.

The sky was back to normal. The fire had vanished. The sun—just the one sun—shone down from a serene azure vault. All was as it had been before.

"Where did it go?" he said. "A moment ago there were flames as far as the eye could see, and now..."

"Now," Reed finished, "they're gone without a trace."

Gradually the tension ebbed out of the crowd. Nervous laughter broke out. People started chatting to one another, comparing notes about their recent hair-raising experience. Like the fire, their hysteria had evaporated. Slowly, in dribs and drabs, everyone began to disperse.

"It's almost as though they weren't there in the first place," Reed said.

"What do you mean, Stretch?" Ben asked. "I saw it. That danged fire was everywhere. It's why I left Alicia and came racing back here. I was expecting you'd already be whippin' up some sort of doohickey that'd be able to put it out, some big old piece of machinery you'd maybe want me to hoist up onto the roof of the Baxter Building so's you could set it going."

"Not needed, old friend," said Reed. "The fire was fake."

"I thought that too," Johnny said. "I know fire, and that fire wasn't behaving like real fire does."

"The question remains, though," said Reed, stroking his chin, "if it was fake, what was the point of it? Was it simply to scare people? Or was it to send some kind of message? And if so, what message?"

"More importantly," Sue added, "who's responsible? Is it one of our old foes? Or is it someone new?"

"I'd bet my last buck it was Doc Doom," Ben said. "It's just the kind of stunt he would pull."

"Or the Wizard," Johnny chimed in. "He was a stage magician once, and this reminded me of a conjuring illusion, but, you know, on a massive scale."

"It doesn't really feel to me like something Victor would do," Reed said. He and Doom had been friends at college, and he still referred to the other man, now his sworn enemy, by his forename. "It's too nebulous, too arbitrary, for him."

"Yeah, I guess so," said Ben. "Plus, he ain't braggin' about it already, and old Doomsie—he wants you to know, soon as possible, when it's him who's jerking you around."

"He does like to sign his handiwork, yes. As for the Wizard, he's ingenious, to be sure, but a feat like this is beyond even his capabilities. No," Reed went on, musingly, "the mind behind this is formidable, with powers on a level that's almost incomprehensible."

"But who?" Sue insisted. "And what did they hope to accomplish?"

"I suspect," her husband replied, "that once we figure out the *why* part, the *who* part will quickly follow."

SEVENTY-TWO HOURS LATER

A DYING star went supernova.

After bloating into a red giant over the course of millennia, it had shriveled back down to a tiny, bright core, the white dwarf stage of its lifespan. Having collapsed in on itself, and no longer able to support its own mass, it fell victim to a runaway nuclear fusion deep within its heart. Enough energy was unleashed all at once to unravel the dense fabric of the star, and it exploded.

The Silver Surfer stood ready, poised on his surfboard.

As the shock waves from the supernova reached him, he tilted his board and let them carry him.

He rode them.

Knees bent, arms outstretched, the Surfer jetted through space, powered along by the shock waves alone.

He kept going until their motive force finally faded.

Just perceptible on his usually impassive face was a smile—the tiniest lifting of the corners of his mouth.

Then, with this brief and pleasant interlude over and done, he resumed his quest.

THE SUPERNOVA propelled him deep into the spiral galaxy he had been aiming for after leaving Kree territory.

The Surfer's keen gaze alighted on a solar system within that galaxy which had a G-type main-sequence sun as its star.

Such a sun, one in the prime of life, all but guaranteed life-bearing planets in orbit around it.

The Surfer veered towards it, and as he did, a dim memory bubbled up from the deepest recesses of his mind.

Another, similar sun.

A world nestling in that sun's circumstellar habitable zone.

A civilization whose golden age had passed. Who no longer appreciated the wonders of their technology. Who had grown listless and apathetic, inward-looking, dull.

Their every need and whim catered for by machines.

Their autonomy surrendered to the computers that governed them.

Their lifespans greatly prolonged by their science, so that the years passed aimlessly and time began to lose meaning.

Their days spent indulging in mindless pleasure and recreation.

This world's name…

Its name…

But he had forgotten what it was called. He assumed the world had been his home once. But that was eons ago.

He assumed, too, that he used to have another name, before he became the Silver Surfer. Whatever it was, though, he had forgotten that also.

The Silver Surfer perceived eight planets circling in great elliptical sweeps around the sun ahead of him. His eyes, though pupil-less, seemingly blank, could perform incredible feats of long-distance analysis. They surveyed each planet in forensic detail, assessing chemical composition, temperature, gravitational strength, atmospheric makeup.

Two of them were too close to the sun.

Two were gas giants.

Two were much too far out.

That left two that were neither too hot, nor too vaporous, nor too cold to support complex life.

One of those two, the third planet from the sun, looked very promising indeed, and worthy of further investigation.

MEANWHILE, ON THAT THIRD PLANET FROM THE SUN...

SUE RICHARDS had not seen her husband for three whole days.

She was not happy about this.

Immediately after the incident of the burning sky, Reed had taken himself off to his laboratory, which filled practically an entire floor of the Fantastic Four's skyscraper headquarters. He had remained there ever since. He hadn't come out to eat. He hadn't communicated with Sue or any of the rest of the team. He had shut himself away in the lab for all that time, getting up to who-knew-what.

Sue had had enough.

She understood that whatever Reed was doing in there, it must be important. She understood, too, that it must be related to the burning sky. There couldn't be any other reason.

She had left him to it, accepting that he did not want to be interrupted. Patiently she had waited, expecting him to emerge at any moment.

Sue gave Reed a lot of latitude. He was a genius, no question. By any benchmark, he was one of the cleverest people who ever lived. And when he was engaged in research and inquiry, particularly in a matter as important as this one obviously was, he needed to be left alone. He would not welcome her, or anyone, butting in.

But three days?

Enough was enough.

Time for an intervention.

Sue pressed the button on the video intercom at the laboratory entrance. The lab was sealed off behind a set of adamantium-reinforced doors. The whole of the lab, in fact, was enclosed within a bulwark of similarly reinforced walls, which also boasted honeycomb layers of sonic and kinetic insulation.

The high level of protection, Reed said, was to ensure that if anything went wrong—be it an accidental spillage, an explosion, or the escape of something undesirable—the problem would be contained and could not get out. But it was also to hinder anyone trying to get into the lab and plunder his array of extraordinarily sophisticated high-tech equipment.

Sue pressed the button several times before her husband finally answered.

The face on the video screen was gaunt and haggard. Three days' growth of stubble adorned Reed's chin. His hair was awry. His eyes were hollow pits.

Sue could barely keep herself from gasping.

"Reed!" she exclaimed. "You look awful."

"Sue." Reed spoke wearily, without enthusiasm. "What do you want?"

"What do I want? What do I *want*?" Her voice rose. "What I want, Reed Nathaniel Richards, is for you to come out here this instant, go eat something, and then head straight to bed. Have you slept at all these past three days?"

"Now and then. The occasional catnap. Listen, Sue, I understand that you're worried about me. I appreciate that. But the work I'm engaged in is vital. I can't stop now. I'll… I'll be done soon, I swear. I just need a little more time."

"What are you even up to in there?" Sue asked.

"I can't… It's not easy to explain. Just trust me, Sue. Everything's fine. *I'm* fine. What I'm doing—it's for everyone's benefit."

"So tell me what it is. At least do that for me. If you're not going to take my advice..."

"I can't tell you just yet. I will, I promise."

"You know I can find out for myself," Sue said. "I can turn a section of the wall invisible and look in."

"I know. I'd rather you didn't though. Things are... at a delicate stage. Please, leave us be for now."

"Us?"

"Me. I meant me. All will become clear in due course."

Sue hesitated. She was ready to make good on her threat to open up a window of invisibility in the wall.

But Reed's expression was so pathetic and imploring, she couldn't bring herself to do it. It would only irritate him and suggest she lacked faith in him.

And one thing Sue Richards had was faith in her husband.

"You," she said, "are the most aggravating man alive."

"True," Reed said, with a bleak smile. "And I'm sorry about that. For what it's worth, I love you, Sue."

"It's not worth very much, right this moment," she said. "But yes, I love you too, Reed. Just... Just look after yourself, please. Promise me that?"

"I will. Thank you, Sue."

"Thank me later. And it had better be the greatest thank-you any man gave his wife."

She cut the intercom connection.

Then, fuming with exasperation but also filled with a sense of pride, she strode off.

o———o

REED TURNED away from the intercom, feeling both guilty and relieved.

He loved Sue more than he could say. What a woman she was! His equal in so many ways, and his superior in so many others. His guiding light and his sanctuary. Without Sue tethering him to the real world, grounding him, he might long ago have floated off into the realms of abstract thought, never to return.

He hated shutting her out like this. It pained him to push her away.

But he had to. There was too much at stake. He couldn't put his own interests first, or Sue's, for that matter. Not when the fate of the whole world hung in the balance.

He was about to resume his work when the lab's communications screen chimed. A computerized voice said, "Incoming call."

"Origin?" said Reed.

"S.H.I.E.L.D. Helicarrier."

"Caller?"

"Colonel Fury. Accept or refuse?"

Reed paused, then sighed. "Accept."

From past experience, he knew that Nick Fury did not take no for an answer. If Reed did not pick up, he would persist in calling, and if Reed still kept not picking up, he would simply come to the Baxter Building and demand to be seen. And he would be angry, and Fury when he was angry... Well, he had been known to make grown adults cry. And included among those grown adults were chiefs of staff, senators, Supreme Court judges and even presidents.

To put it another way: never was there a clearer case of nominative determinism than that man's surname.

"Richards," Fury said. "You look awful."

"So people keep telling me."

The face filling the screen in front of Reed was tough, square-jawed and grizzled, an impression heightened by the patch Fury wore over his right eye, which lent him an almost piratical look. The hair at his temples, like Reed's, had gone white, but he showed few other signs of age—surprising in someone who had fought on the front lines in World War II, leading a scrappy band of troops called the Howling Commandos.

But then Nick Fury was known to take regular doses of a rare, special serum called the Infinity Formula, which significantly slowed the aging process. He appeared to be in his early forties, but chronologically he was much, much older.

This was the head of spy agency S.H.I.E.L.D.—Supreme Headquarters International Espionage Law-enforcement Division—and America's top intelligence operative.

The stub of an unlit but well-chewed cheroot was gripped in Fury's teeth, jerking up and down like an admonishing finger as he spoke. "I'm going to assume you've been burning the midnight oil, lookin' into that whole inferno-in-the-sky thing of a few days ago."

"You would assume correctly."

"Good. 'Cause I've had our S.H.I.E.L.D. techs bludgeoning their brains about it, and they've come up with the square root of diddly-squat. So I reckoned I'd better touch base with the eggheadedest guy I know and see what he thinks. That's you, by the way."

"I gathered," said Reed.

"And in case you're wondering, I've approached you before Stark, Pym, any of 'em other brainiacs. Even Banner, not that he's ever easy to find."

"I'll take that as a compliment."

"You should. So, what's the answer? How come the whole of New York got the bejeezus scared out of it for half an hour? It's not just me who wants to know either. I've been fielding calls from the Pentagon, the State Department, the Oval Office, even the goldarned Kremlin. Just about the only people who haven't got in touch are the Shriners."

"The truth is, Colonel," said Reed, "I'm close to making a breakthrough on the problem. It won't be long."

"Is that supposed to reassure me?"

"It's all I can offer, for now."

Fury scowled at him, chomping hard on the cheroot. "Okay. Well, better'n nothin', I guess. Still doesn't leave me much to tell the bigwigs."

Reed shrugged apologetically. "I know."

"Ahh, it ain't your headache, it's mine. Sorry if I'm bein' hard on you. It's just been a hell of a few weeks for us at S.H.I.E.L.D., is all. We tangled with Hydra, big time. And then, as if that weren't bad enough, a couple of crumbs by the name of Mentallo and the Fixer tried to take over our HQ—manacled me to a flamin' H-bomb, even! Now there's this. I tell you, it's a lot to deal with, even for an old warhorse like me. Got me wondering whether I should bail out of the spying racket and go live on a beach in Cancún."

"I very much doubt that will happen," Reed said. "You, Colonel Fury, are destined to die with your boots on."

Fury grimaced. "Yeah. Ain't that a fact." His good eye narrowed. "Hey, is there someone there with you?"

"No."

Fury peered closer into his camera. "Could've sworn I saw someone moving in the background there. Big fella too."

Reed glanced over his shoulder. "I'm quite alone here, Fury. Our transmission *is* a little distorted. Perhaps it was some visual artifact on your screen."

"Hmmm. Could've been, I guess. Anyways, I'll leave you to get on with it. I want to hear from you, soon as you've got something for me. Okay?"

"You will, Colonel Fury."

As the call ended, Reed looked round.

That made two people he had lied to now—Sue and Fury. Two people he greatly respected and didn't like keeping the truth from.

He wasn't alone in the lab, and hadn't been since yesterday evening.

"Well," he said to the towering figure who had been lingering in one corner while Reed had been in conversation with his wife and then the S.H.I.E.L.D. head honcho. "Hopefully that's the last of the interruptions. For the time being, at least."

"I apologize for my carelessness," said the other. "I did not realize I had strayed into Fury's eyeline."

"Not much gets past Nick Fury," Reed said. "I don't think he believed what I was saying about a visual artifact. But he's wise enough to give me the benefit of the doubt."

"That is good."

"So then, where were we?"

The giant gestured at the vast, baroque contraption he and Reed had been constructing together. "The Matter Mobilizer is almost ready."

Reed stifled a yawn. He was exhausted but knew he could not afford to be. Not when things were at such a crucial stage.

"Then, Watcher, let's get on with it."

"Why not call me by my given name, Dr. Richards? I feel we know each other well enough by now."

"Very well… Uatu."

UATU THE Watcher had appeared in Reed's laboratory the previous day.

He had teleported in without warning, startling Reed—although his arrival had not come as a *complete* surprise.

He was an imposing figure, nearly twice as tall as any human, with a disproportionately large head. He was clad in a kind of high-collared toga which lent him the air of an Ancient Roman statesman. His bald pate almost scraped the ceiling of the lab.

The Fantastic Four had first met him a few months earlier on the moon, where they had been fighting the Red Ghost—a monomaniacal Russian villain with the ability to turn intangible—and his trio of sinister, super-powered pet apes.

The Watcher dwelled in an air-filled pocket on the lunar surface known as the Blue Area. From this vantage point he had been observing the goings-on of people on Earth for centuries, compiling a record of humankind's exploits from its earliest days.

He belonged to an extraterrestrial race of near-immortals, committed since the dawn of time to monitoring and studying all aspects of the universe and accumulating knowledge.

Watchers watched and never interfered. That was their one abiding credo. They permitted themselves only to document events, and vowed not to influence or alter them in any way.

Uatu himself had taken this solemn oath.

And, in Reed's presence, had broken it more than once.

The first time was during the aforementioned battle between the Fantastic Four and the Red Ghost, when Uatu had shifted both warring parties elsewhere on the moon so that their conflict wouldn't endanger his gleaming, futuristically palatial home.

The second time occurred when the Red Ghost inveigled the team into a rematch, also on the moon. The Fantastic Four were left marooned after defeating him, but Uatu volunteered to transport them back to Earth.

Now, for a third time, Uatu was involving himself in human affairs, and far more seriously than before.

Upon manifesting in Reed's laboratory, he had announced that he was responsible for the burning sky incident.

"Yes, I was already coming to that conclusion," Reed had said. "For the past couple of days I've been racking my brains as to who would have the knowhow and the technological wherewithal to accomplish a feat like that. Both my colleague Johnny Storm and I spotted that the fire was only an illusion. I asked myself how it was done and who could have done it, and my findings pointed inescapably in one direction. You."

Uatu nodded.

"You did something with the world's telecommunications satellites," Reed continued. "I tracked their orbits and saw that many of them had been repositioned, without the involvement of their respective owners. I hacked into a number of them and discovered they had had their programming altered. Would I be right in thinking you re-tasked them and used them as a kind of holographic projection system?"

"You would."

Reed allowed himself a brief moment of intellectual triumph. Hypothesis followed by research and experiment, leading to a conclusion, now confirmed by fresh data and peer review.

"The fire," he went on. "You planned to encircle the whole of the world with it."

"Yes."

"So that, from the outside, Earth would resemble a small sun."

"Yes," Uatu said. "I drew inspiration from the Krr'ilth Protocol."

"The name sounds Skrullian to me."

"Well deduced, Dr. Richards. The Krr'ilth Protocol is a technique used by the Skrulls in times of crisis to camouflage their homeworld Skrullos. I mimicked it, reconfiguring Earth's satellites so that they would aid in casting a false fiery screen around the entire planet. However, no sooner had I initiated the process, starting above your city, than I noted the fear and alarm it was causing among the populace. This was a byproduct I had not foreseen."

"So you halted it almost as soon as it began," Reed said.

"Indeed. I could see it was doing more harm than good. Your people were unprepared, and their adverse reaction led me to understand that I had made a grave error."

"Imagine what happened in New York, but on a worldwide scale."

"Exactly. It would have been disastrous, potentially cataclysmic. Your more bellicose nations, mistaking the fire-filled sky for some existential threat instigated by their opponents, might conceivably have launched nuclear strikes. I carried out the procedure more as a test than anything, but given its unfavorable outcome, I was obliged to rethink and come up with a better scheme. I believe I have, but I wish to consult with you first, Dr. Richards, before implementing it."

"I'm happy to do that," Reed said, "but I'll need to know why. Why are you doing this for us, Watcher?"

"There is great danger coming," Uatu replied. "I hope to forestall it."

"Great danger?"

"Your planet is facing a peril unlike any it has ever known. I wish to protect it. To that end, I intend to shield it."

"But what is this peril?"

Uatu declined to elucidate. "You will have to take it on trust, Dr. Richards. Rest assured, I have your world's best interests at heart."

Reed pondered this. In their encounters so far, Uatu the Watcher had done nothing to show that he was humankind's enemy. Quite the opposite. Behind that stern, forbidding countenance of his, Reed sensed a kind of abiding affection for the people of Earth. Over the long period he had been observing the planet, Uatu had come to admire its inhabitants and wanted what was best for them.

Reed thought of him as a zoologist who, against every scientific instinct, had developed a great, if unspoken, fondness for the species he studied.

This affinity had led Uatu to betray the fundamental tenet of Watcher existence three times now.

Trusting him seemed the only sensible option.

However, having collaborated with him unquestioningly for several hours, helping him build, develop and refine this Matter Mobilizer device of his, Reed felt a full explanation was long overdue. Not least since he had just had to be so regrettably evasive with both Sue and Nick Fury.

He said as much, even as he and the Watcher began making a last few fine calibrations on the Matter Mobilizer.

"I've been patient, Uatu, but I think it's high time you told me what we need the Matter Mobilizer for. Don't get me wrong, I understand its function. I understand that it has to be operated from somewhere on Earth, and the Baxter Building is as good a location as any. What I don't understand is why it's required in the first place. This 'great danger' you spoke of—I'd be grateful if you elaborated on that."

Uatu half-smiled. "Your irritated tone of voice is forgivable, Dr. Richards, given your lack of sleep and nourishment. It is perhaps also warranted. If I seemed elusive, it is merely because my priority was the Matter Mobilizer—siting it and assembling it. Now that it is ready for use, I feel I may expound on its purpose."

"Then go ahead."

After a pause, Uatu said, "Do you know of Galactus?"

Reed shook his head. "The name doesn't ring a bell. What is it?"

"It is a 'who', but equally could be deemed a 'what'. Galactus is a being of nigh-omnipotence, but also one of the fundamental forces of the universe. There are those who posit the existence of a divine creator, someone who brought the cosmos into being and shaped it. Galactus is, if anything, the opposite. He is an un-creator, a ravager, a destroyer. Where there is life, he undoes it. Where there is energy, he claims it as his own."

"For what purpose?"

"For sustenance. So powerful an entity requires the input of vast quantities of raw energy to live. His preferred source is worlds."

"He siphons worlds of their energy?"

"Siphons is too weak a description for what he does. He *consumes* worlds. He drains them of their every last erg of vitality. When he has finished with a planet, all that remains is a dry, crumbling husk. Every elemental constituent is gone—its biomass, its water, its magma. He leaves behind nothing but a cluster of dead rocks floating in space."

Reed felt a chill go through him. "This entity—this Galactus—he's a monster."

"Is he?" said Uatu. "By his lights, he is merely a creature who wants to live. Does a blue whale care about the millions of krill it swallows to survive? Does it trouble an aardvark that it devastates an entire termite mound in its quest for food? Galactus knows simply that he hungers, and that his hunger must be assuaged in the only way it can."

"And you believe he has Earth lined up as his next meal?"

Uatu looked somber. "It seems almost certain, for Galactus's herald, the Silver Surfer, is on his way hither."

"He has a herald?"

"It might be more accurate to call him his scout. The Silver Surfer seeks out planets that meet Galactus's criteria for consumption, and Earth is perfect for his master's needs. Although you humans have sullied its biosphere through industrialization and the careless disposal of waste products, it is not so polluted as to be unpalatable. It is vibrant with life. Teeming oceans. Dense forests. Not to mention billions of people."

"Galactus would eat us all?"

"A simplistic way of looking at it," said Uatu. "Galactus would reduce you down to your component molecules, the form in which he may most easily ingest you."

"My God." Reed rubbed his face. "What does an entity like that even look like? I can't begin to imagine."

"Galactus's true form has always been unknowable and unfathomable. He appears to sentient beings in a shape that is recognizable to them. A Skrull will perceive him as a Skrull. A Dire Wraith will perceive him as a Dire Wraith."

"A Dire…?"

"You have not encountered them yet, Dr. Richards. Pray you never will."

"So you're saying a hominin like me will see Galactus as a hominin."

"More or less. He will manifest to you as a larger, superior version of your own species. It is the only way that your five senses can, well, make sense of him."

"So, how do we stop him?" Reed asked.

"You cannot," Uatu the Watcher replied. "What you can do—what *we* can do—is try to prevent the Silver Surfer from summoning him to Earth in the first place."

"Which is where your Matter Mobilizer figures in."

"That is my hope."

"Your... hope?"

"I can promise nothing. The Silver Surfer is imbued with the Power Cosmic. Though but a tiny fraction as powerful as Galactus, he is nonetheless formidable. I do not even know if my plan to camouflage Earth with fire would have succeeded in masking it from his keen perceptions. In all probability he would have seen through the imposture. It was a desperate measure, with a slim chance of achieving the desired result."

"In football it's what's known as a Hail Mary pass."

"I am aware of that phrase. It applies just as aptly to what I intend to do with the Matter Mobilizer. It may work. Far likelier, it will not. But it must be attempted nonetheless."

Reed sat with his head in his hands for several moments, contemplating the information Uatu had just given him.

It was hard to take in. Harder still to accept.

Earth faced the possibility of being consumed by a godlike cosmic entity, just to slake his hunger.

Reed could not recall feeling so small, so insignificant, so helpless.

"Why?" he said eventually.

"Why does Galactus wish to devour your world? I thought I had covered that already. It is not out of malice or hostility. Those concepts are alien to one such as him. He merely needs to––"

"No," said Reed, cutting in, "why are you bothering to help us, Uatu? Why abandon your policy of non-interference to try to save Earth? When you've intervened before, it's been small-scale—nothing that would change the outcome of events in any significant way. This is orders of magnitude different. What would your fellow Watchers think if they knew?"

"If they found out, they would abominate me. They would put me on trial and undoubtedly find me guilty. Then they would strip me of all I hold dear and shun me forever after. I would be an exile and a pariah. I would live the rest of my days in a state of the utmost shame."

Although his tone was matter-of-fact, there was clear pain in Uatu's eyes as he considered this fate.

"And you would risk that much," Reed said, "all for us?"

Uatu hesitated. "I would. I am indeed doing so. And the reason is twofold. Firstly, I cannot deny that I have a great liking and esteem for the people of Earth, acquired over my many, many years of watching you. Granted, you are capable of vile wickedness, you are warlike, you despoil your world, you often treat your fellow beings with cruelty and even savagery..."

"I wish I could disagree."

"Yet you are also capable of remarkable feats of invention and compassion and nobility and love. You strive to create and improve. You yourself, Dr. Richards, with your three teammates, have constantly done your best to help others and defend those less fortunate than you. I have seen how willing you are to fight in the name of what's good and right, often at the expense of your own safety and happiness. The same applies to all those like you who are dubbed 'super heroes'. You are valiant and true and self-sacrificing, and you set an example for others."

"We try to."

"And one day, perhaps, all humans will follow it, and then shall you as a species truly come into your own. For in your race lie the seeds for true greatness. You have the potential to become a positive force throughout the galaxy, spreading your better traits wherever you go. And I—I do not wish to see all that promise snuffed out."

"It's good of you to say so."

"It is no more than the truth."

"And what's the second reason for helping us?"

"Ah, as for that..."

Uatu lowered his head, and Reed detected a certain guiltiness in his bearing, a hint of remorse.

"That," he said, "relates to something one of my kind did, long, long ago—a deed for which I feel all Watchers must bear the blame and the stigma. You see, Dr. Richards, in many ways my people are responsible for Galactus."

"What! How?"

"I believe the Matter Mobilizer is ready," said Uatu, stepping away from the machine. "So now is as good as time as any to explain things."

And he did.

BACK IN THE VERY DIM AND DISTANT PAST

THE NEW universe was still in its infancy, having only recently arisen, phoenix-like, from the ashes of the old.

The cosmic dust was still settling.

The echoes of the Big Bang could still be heard, rippling like far-off thunder.

Yet even then, in those early days, there were Watchers.

They were one of the first truly advanced species. Whereas almost everywhere else, lifeforms were limited to microorganisms, or slime molds, or ocean-dwelling worms, or the occasional crouching, grunting primate, the Watchers were a fully developed, highly sophisticated humanoid species.

They already possessed mighty technology and the capacity for interstellar travel. They also had an insatiable curiosity that compelled them to fan out across the universe and conduct their endless studies.

One Watcher was visiting a remote planet where plant life grew in abundance but the furthest-evolved multicellular animals were simple sponges crawling across the seabed.

This Watcher's name was now lost to history. Either it had slipped from memory over the march of countless eons, or it had been deliberately forgotten, stricken from all records because of the consequences of his actions—or rather, his inaction.

While exploring the primordial planet, he stumbled upon what appeared to be the remnants of a crashed starship.

On closer inspection, the wreckage proved to be more complicated than that. What had once clearly been a starship had been re-formed by some unknown hand into a life-supporting apparatus.

And within this—the only word for it was *cocoon*—lay a living being held in suspended animation.

The Watcher busied himself taking readings of both the reconfigured starship and the dormant creature it contained. The ship's design was unfamiliar. As for the creature, the Watcher determined that it was suffused with energies so immense and strange, they all but defied comprehension.

He spent day after day in fascinated absorption, subjecting this new find of his to every form of analysis available to him.

And the more he discovered about it, the less he understood. The starship's origin lay outside of this universe, while its lone inhabitant, swathed in its patchwork metal casing, exhibited none of the standard markers of sentient life. Its body was saturated with such immense power that the Watcher's instruments struggled to quantify it, let alone identify it.

For a Watcher, detachment from the subject of study was customary. In fact, it was obligatory.

Yet this Watcher could not help growing ever more intrigued, and even excited. In all his long life, he could not remember being as baffled as he was now, and it delighted him.

Then came the time when the cocoon hatched.

IT STARTED to tremble. Its component parts shuddered and rattled. Cracks appeared in its surface, through which shafts of uncanny, coruscating light burst through.

Then, right before the nameless Watcher's eyes, it broke wide open.

What emerged all but defied description. In its earliest moments, it was just a mass of pure energy. Balls of sizzling, crackling plasma rippled across it. All around it, trees were scorched. Grass burned. The ground underfoot shook.

Were the Watcher any less mighty a being, he himself would have suffered injury simply through proximity to this phenomenon. He was buffeted by hurricane-strength winds. Searing heat coursed over his body. The brilliance the energy mass exuded was near blinding.

Gradually, the entity from the cocoon began to adopt a shape. Or rather, its form became comprehensible to the Watcher's perceptions. Vaguely humanlike features developed—arms, legs, a torso, a head.

The Watcher's suite of analytical devices registered not just this being's colossal power but also the fact that that power was depleting at an extraordinary rate. Already its dazzling glow was dimming and the tumultuous forces radiating around it lessening.

Merely by existing, the entity was burning through its own energy reserves with remarkable speed. If it didn't find some means of replenishing them, it would swiftly expire.

The entity itself seemed aware of its predicament. It reached out one armlike extremity, and a tree close by was reduced to a heap of dust, all life sapped from it.

Within an hour, there was no greenery left in a mile radius around the entity.

The Watcher had by then retreated to the safety of his starship. He knew all too well that his own life force was in danger of being absorbed by the entity if he did not seek shelter. He took off and continued to monitor the creature's progress from a safe distance.

This was the moment when the Watcher could have, and perhaps should have, acted. The entity was still in a confused and unsteady state. What sentience it had was as yet imperfectly developed. It was only just beginning to grasp the fact that it lived, and it moved clumsily and at random, a thing of instinct rather than direction.

Nonetheless, the Watcher was in no doubt that, given time, it would evolve into a being of unparalleled greed and rapacity, posing a danger not simply to the world on which it stood, but *all* worlds.

Aboard the Watcher's ship there were defensive devices which, while not strictly weapons, were capable of rendering inert anything that might threaten him. He could have turned one of these on the entity and snuffed out its nascent existence then and there.

He was sorely tempted to do just that. His hand hovered above the relevant activation panel on his control console. At the touch of a couple of buttons, the throw of a lever, the creature's life would be over almost as soon as it had begun.

But the Watcher was beholden to the vow every member of his race took.

He must not tamper with the affairs of living beings.

Whatever he witnessed, however dreadful it might be, however terrible its possible ramifications, he must leave it to run its course.

With a heavy heart, the Watcher withdrew his hand from the activation panel.

What must happen, must happen.

It was in the lap of fate.

o———o

THE WATCHER continued to observe the entity over the next few millennia.

He did his solemn duty, though his soul remained troubled.

He watched the entity grow in stature and solidity, drawing

on the resources of the planet it resided on, piecemeal, in order to sustain itself.

He watched it restructure the starship that had been its cocoon, turning it into a space-going craft once more.

He watched it fashion attire for itself, a suit that betokened majesty and grandeur.

He watched it announce its name, its very first words.

"I... am... Galactus."

WHEN THE planet was finally devoid of all life and energy, Galactus departed in his starship, and the Watcher, maintaining his distance, followed. Whether Galactus was even aware of his presence, he did not know. Did the shark notice the pilot fish that swam in its wake? Did the tornado care about a mote of dust caught in its swirling slipstream?

World after world was visited by Galactus, and world after world succumbed to his appetite. The primitive lifeforms he encountered could offer him no resistance. They were swept up helplessly in the vortex of his nigh-insatiable appetite.

Eons elapsed before Galactus came across a civilization sufficiently advanced to present any sort of opposition.

This was on a verdant world named Archeopia. No sooner did his ship move into orbit above it than the Archeopians recognized it as a threat. Unhesitatingly they launched a fleet of spacecraft to do battle.

The Watcher made sure to hang back, far enough away to ensure that he himself did not inadvertently become embroiled in what was about to happen.

The Archeopians' corvettes, interceptors, and long-range bombers unleashed an awesome amount of firepower upon Galactus's starship. They pummeled it with ion cannons, particle beams, and mass-driven kinetic projectiles. They rained thermonuclear hell down onto it.

They barely put a scratch in it.

Galactus retaliated by stepping forth from his vessel and personally dispatching every last one of the Archeopian ships with blasts of raw power from his hands.

Then he turned his attention to the planet below.

Holocaust ensued.

It was not the utter obliteration that he would visit upon subsequent planets, but it left Archeopia scoured and bare, stripped of anything that had given it vitality.

And when he was done, his hunger sated, Galactus beheld the carnage he had wrought.

And the Watcher beheld him beholding it.

Galactus descended in person to the surface of Archeopia and flew among the ruins of once-great cities. He passed across dried-up oceans and devastated farmland, across jungles that were now deserts and great rolling plains of dustbowl emptiness.

And the Watcher, observing from a very long range, thought he spied something unusual on the habitually expressionless face of the Devourer of Worlds.

Something akin to a look of regret.

He sought to understand why, and came to the only conclusion he could.

Here, for the first time, Galactus had destroyed, not merely plants or crude lifeforms, but people. People with dreams and ambitions, people who created and loved, quarreled and strove.

Could a god feel sorrow? Could a force of nature rue the chaos it had wrought?

If so, Galactus did not indulge in the sentiment for long.

He embarked on the construction of a new starship for himself, this one larger and infinitely more sophisticated than the previous. It was as big as a world—bigger, even—and took the form of that lemniscate-shaped, twisting-in-upon-itself figure known on Earth as a Möbius loop.

It was the work of centuries, and when it was completed, Galactus looked upon what he had done and thought it good.

He christened his new vessel *Taa II*.

Perhaps, the Watcher reasoned, Galactus built himself such a ship as a kind of apology for the annihilation of Archeopia. An act of supreme creation to compensate for an act of supreme destruction.

Or perhaps Galactus had decided that a being such as himself needed a vehicle befitting his quasi-divine status.

If *Taa II* was meant as contrition, it certainly seemed to absolve Galactus of any twinge of conscience he might have experienced over Archeopia.

Because thereafter he consumed worlds without a hint of compunction, and unlike Archeopia, he left nothing whatsoever behind. Not a scrap of habitation, not a single organism, not the least trace of a chemical compound. No evidence that life had once flourished there, or indeed that the planet had been a planet at all.

Better to wipe things clean and move on. That must be his thinking.

So the Watcher surmised, but who could truly say what went on in the mind of a creature like Galactus?

All the Watcher was certain of was that if Galactus ever felt guilt about what he did, it was nothing compared with the guilt he himself felt about what he *hadn't* done.

BACK TO THE BAXTER BUILDING

UATU ENDED his account of Galactus's origins with these words.

"Although it was not I who spared the life of Galactus when it could have been taken," he said, "I cannot help but shoulder some of the blame for the devastation the Devourer of Worlds has wrought since. Trillions of lives have been lost to him and countless worlds eradicated, and these could all have been spared if my fellow Watcher had only stirred himself to deliver a fatal blow."

"Would you have?" Reed asked. "If you'd been in his position?"

Uatu bowed his head. "It is hard to say. Our vow as Watchers is so entrenched in our psyches, so intimately bound up in everything we do and are, that to go against it is to defy our very natures. It is a betrayal of all we hold dear."

Reed motioned at the Matter Mobilizer. "But you're doing just that right now."

"Believe me, Dr. Richards, I have agonized greatly over my decision."

"For what it's worth, Uatu," Reed said, "I'm grateful. I think everyone on Earth would be grateful, if they knew. Your personal ethics have overcome a moral stance that many would see as indefensible."

"That is good to hear, even if it does little to assuage my unease. Now then…"

From the folds of his toga-like robe, Uatu produced a handheld device festooned with knurled knobs, overlapping zigzag patterns and a host of angular protrusions that resembled aerials or antennae.

"This visi-communicator is slaved to the long-range monitors in my home on the moon. With it I can track the Silver Surfer's position in space to within a kilometer. Should he approach Earth, we may initiate the Matter Mobilizer and begin our attempt to repel him."

"Where is he now?"

Uatu consulted the hexagonal screen inset into the face of the device. "I place him within the asteroid ring you humans call the Kuiper Belt."

"In other words, somewhere between Neptune and Pluto. Around thirty astronomical units away. In galactic terms, that's not far at all."

"He is moving at roughly 170 million miles an hour," Uatu said, "which, for him, is quite slow. One might call it cautious, even."

Reed made a mental calculation. "At that rate it'd take him around sixteen hours to reach us."

"Unless he accelerates, yes."

"How fast can he go?"

"A little short of lightspeed."

"So he could be here in under four hours, if he wished."

"He could."

Reed looked over at the Matter Mobilizer. "Then we'd better get this thing up onto the roof, don't you think? So that we'll be good and ready for him. I'll give Ben a buzz and get him to come to the lab. Lugging large pieces of machinery around is his least favorite job, but he'll do it. He'll grumble a lot, but he'll do it."

Ben, however, did not answer when Reed called him on the internal intercom. He tried Ben's rooms, and the purpose-built gym where Ben liked to work out, and the communal recreation area. He wasn't in any of those.

In the end, Reed called Sue, who was in the suite of rooms he and she shared.

"Darling, have you seen Ben?"

"He's gone out," Sue said, "as you'd know, if you'd not been such a hermit. He headed over to Alicia's about an hour ago in the Fantasti-Car—not the fancy new one, the older model. 'Got a date with my best gal,' he said. 'Wouldn't do to leave her hangin'.'" Her impression of Ben's gruff tones was dead-on. "He also said, 'And another thing, Suzie. You can tell Stretcho that if he don't come out of his playpen soon, we're going to bring in the Impossible Man as a substitute leader.' I think he meant it too. Anyway, what do you need him for?"

"Some heavy lifting."

"Well, in his absence, will a woman with the power to project remarkably strong invisible forcefields do?"

Reed had to agree with her that, as a Ben substitute, she would be more than adequate.

OF COURSE, there was some explaining to be done after he admitted her into the laboratory.

It took around five minutes, with both Reed and Uatu sharing the narration.

Another minute or so passed as Sue let the grim news sink in.

Then she clapped her hands purposefully together.

"Right," she said, going over to the Matter Mobilizer. "Let's get this great hunk of metal into the freight elevator, shall we?"

She slid a paper-thin forcefield beneath the machine and

expanded it vertically until the Matter Mobilizer was hoisted a few inches off the floor on a cushion of pure psionic force.

Then, brow knotted in concentration, she shunted the forcefield and its burden towards the elevator doors.

"That's it," Reed said. "Hold it steady. You're doing great, Sue."

"Not patronizing at all, Reed."

"It wasn't meant to be."

"Well, even so, I don't appreciate you speaking to me as though I'm Ben."

"Is that how I talk to Ben?"

"You'd obviously prefer it was him doing this than me. If it helps, I can always refer to this thing as a 'gizmo' or a 'frammistat', like he would."

"Just keep it moving, my dear. *Please.*"

The freight elevator ferried the three of them and the Matter Mobilizer all the way up to its rooftop exit.

There, Sue repeated the process, gliding the machine out onto the Baxter Building's flat summit. She maneuvered it past the observatory dome, around the swimming pool and onward to the helipad.

"Almost there, Sue," Reed said. He was hovering close to the Matter Mobilizer with his hands held out on either side of it. He had expanded them to the size of umbrellas, large enough to catch it if it toppled. "Be careful now."

She lowered the Matter Mobilizer onto the helipad. It came to rest gently as a feather.

She exhaled. "Well, that would have been a great deal easier," she told her husband, "without you clucking around the whole time like a mother hen."

"The Matter Mobilizer's workings are very delicate."

"They're not. That's what you always say about the things you've built—they're delicate—but if I know anything about you, you make them to the highest of specifications and with the most precise of tolerances. Robust enough that even if Ben dropped one of them, it'd be fine. And I can't imagine a Watcher's quality threshold is any lower than yours. Eh, Uatu?"

Uatu's only answer was a small, enigmatic smile.

"You treat your inventions like they're your children, Reed," Sue continued, "and perhaps they are, in a way. But children are a heck of a lot tougher than you might think. Maybe you'll find that out for yourself someday. Possibly sooner rather than later."

Reed peered at her.

Sue stared back.

Then she grinned.

"Don't look so alarmed," she said. "I'm only teasing. Children aren't in our future. Yet."

Uatu retreated to a corner of the rooftop, where he stood consulting his ornate handheld device. It was almost as though he was trying to be discreet, giving Reed and Sue a little space and privacy.

Which was ironic, Sue thought, for someone whose life's work was viewing practically everything that happened on planet Earth.

On the face of it, the idea of a Watcher constantly observing humankind was unsettling, to say the least. Some would even say it was downright creepy.

However, having met this particular Watcher, Sue could set such misgivings aside. He was an aloof character, with a stiff, even haughty manner. But, for all that, he seemed benign.

And if, as now, he was willing to set aside a long-ingrained prohibition in order to help out, that spoke volumes about him.

Lowering her voice, she said to Reed, "You know you could have told me you had the Watcher in your lab. You didn't have to pretend you were alone."

"Uatu and I—"

"Oh, so it's first-name terms, is it? Should I be jealous?"

Reed disregarded the remark. "Uatu and I," he repeated,

"were close to finishing our work on the Matter Mobilizer. I just wanted to get it over the line. I suppose I wasn't thinking straight. I was—I *am* just so very tired, Sue."

He let his arms stretch and droop until they dangled at his feet, coiled like two strands of limp spaghetti.

"That's how tired I am," he said with a wry smile.

"Not so tired you can't clown around," Sue said, "which is good to see. But..." Her mood darkened. "Tell me, Reed. And be honest. This—what's he called again?—Silver Surfer. What chance does your machine have of seeing him off?"

"Not great," Reed replied, snapping his arms back to their default dimensions. "If Uatu's right about him, and there's no reason to think he isn't, then we've never faced anyone whose power is on a comparable scale. And then there's Galactus, who is in a whole other league beyond that. I... Frankly, darling, I don't hold out much hope. You were talking about 'our future' a moment ago. I'm not sure there *is* a future—for any of us."

"No."

The severity in her voice took him aback. She wasn't speaking with denial; she was speaking with passion.

"What do you mean, no?"

"I mean," Sue said, "that we are the Fantastic Four. We take on the biggest threats known to man, and we prevail."

"Well, if our track record is anything to go by, yes. But Sue, this is a crisis like no other we've experienced."

"Reed, listen to me, and listen well. I won't hear this defeatist talk."

"It's hard not to be defeatist when you're looking at possible global extinction."

"We'll find a way," Sue insisted. "We always do. You, with your brain. Ben, with his refusal to ever give up. Johnny, with his sheer self-confidence. And me... Well, I'm the kind of girl who moves immovable objects."

"That's true enough," Reed said, nodding. "I've never known you to let anything stand in your way."

"So, shape up, Mister Fantastic. *Be* fantastic, like I know you can. We're going to get through this, Reed. We're going to save the day, come what may. It's what we do."

Sue only wished she felt half as confident as she sounded.

BEN EXITED the pizza joint with a takeaway box in one hand and Alicia's hand hooked in the elbow of his other arm.

"I got to say, 'Licia, I'm a New York slice guy through and through," he said. "Accept no substitutes. But sometimes only your Chicago deep-dish hits the spot."

"Really, Ben?" said Alicia. "From the way you've just wolfed down two whole ones in a row, and the fact that you ordered a third to go, I'd never have guessed."

"Hey, you don't get muscles like these out of nowhere, baby. They need fuelin'!"

"Is that why you also ate half of my pizza?"

"You were going to leave it. Waste not, want not." Ben chortled. "I mean," he said, returning to his theme, "it ain't like I'm considerin' moving to the Windy City or nothin'. I'm not crazy. All I'm saying is, if I *had* to, it wouldn't be the end of the world."

"I'm sure millions of Chicagoans appreciate your ringing endorsement of their hometown."

"They ought to."

Alicia leaned in close, nuzzling her head against his shoulder. "This really has been a lovely day so far, Ben."

"And it ain't over yet, neither."

"What else do you have planned?" Alicia inquired.

"I was thinkin' we could head on over to the Guggenheim, and I could describe the artworks to you, like we done before."

"Ben, I'd love that! There happens to be a Henry Moore exhibition that I've been meaning to get to. You know how much I like his work. Is that why you suggested it?"

"Uh, sure, babe," Ben said.

"And it's not just a lucky coincidence?"

"'Course not. Would I lie to you?"

"Well, Benjamin Jacob Grimm, I'll believe you, though thousands wouldn't."

Happiness suffused Ben. Could this day get any better?

Earlier, he and Alicia had wandered round Central Park, listening to the buskers.

Then they'd visited a movie theater in the Village showing *Casablanca*, with audio description available on headphones for the sight-impaired. Afterwards, Ben had kept sniffing and rubbing his eyes and complaining about allergies. Nothing to do with the film, of course, and its poignant final scene.

Now, to cap it all off, he had a belly full of primo pizza, and he'd lucked into taking Alicia to a show by one of her favorite sculptors.

It felt like nothing could go wrong today.

"One thing," Alicia said. "Promise me you won't make snarky comments about any of the more avant-garde pieces we come across."

"Not even if it's one that looks like somebody dropped their Erector Set and splashed paint all over it?"

"No."

"What about if it's just a pile of clothes dropped on the floor? I mean, that ain't art—that's a thrift shop donation."

"Not even then, Ben."

"Aw, you ruin all my fun, sweetie."

Alicia slapped him playfully. "Why do I even go out with you? You're such a philistine."

"Phillies fan? How dare you! Yankees till I die."

The most direct route to the Guggenheim meant cutting through an alleyway—the kind of alleyway that the average, law-abiding New Yorker would think twice about before going down. Dark, narrow, lined with dumpsters and overshadowed by tall buildings on either side, it was the perfect spot to ambush some unsuspecting victim and steal their valuables.

But the Fantastic Four's Thing wasn't in danger of being held at knifepoint or gunpoint by muggers. They'd take one look at him and flee in the opposite direction.

Which was what happened now, more or less.

BEN AND Alicia had just turned into the alleyway when two youths came sprinting full tilt towards them from the other end. They wore hoodies with the hoods pulled up over their baseball caps and had bandanas tied around the lower half of their faces, so that only their eyes showed. One was carrying a semiautomatic pistol while the other had a machete.

"'Licia?" Ben said. "Get behind me, babe."

"What is it, Ben? I hear people running."

"Trouble. But don't you worry. I got this. And I won't even have to put this pizza box down."

The two armed youths suddenly caught sight of Ben, and skidded to a halt. Both of them looked over their shoulders, then back at him.

"Cripes!" one exclaimed.

"This just ain't fair," the other lamented.

In unison, they turned on their heels and started running the other way.

They halted again almost immediately.

Behind them, standing on the lid of a dumpster, legs akimbo, was a masked man clad entirely in red. He had seemingly appeared out of nowhere. He was athletically built, lithe and thin, and in his hands he was holding a matching pair of billy clubs, each a foot long. Crowning his cowl was a pair of short, curved horns, while his chest sported a logo consisting of a capital D entwined with another capital D.

"Gentlemen," he said to the two youths, "you may as well give yourselves up. That's none other than the Thing over there. Between me and him, you don't have a prayer."

"Oh yeah, Daredevil?" said the one with the handgun. "We'll see about that."

He started loosing off rounds at Daredevil. Alicia shrieked in alarm and covered her ears. Ben made sure he was standing directly in front of her, in case a stray ricochet came their way. His rocky hide was effectively bulletproof.

As for Daredevil…

He danced around the shots. He seemed to know where every single bullet was about to go and twisted nimbly out of the way. In next to no time, the pistol's magazine was spent, and the shooter hadn't even come close to hitting his target once.

The same could not be said for Daredevil. No sooner had the gunfire ended than he launched one of his billy clubs into the air. It bounced off a wall, then off the base of a fire escape, then off the ground, finally striking the shooter dead in the center of his forehead.

The youth went down like a bowling pin, out cold.

The other youth let out a guttural cry that was a mix of rage, fear and bravado. He ran at Daredevil, waving his machete aloft. As he brought the weapon down, Daredevil turned the blade aside with his other billy club, almost casually, as though batting away a butterfly. He did this twice more, scarcely moving his body, just accurately deflecting the machete with the least amount of exertion possible.

"Ben, what's happening now?" Alicia asked.

"Nothin' much," Ben replied. "Just a surgeon at work."

The fourth time the youth swung the machete at him, Daredevil ducked under it and came up again at lightning speed. He drove an uppercut into the youth's chin that practically lifted him out of his sneakers. The guy spun around a couple of times on the spot, much as though performing a pirouette, then teetered and slumped to the grimy floor of the alleyway.

Ben cheered and whistled.

Daredevil gave a little bow.

"Thank you for being such an appreciative audience, Mr. Grimm," he said, stooping to retrieve the billy club he'd thrown. He slotted it and its counterpart into holster loops strapped to his thigh.

"Nah, pleasure's mine, Hornhead."

"And thank you, too, for not getting involved. I needed the exercise."

"I knew you had it sewn up. Didn't need no help from me, not with a couple of lowlife bottom-feeders like these."

"And who is this lovely friend of yours?" Daredevil said, turning to Alicia.

"Oh yeah, you guys ain't met. Daredevil, this is Alicia Masters, the love of my life. Alicia, Daredevil."

Daredevil took Alicia's hand in his, bent from the waist, and kissed it, like some swashbuckling character from an old movie. "Ms. Masters. The famous sculptor, no less. Delighted to make your acquaintance. And may I say your perfume is exquisite. Chanel, am I right?"

"I told you about Daredevil, didn't I, hun?" Ben said. "How he saved me and the others a few weeks back, when we lost our powers that time and Doc Doom took over the Baxter Building?"

"I remember," Alicia said. "According to Ben, Daredevil, you took on Doctor Doom all by yourself. That was incredibly brave."

"They don't call me the Man Without Fear for nothing," Daredevil said.

"More like the Man Without Sanity," Ben joshed. He jerked a thumb at Daredevil. "This guy, 'Licia, don't got no super-powers that I know of. Just guts and skill. A glorified acrobat, basically. No offense, DD."

"Some taken."

"And still," Ben continued to Alicia, "he stood up to Doom, and came within a hair of gettin' killed for it. Luckily Reed got the four of us our powers back just in time and we sent old Dooma-roonie packing. It was a close-run thing."

Ben studied the two unconscious youths at their feet.

"So tell me," he said, "what'd this pair of bozos do?"

"Held up a liquor store," Daredevil replied. "You'll find they each have a few hundred dollars stuffed in their pockets. I was out on patrol and happened to swing by on my billy club cable just as they came running out of the store."

"Don't you normally patrol at night?"

"I do, but since the whole sky-on-fire thing the city's been spooked and on edge, and that tends to bring the lowlifes out of their hidey-holes. Unrest is catnip to them. So, I've stepped up my rounds and been keeping an eye on things during the daytime as well as after dark. Anyway, as I said, I came across these two scurrying out of that liquor store, and they took one look at me and scrammed. I chased them down this alleyway, and you know the rest. I'm going to haul them to the nearest police station, then return the money to the store owner."

"You're a regular knight in shinin' armor."

"Not all heroes wear capes, Mr. Grimm. In fact, I think only Thor does. Otherwise it's the villains."

"That's another thing about this guy, Alicia," Ben said. "He's a wisecracker, like Spider-Man. Though, if you ask me, DD's a whole lot funnier. That web-slinger's constant yammerin' just gets on my—"

"Ssh!" Daredevil cut in.

"What's up?"

"Do you hear that?"

"Hear what?"

"It's..." The Man Without Fear cocked his head to one side. "A low hum. Like nothing I've heard before."

"You see ears on this head of mine?" said Ben. "They're there but they're tiny. Can't say hearing's what I do best. Now, eyebrows I got in spades, but ears? Not so much."

Daredevil laid a hand on the nearest wall. "It's so deep and reverberant, it's making the brickwork tremble."

"You sure it ain't the subway?"

"There aren't any lines running nearby. This is something else. It's more a pressure in the air."

"I'm hearing it too, Daredevil," Alicia said. "You're right, it's sensation more than sound."

Daredevil moved off towards the alleyway entrance. "It's coming from this direction."

Alicia slipped a hand into the crook of Ben's elbow and gave a tug, which he knew meant she wanted him to help her follow Daredevil.

As they emerged onto the street, Ben saw that Daredevil was hunched over, peering around, clearly trying to pinpoint the source of the mysterious hum. How the guy could distinguish a single sound amid the overall racket of daytime midtown Manhattan, Ben had no idea. For that matter, he was unsure how Daredevil could see through the eyeholes of his mask, which were covered by opaque red lenses. He presumed they were made of some kind of material with one-way transparency, much like the all-white eyeholes in Spider-Man's mask. They just looked way less penetrable than Spidey's, somehow.

"There." Daredevil was pointing. "That's the origin of the noise."

Ben squinted. "But that's..." The man's finger was aimed at

a structure he knew all too well. "That's the dang-blasted Baxter Building."

"Well, what do you think might be happening there to cause it?"

"Ten-to-one it's Reed. Fact is, Stretcho's been hunkered down in his lab lately, beaverin' away on a project. I ain't seen hide nor hair of him."

"Then I would submit that, on the available evidence, whatever Dr. Richards has been working on is now operational."

"You know that sounds like lawyer talk?"

"I've been told I do that sometimes," Daredevil said.

"Just a moment." Ben shaded his eyes. "Is that…? Nah. Can't be. My eyes must be deceivin' me."

"What, Ben?" said Alicia. "What can you see?"

"Tell me you see it too, Hornhead."

Daredevil looked briefly nonplussed. "Some kind of mass?" he hazarded. "Above the building."

"'Mass' is the word," Ben said. "It's a huge boulder, from the looks of it. It's just moved into place and is hovering there. Oh wait. Now there's another. Sailin' in from over the East River. The heck is this? And here comes yet another."

"Boulders, Ben?" said Alicia.

"Real big ones. They're coming in from all directions now. Dozens of 'em, flyin' through the air, gatherin' over the Baxter Building. It's like birds flocking. I don't like this. Not one bit."

"Do you think it's Reed's doing?"

"If it ain't, we're in trouble. And if it is, I want to know what he's up to. DD? Can I ask you a favor?"

"Name it, Mr. Grimm."

"For starters, it's 'Ben'. And for seconds, I'd like you to escort Alicia to her apartment, while I head for the Baxter Building to take a look-see. Will you do that for me?"

"Ben," said Alicia, "I'm perfectly capable of getting home by myself."

"I know that, babe. But remember what happened when the sky caught fire? The whole city went bananas. I'm worried the same thing's going to happen again, once people glom all those big rocks floatin' around up there. I don't like the idea of you out on the streets alone if there's another panic."

"You make a compelling case, Ben," Daredevil said. "It would be my honor to see Ms. Masters safely to her house."

"I'm trusting you with the one person who matters to me more than anythin', DD. And also this pizza." He handed the takeaway box to Daredevil.

Daredevil hefted it in his hand. "Feels like Chicago deep-dish, from the weight of it. Heavy on the pepperoni. The anchovies too. And also… spinach?"

"If it works fer Popeye, it works fer me," Ben said. "What are you anyway? Some kind of pizza savant?"

"I have a sensitive nose."

"Well, goody fer you. Just look after 'em, will you? Alicia *and* the pizza. Not that the pizza's anywhere near as important as she is, but I'd still be obliged if you'd get 'em both home in one piece."

"I won't let you down. On either count."

"You'd better not. Honey?"

"I'll be fine, darling." Alicia went up on tiptoe and kissed him. "You go."

Ben had left the Fantasti-Car parked on the roof of Alicia's apartment building, which was farther away than the Baxter Building was. His quickest option was simply to travel on foot.

With one last wistful glance at Alicia, he set off at a loping jog.

o———o

DAREDEVIL TUCKED the pizza box under one arm and bent the other towards Alicia.

"My elbow is a few inches in front of your right hand," he said.

Alicia slipped her hand into the crook of his elbow and took ahold.

"Please," he said, "lead the way."

"We're on Thirty-fourth, correct?" she asked.

"Correct."

"And judging by the feel of the sun on my face, west is that direction. Which means we need to turn round and go east, then head south when we hit Sixth Avenue."

They began walking.

"Don't take this the wrong way, Ms. Masters..."

"It's Alicia. And I'd like to call you something else other than Daredevil, but I realize how it is with you super heroes and your secret identities."

"Well, Alicia, all I was going to say was that I know a thing or two about blindness. I have a... a close friend. Matt Murdock."

"The attorney."

"The same."

"I know about him. He has sight loss, like me."

"He does. He's mentioned you more than once. And if he were here right now, I'm sure he would want you to know that he thinks you're a shining light among the blind community, an example to the rest."

"As Mr. Murdock himself is," said Alicia. "The truth is, Daredevil—him and me and those like us, we're just people, getting by with what we've got. Yes, we have to make adaptations, and we trust that others will make allowances for us. But then that's true of everyone, isn't it? In a way, all of us are groping through life in the dark, trying not to bump into anything, reaching out to touch others, hoping to make connections."

"I couldn't have put it better myself, Alicia."

"The trick is never to be afraid. Never to let the thought of what you lack get you down. Never to give in to the expectation that you might be 'less' in any way."

She patted his arm, feeling the taut, sinewy strength of the muscles beneath the fabric of his costume.

"What do you think to that, Daredevil?" she said.

"I think," said Daredevil with a smile, "that the Man Without Fear has just met the Woman Without Fear."

THE SILVER Surfer was coming.

It was indisputable.

Uatu the Watcher's visi-communicator had registered that the Surfer was on the move—no question about it, he was making a beeline for planet Earth. He was now less than an hour away, and Uatu and Reed Richards had duly gone ahead and activated the Matter Mobilizer.

A last-ditch effort.

A final throw of the dice.

Perhaps the only hope of preventing the end of the world.

The machine was attracting enormous boulders towards itself from all points of the compass. In national parks, in wildernesses, in remote rural regions all over the northern USA and Canada, the rocks were tearing themselves out of the ground and levitating across the countryside at a steady, rapid pace, to converge on New York City—specifically on the Baxter Building.

The Matter Mobilizer had been programmed so that the boulders did not enter civilian or military airspace, and stayed low to the ground so as not to show up on radar systems and trigger unnecessary alarms in air traffic control centers. They swerved around tall structures and hurdled mountains.

More of them, and yet more, amassed in the air above the Fantastic Four's headquarters. They formed a huge swarm overhead, casting the Baxter Building into shade. The Matter Mobilizer thrummed mightily as it kept all the boulders in suspension. It alone was holding many thousands of tons of mineral aloft.

Reed could only marvel at the technology involved. Even though he had assisted Uatu in setting up the Matter Mobilizer, he had only the merest inkling how it worked. He theorized that it generated a wave which repelled the massless elementary particles known as gravitons—the force of nature that mediated all gravitational interactions. This would mean that the Watchers had resolved quantum field theory and thereby proved that gravitons, which human scientists still considered hypothetical, did actually exist. Even for someone such as Reed, the implications were mind-boggling.

One day he would quiz Uatu on this topic. Assuming Uatu was allowed to answer his questions without it impinging on the Watchers' vow, it would help him learn so much. It would give him insights into the fundamental underpinnings of the universe and surely lead him to world-changing scientific breakthroughs of his own.

One day, yes. But that day was not today.

Today, Reed knew he must focus solely on warding the Silver Surfer away from Earth.

Otherwise there would be no call for world-changing scientific breakthroughs, ever.

Because, in all likelihood, there would be no world left to change.

JOHNNY STORM flamed on and flew out of the window of his room, up to the roof of the Baxter Building.

Moments earlier, he had been mulling over his college acceptance letter for the umpteenth time since receiving it. So far, he hadn't mentioned getting a place at Metro to anyone, not even Sue. He knew he wanted to go, and he knew he had to inform Sue, Reed and Ben of his decision, but he hadn't been able to figure out how.

Besides, Reed had been a recluse these past three days, squirreled away in his lab. That had put Sue on edge, and Johnny wanted everyone to be in a calm, open frame of mind when he made his big announcement. It wasn't the kind of news you broke casually. It needed to be at the right time, in the right circumstances.

He rubbed the back of his head absently, his fingers chancing upon the lump left by the chunk of concrete that had been hurled at him the other day. The bruise had gone down but the area of scalp was still tender. Johnny wondered what would have happened to him if Ben hadn't turned up in the nick of time. He knew that the people who had attacked him were just frightened and angry, but still, you sometimes had to ask yourself if the human race really was worth saving.

Maybe the Inhumans were better off staying isolated from *Homo sapiens*, he thought ruefully.

Not that he wanted that. The opposite. He wished Crystal was here right now, next to him. She, he was sure, would have listened to his woes with a patient ear. Some people you just knew you could pour your heart out to. She was one of them.

Not a day went by that Johnny didn't think about Crystal. Was she missing him as much as he missed her? Nah. Not possible. *No one* had ever missed anyone as badly as he was missing Crystal. That gorgeous face, those empathetic eyes, the way her hair hung in a glossy swoop, the cute accent she spoke with, her liveliness, her spark…

A girl like that came along once in a lifetime. The feeling of being separated from her was a physical pain, a constant gnawing ache in the pit of Johnny's stomach, almost like a hunger.

At least Reed was trying to figure out how to bring down the Great Refuge barrier, meaning the two of them could one day get back together. Johnny was pinning his hopes on his genius brother-in-law finding the answer, and soon.

He'd been so absorbed in these thoughts that he didn't notice, at first, the deep, droning vibration that was passing through the Baxter Building. It wasn't until the daylight outside the window started darkening—well before sunset—that he was alerted to something weird going on. He looked out to see rocks collecting in the sky overhead.

Now, he alighted on the roof. There was Reed. There was Sue. And… the Watcher? And some kind of large mechanical thingamajig, humming and shimmering and whirring. Not to mention about a kajillion boulders floating directly above the building.

"Oh boy," Johnny said, flaming off. "Obviously a lot has been happening that I don't know about. Somebody bring me up to speed, *please*."

"There isn't much time, Johnny," said Sue, "but I'll do my best."

Johnny listened as his sister filled him in on everything, from the nature of the large mechanical thingamajig to the dire reason why the Watcher was present.

His blood ran cold.

"Couldn't you have told us about it sooner, Reed?" he said. "Given us a bit of a heads-up?"

"I'm sorry, Johnny," Reed replied. "Once Uatu showed up last night, all I could think about was solving the problem. Nothing else seemed to matter."

Resolutely Johnny clenched his fists, and his teeth. "But we can fight off this Surfer guy, surely."

"By the sound of it, no," said Sue. "He's too much, even for us. We just have to cross our fingers and hope Uatu's plan succeeds."

"But if it doesn't…"

"Then we *will* face off against the Silver Surfer, and we'll give it all we've got."

"Where's Ben? Seems like we could do with the Thing right now."

"Somebody mention my name?"

Ben emerged from the elevator, striding purposefully across the rooftop towards his teammates.

"'Cause if it's a certain blue-eyed idol of millions you're lookin' for," he went on, "look no further. I came as soon as I saw all that floating-rock craziness going on up there. Anybody care to tell me what in blazes this is all about? And why's the Watcher hangin' around?"

Sue repeated what she'd told Johnny.

"Ah, for the love of Mike!" Ben groaned. "I guess I should've known the moment I laid eyes on old Cueball that it was something serious. He wouldn't've come down from the moon for anything less. The fate of the world hangin' in the balance? Again? Sheesh! Don't we ever catch a break?"

"I'm not sure this is the time for flippancy, Ben," Reed said. "We've never been confronted with so serious a threat before."

"Which is exactly why it *is* the time for flippancy. Or would you rather see a grown man fall to his knees and start sobbin'?"

"The Silver Surfer is almost upon us," Uatu the Watcher said, looking up from his visi-communicator. "He is just passing Jupiter. We must send the boulders into space to intercept him."

He and Reed bent over the Matter Mobilizer and began manipulating dials and switches. The thrum from the machine deepened further to a tremendous, whalesong-like moan, and the massed boulders above began to rise, as one.

In a rough sphere, the enormous agglomeration of rocks ascended heavenward. Soon they were at so high an altitude, Johnny could blot them from his sight simply by holding up a hand.

"What happens now?" he asked.

"Now," said Uatu, "the boulders will move into a low-orbit position whereby they meet the oncoming Surfer. They will surround him, bombard him from all sides, and, it is hoped, baffle him. The aim is to disorient him sufficiently that he is thrown off course, away from Earth. If, by this means, he can be diverted to another solar system altogether, so much the better."

"What are the odds on it workin'?" said Ben.

"I'm optimistic," Reed said.

"No disrespect, Stretcho, but I want to hear it from the big guy." Ben jabbed a stubby forefinger at Uatu. "He seems to know more about this Surfer fella than anyone. So, what do you say, Watcher?"

"The odds of success?" Uatu's voice was as devoid of expression as ever, but his face betrayed concern. "Not even low. Vanishingly remote."

"Okay. Great," said Ben. "Well, leastways you're bein' honest."

Johnny Storm was not normally the praying kind. At that moment, however, he sent up a brief entreaty to his maker.

To think that, half an hour ago, his biggest worries had been an absent girlfriend and how to break it to his teammates that he was going to college!

AS THE Silver Surfer neared the inhabited planet, he scanned it carefully and intently.

It was a great, shimmering green-and-blue orb, teeming with life. Over two-thirds of its surface was covered in ocean, whose tides were swayed by the presence of a barren, airless moon. The rest was an array of different terrains ranging from frozen waste to arid desert, dense forest to grassy plain, steaming swamp to rugged mountain. Each of these environments was, in its own way, dramatic and spectacularly beautiful.

The dominant species on this world was humanoid, like the Surfer himself, and numbered several billion. They had developed huge swathes of land for a variety of purposes: agricultural use, urbanization and industrialization.

A byproduct of their handiwork was a higher level of atmospheric carbon dioxide than was safe. Already this was having an effect on the planet's climate, triggering unpredictable and sometimes devastating weather events. Unless curbed, the harm would only increase exponentially, until in due course the ecosphere would become uninhabitable for higher lifeforms.

Still closer to the planet, the Silver Surfer attuned his senses to pick up telecommunication signals radiating from a host of sources, on a range of wavelengths. Information flooded his mind. He processed words spoken in countless different languages, all of which he learned fluently in an instant.

The world had a name, a rather prosaic one: Earth.

And Earth was, the Surfer soon ascertained, an embattled place. The dominant species, who referred to themselves as human beings, were deeply tribal and corralled themselves in nation-states that were organized largely along racial, religious and ethnic lines. Countries warred against other countries, with conflict such a global commonplace that there had, by all accounts, never been a single day of peace since recorded history began.

Not only that, on an individual level these human beings routinely murdered, robbed and assaulted one another. A few had wealth, many did not, and the disparity between rich and poor fostered tension and unrest. Some populations were well fed, others starved. It wasn't unusual for those with power and influence to exploit those who had little or none. Few people, if any, seemed truly content with their lot.

All this the Surfer gleaned in a matter of moments from the reams of data that Earth was giving off like a burning coal shedding heat. He noted, too, that the humans were also capable of generous acts, kindness and compassion. There were loving families, and communities who worked together to make things better for themselves and their neighbors. He identified some marvelous specimens of creativity and inspiration—music and architecture and entertainment and suchlike.

Yet mostly the denizens of Earth were an unevolved lot. Their scientific prowess outstripped their emotional maturity. They had devised weapons of such unimaginable mass lethality that they could easily obliterate themselves with them, and on several occasions had come close to doing just that, whether through misunderstanding, miscalculation, or military misadventure. Their future survival teetered on a knife edge.

None of this really mattered, however. Not if Galactus was to consume the planet. The Devourer of Worlds could, in the space of just a few hours, bring down the curtain on the human race's precarious existence. Some might argue he would merely be hastening the inevitable.

Nor would Galactus spell the end of just humankind. He would scour the planet clean of every last scrap of life, until there wasn't so much as a bacterium remaining.

The Silver Surfer did not question the morality of this action. The Surfer served only to find sustenance for his master.

And Earth, in his judgment, afforded Galactus a veritable feast.

BEING SO preoccupied with the wonders and tribulations and contradictions of the world before him, the Silver Surfer failed to detect the multitude of boulders sweeping towards him at lightning speed.

Not until the last moment, at least.

The first boulder almost collided with him, but the Surfer was alerted to the imminent impact by his spacefaring senses, which were as finely tuned to danger as a cat's. He ducked aside, and the massive, rugged hunk of rock whooshed past, missing him by nanometers.

Likewise, the next boulder almost struck him, but the Surfer twisted nimbly out of its path.

More boulders came, and yet more, a torrent of them, flung up from Earth. By now the Silver Surfer was well aware this was no natural phenomenon—he was under attack. Poised perfectly on his surfboard, he darted this way and that as the rocks came at him. Man and board were as one, the Surfer scarcely having to think as he swerved, slalomed and side-slid, his given mode of transportation responding instantly to his every mental command.

Even as new boulders cannoned towards him, the ones that had passed him wheeled round and hurtled back at him from the opposite direction.

Reaching out with both hands, the Surfer let loose with the full force of the Power Cosmic. Bolts of scintillating energy poured from his fingertips, blasting the boulders and reducing them to dust.

The Surfer dodged and evaporated boulders simultaneously. It was a spaceborne ballet of evasion and destruction, conducted with grace and contemptuous ease. He who could weather meteor storms, who could zoom around speeding asteroids, who could race untouched through the debris fields that made up planetary rings, had little difficulty dealing with the threat the boulders presented. The tiniest frown of concentration creased his gleaming, silvery brow as he methodically whittled away at the salvo of rocks, until at last none remained.

Briefly the Surfer paused, taking stock. Around him a great gray cloud swirled and billowed—several thousand tons of solid mineral, pulverized.

Who had launched this assault against him? What purpose had they hoped it would serve? To repel him? Redirect him?

Did they not know who he was? *What* he was?

The boulders had been sent from Earth and controlled by someone down there on its surface. Someone had the ability to marshal and manipulate the very fabric of the planet, and has employed it in an offensive capacity.

Such a level of technological proficiency was beyond the human race, in the Surfer's assessment. There was an anomaly here, and it bore investigating.

Before he summoned Galactus, the Surfer would find out the answer to the mystery. It wouldn't take long, for one gifted with the Power Cosmic.

He detected the source of the boulders. The trail left by the particular form of energy used to maneuver and aim them—imperceptible to most, but perfectly visible to the Surfer's eyes—led back to a continent that straddled Earth's equator. There, in a sprawling coastal city in the continent's northern region, was where the rocks had originated.

o———o

GRAVELY, RUEFULLY, Uatu the Watcher shook his head.

"Our ploy," he said, "has not met with success." He indicated his visi-communicator. "The Silver Surfer was scarcely hindered by the boulders."

"Where is the Surfer now?" Reed asked.

"On his way here."

"Here? You mean to Earth?"

"To this very spot, I would judge. He surely seeks to learn where the boulders were sent from."

"So all we've done," said Sue, "is alert him to the Fantastic Four's presence and bring him right to our doorstep."

"I'm afraid so," said Uatu.

"Then let's get ready," said Johnny, flaming on. "We'll roll out the welcome mat for him."

Ben clenched a fist and thumped it into the palm of his other hand. "Well said, Matchstick. When he gets here, this Surfer guy's going to find out what time it is."

o———o

THE SILVER Surfer hit Earth's atmosphere somewhere over the mid-Atlantic, at an altitude of roughly sixty miles above sea level.

His speed slowed fractionally as he exchanged the vacuum of space for atmospheric friction. Rapidly a glow formed around him, the pressure wave generated by his sheer velocity ionizing the air molecules and surrounding him in a sheet of incandescent, electrostatically charged plasma. He barely registered the intense heat through his silvery skin.

The Surfer bent forward until his torso was parallel with his board, lowered his head, and stretched his arms out behind him. The posture sharpened his aerodynamic profile and reduced drag. The plasma glow faded, and the Surfer became a clean quicksilver streak in the sky, soaring across the ocean towards the east coast of a nation he knew to be called the United States of America.

Towards a city he knew to be called New York.

Towards a structure he knew to be called the Baxter Building.

THE FANTASTIC Four stood poised on the rooftop. Mister Fantastic stretched his limbs and trunk to make himself taller, broader and more imposing. The Invisible Woman erected a shield-like forcefield, in case of need. The Thing crouched with his fists up, like a boxer waiting for the bell to ring and the round to start.

Johnny flamed on. His every nerve tingled with anticipation. He felt fire crackling and rippling around his body, and reveled in the power he possessed. All thoughts of Crystal and college were banished from his mind. He was focused only on what was about to happen. A battle, no doubt. Against a foe who—if the Watcher was to be believed—was all but unbeatable. And the fate of the world at stake.

These were the moments Johnny lived for.

Some people called him a hothead. He was cool with that. Sometimes it was better not to think too much, just react. It got things done.

Some people also called him a showoff. He didn't mind that either. It was true. His powers were flashy and flamboyant, and he enjoyed using them. Who wouldn't?

But, all said and done, there was a lot more to it. To *him*.

When duty called, Johnny Storm never shirked. He had a sense of obligation as a member of the Fantastic Four and he always tried to live up to it, even when, as now, it might put him in grave danger.

He was still only a kid—much though it pained him to admit it—but he had done a heck of a lot more than other kids his age. He had helped see off extraterrestrial invasions. Time-traveled into the far-flung past. Journeyed to an undersea kingdom, and a subterranean one as well. Been in space. Met gods and monsters. Gone toe to toe with the most menacing super villains the world had to offer. That sort of thing made a guy grow up fast.

Just about the only teenager he knew who'd had similar life experiences was Spider-Man, which was why the two of them got along pretty well. They hadn't hit it off the first couple of times they met, but since then they'd formed a bond. Johnny still didn't know the real name of the person behind that slightly creepy web-patterned full-face mask, but he and Spidey had nevertheless hung out together now and then, usually on top of the Statue of Liberty, and chewed the fat; and it was nice having someone to compare notes with, someone who understood what it was like to be a young super hero—the risks, the pressures, the responsibilities.

Johnny scanned the skies now, braced for the Silver Surfer's imminent arrival.

He burned.

With dread.

With hope.

With literal fire.

He burned.

THE SILVER Surfer appeared almost out of nowhere.

One moment, the sky above Manhattan was empty.

The next, a figure on a flying surfboard manifested, drawing close to the Baxter Building, performing an exploratory circuit around the famous skyscraper.

The Human Torch leapt into action. Without hesitating, he launched himself aloft from the rooftop, rocketing towards the Surfer, leaving a blazing trail behind him.

Moving at top speed, he was on a course to intercept the Surfer.

The Surfer dodged. He and his board darted aside so swiftly, so handily, it was as though the Human Torch was going at a snail's pace.

The Torch made a U-turn in midair, looking left, right, up and down to see where his quarry had got to.

The Surfer was several hundred yards away, hovering. He cocked his head to one side. Those blank, pale eyes of his seemed to be studying the Torch, making assessments.

"Got to say, pal," the Torch said, "you're quick. But are you quick enough to avoid *this*?"

The Torch hurtled straight at the Surfer, at the same time discharging a powerful flame burst from either hand.

Again—with barely any effort, or so it seemed—the Surfer evaded the attack. He grabbed the tip of his board and barrel-rolled around the twin flame bursts. They petered out uselessly into nothingness.

"Okay," the Human Torch said, sounding more than a little peeved. "Now you're really starting to tick me off. Will you hold still just one second?"

He began hurling fireballs at the Surfer. Each was as big as a grapefruit, conjured up thanks to Johnny's talent for pyrokinesis—his ability to shape and manipulate flame through thought alone, and if necessary, wield it offensively.

None of the fireballs even came close to making contact with its target.

Meanwhile, down below on the roof of the Baxter Building,

Mister Fantastic and the Invisible Woman exchanged looks.

"The Silver Surfer is just toying with Johnny," Mister Fantastic said to his wife. "It's obvious Johnny is no threat to him whatsoever."

"I know, Reed," the Invisible Woman replied. "But give him a chance. He's still getting the measure of him."

The Thing looked on as the one-sided aerial combat continued, one hand raised to shade his eyes. His craggy face displayed a sense of misgiving similar to that of his two teammates. The Silver Surfer was running rings around the Torch. What would happen when eventually, inevitably, the Surfer retaliated?

The answer came the very next moment.

The Human Torch paused to regroup, considering a different approach. The Silver Surfer lifted a hand and unleashed a bolt of bright white energy. It struck the Torch with such force that he was sent pinwheeling through the air. His flame was partly extinguished, and it was only thanks to some desperate maneuvering that he was able to land safely on the top of an adjacent skyscraper. He lay there stunned, a few small tongues of fire still flickering, licking up and down his body.

"Is he...?" said the Invisible Woman worriedly.

"He looks unharmed," said Mister Fantastic. "Just had the wind knocked out of him."

"That," said Uatu the Watcher, "was the Silver Surfer deploying the tiniest fraction of his full might. He could easily have obliterated young Mr. Storm had he wished to. Count yourselves lucky he chose to be merciful."

"I'll show *him* mercy," growled the Thing. "Hey!" he yelled up at the Surfer. "You! Yes, you, Chrome Dome!"

The Silver Surfer peered down at the thickset, orange-hued being who was calling to him.

"C'mon down here," the Thing said. "I want a word. Three words, actually."

The Surfer descended slowly, with curiosity, to the roof. He skimmed to a halt in front of the Thing and stepped off his surfboard.

"You," he said, "are Benjamin Grimm, also known as the Thing. And you"—he turned to the other two members of the Fantastic Four—"are Reed Richards, also known as Mister Fantastic, and Sue Richards, also known as the Invisible Woman."

"And you," said the Thing, "are the Silver Surfer, also known as dogmeat."

He drew back an arm and threw a punch hard enough to demolish a house.

The Surfer was sent flying. He vanished over the side of the building in a flail of limbs.

The Thing brushed his palms together. "Well, that takes care of that. And I didn't even have to say my catchphrase."

The surfboard suddenly took off, shooting after its owner.

Moments later, both board and Surfer reappeared, rising together from behind the edge of the roof. The Surfer looked none the worse for wear, despite having just taken a blow that could possibly have felled the mighty Thor.

"Aw, man!" the Thing groaned. "That was my best haymaker, and look at him. Not even a dent in that skinny little body."

The Surfer landed once more on the rooftop. "You tried to hurt me, Benjamin Grimm."

"Darn right I did."

"Please desist."

But the Thing simply lowered his head, like a bull about to charge. "I don't do desistin'," he said. "Ain't in my nature."

"Ben..." Mister Fantastic warned.

The Thing, however, was already running. He thundered towards the Silver Surfer, who stood his ground, clearly unperturbed.

"It's clob—" the Thing began, but he didn't get to complete his signature battle cry.

The Surfer gestured, almost casually, as though flicking the air. Another of those bright white bolts issued forth from his hand, halting the Thing in his tracks.

The Thing tottered forward a couple of steps, then sagged to his knees.

He tried to rise, but a further blast from the Surfer brought him low again.

"Urghh," the Thing croaked. "Arms, legs... numb. Feel so heavy. Can't hardly stand. What a... revoltin' development... this is."

Uatu the Watcher addressed Mister Fantastic and the Invisible Woman. "Brute force cannot prevail against the Silver Surfer. You do not need me to tell you that. You have seen it for yourselves."

"Then what do you suggest?" the Invisible Woman inquired.

"Negotiation," said Mister Fantastic. "It's all we've got left. We have to try to talk the Surfer out of bringing Galactus here."

Uatu nodded. "I have interfered enough already. This is up to you now. I wish you luck."

He took a step back, folded his arms over his chest, and watched.

REED UNSTRETCHED his body, reducing his dimensions to normal size. He moved towards the Silver Surfer, passing the immobilized Ben. Sue accompanied him.

He spared a glance for his friend as he went by. He hated to see Ben like this, on his knees, more or less paralyzed. The Surfer must have disrupted his nervous system somehow, causing some kind of neural short circuit and leaving him an enfeebled wreck. And then there was the ease with which he had dispensed with Johnny. This "Power Cosmic" of his, whatever it was, seemed limitless.

"Surfer," Reed said, halting in front of the slender humanoid alien, Sue beside him.

"Yes, Dr. Richards?" said the Surfer. He stood holding his board upright, a pose much like that of a California surfer waiting on the beach for the waves to start breaking just right.

"We know why you have come to Earth. We know what your presence here signifies."

"The Watcher over there has doubtless explained everything to you. I suspect it is he who is responsible for trying to deflect me with those boulders. You, with your civilization's current level of technology, would not have been capable of such a feat. I admit I am curious why a Watcher has permitted himself to meddle in your planet's affairs. It is unheard of. Doubtless he has his reasons, and in due course perhaps I shall discover them, but for now they need not detain me. I have a mission to complete."

"And that's what I want to discuss with you," Reed said. "Your mission."

"What is there to discuss?" said the Silver Surfer. "Your planet is destined for my master Galactus's consumption. All I need do is send a subspace signal to him, and he will come."

"Understood. You have a job to do. But Earth is home to several billion human beings, not to mention a host of other sentient species. By bringing Galactus here, you will be culpable in their destruction."

"I have led my master to countless inhabited worlds," the Surfer said. "Through me, he has annihilated thousands of civilizations. Why is yours any different?"

"It isn't," Reed admitted.

"In many respects," the Surfer continued, "you humans are primitive. Galactus has consumed planets whose populations were far more advanced, far more cultured, than Earth's. Why should you be spared when they were not? What makes you better than them, more deserving of leniency?"

"Do you not have feelings?" Sue said. "Don't you feel guilt over the countless deaths you have been complicit in?"

The Surfer gave her a blank look. "Why should I, Susan Richards? I exist to serve Galactus's needs. He has entrusted me with the task of keeping him fed and alive. My sole motivation is that. All other urges are subordinate."

"You do have other urges, then."

"They are…" The silver-skinned being paused. "Irrelevant. As is this conversation. You cannot dissuade me from my purpose. What must be, will be. The course is set and cannot be deviated from."

The Surfer lifted his free hand, aiming it skyward.

There was no obvious threat in the gesture. Reed intuited that the Surfer was about to communicate with Galactus, initiating that subspace signal he had just mentioned.

Reed elongated both arms and wrapped them like ribbons around the Surfer's arm. He hauled back, straining, attempting to pull the Surfer's hand down.

The Surfer's arm did not budge. He stared at Reed with a mixture of puzzlement and pity. Hard as Reed tugged, the Surfer resisted, keeping his arm aloft effortlessly.

A nimbus of raw energy crackled around his upraised hand. It brightened until it was blinding.

"Stop!" Reed said. "Don't do it." He could feel, via his arms, the sheer awesome power the Surfer's hand was generating. It seared through the sleeves and gloves of his costume, singeing his skin. He held on all the same, doggedly, despite the pain.

"Why do you persist in trying to forestall the inevitable?" the Surfer said.

"Let go of him, Reed," said Sue. "I'll deal with this."

Reed heeded his wife's words. He unraveled his arms, reverting them to their natural length.

At the same moment, Sue conjured an invisible battering ram. She drew it back—a long, thick rod of rock-solid psionic force—and prepared to impel it with all her mental might at the Silver Surfer.

The Surfer's hand ceased glowing.

"It is done," he said. "Galactus has been—"

He didn't get to finish the sentence. Sue's battering ram struck him square in the midriff, like a pool cue smartly hitting the cueball. He was propelled up, out and away from the Baxter Building, still clutching his surfboard. He flew across the Manhattan skyline, limp and helpless, and within seconds both he and board were lost from sight.

Reed and Sue gazed in the direction the Surfer had gone. They expected him to return at any moment.

There was no sign of him.

"That..." Ben struggled to a standing position. "That was a heck of a nice shot, Suzie." He looked groggy and weak, swaying on the spot. "Couldn't've done better myself."

"Ben!" Sue said. "How are you feeling?"

"Embarrassed, mostly. Surfer left me stunned, limbs turned to jelly, and he didn't even pop a sweat doin' it. I'm still weak as a kitten. Should've known it'd be you who finally sent him packing. You ain't just a pretty face. You're the real powerhouse of the team."

"I'll overlook the sexism in that remark, Ben," Sue said, "because I get the point you're trying to make."

"Sheesh. Try and pay a gal a compliment."

"Ben, this 'gal' loves you dearly, but you are such a dinosaur."

Just then, as if to spare Ben's blushes, Johnny returned. He'd recovered at last from the Surfer's assault. He came blazing over from the nearby skyscraper where the Surfer's blast had sent him.

"I saw what happened," he said. "Is the Surfer gone for good? Did we win?"

Reed shook his head. "I'm afraid not. Unless I miss my guess, he's managed to get a message out to Galactus."

"Oh boy."

"You are correct, Dr. Richards," said Uatu. "The damage is done. The Devourer of Worlds is on his way."

"What do we do now?" Johnny asked.

Uatu the Watcher gave a shrug. "There is nothing you can do," he said, "other than accept your fate."

A POINT at the very fringes of the solar system, within the Oort Cloud.

One second, there was nothing. Nothing out of the ordinary. Just a miasma of asteroids, comets and ice bodies—lumpy agglomerations of frozen substances such as methane, ammonia, water and hydrogen cyanide. The detritus left over from the solar system's formation, a trillion pieces of ejecta scattered to its outermost limits. Subject to the gravitational pull not only of the sun, but also other stars, orbiting in a slow-swirling mass around the heliosphere.

Lifeless. Desolate.

Then: *something.*

An enormous starship, big as a planet. A vast, twisted loop, wrought from a thousand different materials. The handiwork of a god.

Taa II.

It manifested in the blink of an eye, space-warping from some unfathomably far-off elsewhere.

There, amid the interstellar wasteland of the Oort Cloud, it hung. Gleaming. Purposeful. As intricate and sophisticated as the Oort Cloud's constituent parts were rough-hewn and crude.

A hatch opened in its hull, and a smaller craft emerged. A shuttle of some sort. A personal vessel for shorter-distance journeys, like a motor launch for a yacht. Predominantly spherical and fitted with thrusters of incalculable power that incorporated a dark matter repulsion system.

This craft propelled itself into the Oort Cloud on pulsing, helical jets of plasma, wending its way through the maze of billions-of-years-old debris.

In no time at all the shuttle was scudding past the Kuiper Belt, that other assemblage of discards from the solar system's birth pangs.

Past Neptune, Uranus, Saturn…

Past Jupiter and Mars…

Decelerating when it reached proximity to Earth.

Slowing further as it entered the atmosphere.

Further still as it homed in on New York.

Zeroing in on the signal sent by the Silver Surfer.

Arriving, almost gently now, at the signal's point of origin.

Coming to a halt not far above the roof of the Baxter Building, where four humans stood in various postures of alarm, amazement and hostility, along with an ever-impassive Watcher.

The shuttle hovered in position, with a doorway in its base immediately adjacent to the skyscraper. The door slid upwards, and a set of large steps extruded from the opening. The steps unfurled like links in a chain, extending down to the rooftop. Each was several feet in length and positioned a full yard above the one below.

The doorway itself was over thirty feet high and about half as wide.

A figure loomed within it. A figure whose colossal proportions corresponded with those of the aperture.

Out he stepped…

GALACTUS

GALACTUS DESCENDED the steps at a measured pace. Calm. Unhurried. A little shy of thirty feet tall. Clad in an outfit that was part armor, part form-fitting bodysuit. Gauntlets. Ribbed boots. A kind of kilt. A chest harness. All in magenta and royal blue. And a helmet that covered most of his face, with a high, flat crown like an Ancient Egyptian pharaoh's and two squared, wing-like plates on either side whose tips projected even higher than the crown.

Down he trod, vastly self-confident, vastly aloof, vastly imposing. His eyes consisted of square, bright blue irises set amid pure blackness. His mouth was held in a grim, mirthless line.

He was majestic. He was terrifying.

He strode across the rooftop, and the Fantastic Four, gathered in a huddle, braced themselves. They had encountered otherworldly entities before, plenty of them. None, though, had exuded such sheer raw superiority as this creature. Galactus was power personified. He moved without hesitation, without fear.

Earth was not his yet.

But, to look at him, it was as though the planet already belonged to him, and he could do with it entirely as he pleased.

IN THE past, Johnny had had doubts about being in the super hero business, times when the drawbacks had seemed to outweigh the benefits. He'd talked about it with Spider-Man during one of their Statue of Liberty meet-ups.

"I don't know," he'd said musingly. It had been a bright fall afternoon, and they had been squatting side by side on Lady Liberty's head, facing north. "I've come close to quitting more than once. For instance, whenever me and the team have fought the Hulk. I mean, jeez, first time we met him, the big green galoot snuffed out my flame twice in a row, without even hardly trying. Just clapped his hands, and poof! I felt like a complete washout."

"Yeah, well, that's what you get for battling old Jade Jaws," Spider-Man said. "I had a run-in with him myself not so long ago—on a Hollywood movie set, of all places. I was lucky to get away with my life. My webbing's designed to be pretty much unbreakable, and the Hulk snapped it like it was cotton candy. Strength-wise, blow for blow, I might as well have been a toddler in the ring with Muhammad Ali. My best punches didn't even faze him. Comparing your own power to the Hulk's is pointless. That's like being sad about being six foot tall because the guy next to you happens to be six five. There's always going to be someone faster, stronger, whatever, than you. That's just life."

"Still, it left me wondering why I bother," Johnny said. "If I can't handle a threat like the Hulk, what use am I?"

"Did the FF beat him that time?" Spidey asked, in a way that suggested he already knew the answer.

"Sort of. And next time we ran across him, we sort of beat him too. Then, it was mostly Ben who did the work. The Avengers got involved as well. Me? Early on, the Hulk laid me flat just by hammering the ground I was standing on. The shock wave knocked me cold, and from then on, I was out of the game."

"Okay, but the good guys won in the end, didn't they?"

"Sure."

"So what's the problem?" Spider-Man said, spreading out his hands. "There's nothing to go beating yourself up about. And believe me, I know about beating yourself up about stuff. I'm the poster child for it. You're remembering a couple of occasions, Torch, when things didn't go your way. What about all the occasions when they did? There's got to be way more of those."

"Yeah, I'd say there are."

"Take the wins, learn from the losses. It's the only way forward."

Johnny studied the youngster beside him who was, he realized, becoming a good friend. "You're not as dumb as you look, you know that, Spidey?"

"I wish I could say the same for you, pal."

Johnny fired a little finger-burst of flame at him. Spider-Man, demonstrating that uncanny prescience and agility of his, somersaulted clear, as Johnny had known he would.

"Yeah," Spidey said, settling back down on his behind. "It's all about perspective, isn't it? The bigger picture. I mean to say, look at this view." He swept an arm to indicate the panoramic vista of New York City in front of them, with the waters of the Hudson glittering brilliantly and the buildings burnished bronze by the autumnal sunshine. "Amazing. Spectacular. You and I both know that corners of this city are a cesspool. But take a step back, see it from a distance, and it can be breathtaking."

"So you're saying, taken as a whole, life is beautiful."

"Messy, complicated, but yes, overall, beautiful."

"Even the New Jersey parts of it?"

Spidey chuckled. "Even those."

Johnny recalled the conversation now as Galactus emerged from his ship and paced towards them across the Baxter Building roof. This, surely, was one of the New Jersey parts of life. The Fantastic Four had struggled to hinder the Silver Surfer, and ultimately had failed. And the Surfer, apparently, was blessed with only a small fraction of Galactus's power. What did that make the chances of the FF being able to take down Galactus himself? Infinitesimally small.

In the event, Galactus walked straight past the team. He showed no interest in them whatsoever. It would be fair to say he did not even notice them.

He went, instead, to speak with Uatu the Watcher.

Insects, Johnny thought. *We're just insects to him. He paid no more attention to us than I would ants in an anthill.*

What was worse than feeling so small, was feeling so hopeless. Johnny and his teammates were, for the moment, reduced to mere spectators. For all their power, for all their accomplishments, they were now relegated to the sidelines.

And that might well be where they remained while Galactus set about devouring Earth.

No longer super heroes.

Just bystanders.

Eyewitnesses to doomsday.

o———o

"WATCHER," SAID Galactus, in a voice like the rumble of distant thunder, the sound of a storm on its way.

He dwarfed Uatu, fully twice his height. The Watcher nevertheless seemed uncowed.

"You are here to observe," Galactus continued, "in accordance with the creed of your race. You will record for posterity the events that are about to unfold."

"That is my purpose," Uatu said.

"You would not be the first Watcher to document the consumption of a planet by Galactus."

"The archives of my people can attest to that. It has been the fate of many a Watcher to watch the Devourer of Worlds at work."

"And not," said Galactus, "to intercede in any manner."

Uatu gave a reluctant nod.

"As you have lately tried to."

Again—but even more reluctantly this time—Uatu nodded.

"The Silver Surfer communicated that fact when summoning me," Galactus said.

"I will admit, Galactus, that in some small way I did seek to disrupt the Surfer's approach. It proved... ineffective."

"This," said Galactus, indicating the Matter Mobilizer, "is the device with which you directed boulders at my herald, in your vain attempt to deflect him."

"It is."

Galactus waved a hand in the air, like a stage conjuror. And like a stage conjuror, he performed a disappearing act.

One moment the Matter Mobilizer was there; the next, it had vanished. Gone in the blink of an eye, as if it had never existed.

If Uatu was perturbed or irritated, he showed it only with the merest pursing of his lips.

"I must ask, Watcher, why you would do such a thing?" Galactus canted his head to one side. "What could you hope to gain?"

"This world, known as Earth," Uatu replied, "is special. I cannot put it more plainly than that. It has intelligent life."

"As do many worlds."

"It also has certain beings with extraordinary gifts, and courage to match. These, for example." He gestured at the Fantastic Four.

Galactus looked at the quartet, seeming to register their presence for the first time. His strange eyes narrowed ever so slightly.

"They do not strike me as particularly rare or unusual," he said. "The universe is littered with super-powered humanoids not dissimilar to these."

"I believe, moreover," Uatu said, "that Earth itself is unique and has more to offer than most worlds. It has been the focus of an above-average amount of outside involvement. Beings from other dimensions covet it and seek to conquer it. Races from other galaxies have visited it countless times, usually with hostile intent. There is a Nexus of All Realities here, in the region known as the Florida Everglades. The Celestials have sent no fewer than three Hosts to Earth, to conduct their tests and experiments upon the inhabitants. It is numbered among the Ten Realms in the cosmology espoused by the godlike entities known as Asgardians."

"All of which makes it a place of some interest," Galactus allowed, "but far from exceptional."

"But I come back to its people. They are creative. They are ambitious. They are intrepid. There is no question that one day they will spread out from this, their home, and settle on other planets. Their space program is still in its infancy, but I can confidently predict that, given time and opportunity, humankind will become a star-spanning empire to rival any in the cosmos."

"Why should that matter to me?"

"Consider it from a pragmatic viewpoint. More human-inhabited worlds will mean more prospective sources of sustenance for you."

Galactus pondered this for a moment. "By leaving Earth alone for now, I store up nourishment for the future, like stocking a larder. That is your argument?"

"It is a valid one."

Galactus fell silent.

"I THOUGHT the Watcher said we were on our own," Sue remarked in a quiet voice. "That he wasn't going to help any further. And yet here he is, making a case for us to Galactus, like a defense lawyer."

"I guess he just can't help himself," Ben said.

"He's trying to appeal to Galactus's better nature," Reed said.

"But does Galactus even have one?" Johnny wanted to know.

"I guess we're going to find out, Hotshot," Ben said. "And if he don't"—he held up clenched fists—"I got a couple of dukes here that'll convince him to change his mind."

"Ben," Reed warned, "aggression isn't going to help us here."

"Says you."

"I mean it. Attacking Galactus will just provoke a response, one that's bound to be to our detriment."

"Is that a fancy way of saying we'll get our butts handed to us on a plate? 'Cause if so, frankly I couldn't care less. We've got to do *something*, Stretcho. We can't just stand around wringin' our hands and wailin'. We're the Fantastic Four, aren't we? People look to us to step up when the going gets tough."

"They do, Ben," Sue said. "But Reed's right. Attacking Galactus would be tantamount to suicide."

"Don't see what difference that makes. We let him go ahead and eat the damn planet, we're dead anyway. Better to go out fightin', I say."

"Let's just give Uatu a chance," Reed said. "Perhaps he can persuade Galactus. A dialog between near-equals, one ultra-powerful being to another."

"Shut up and leave the grownups to talk, you mean?"

Reed nodded.

"Well, I don't like it," Ben grumbled, "but I'll go along with it. For now."

"Good man."

Reed rubbed his face, hand rasping on his stubble-covered chin. His expression was not that of someone convinced by their own standpoint.

It was that of someone eager not to be proved mistaken.

"NO," SAID Galactus.

"No?" Uatu echoed.

"There is no guarantee that the people of this world will develop into a 'star-spanning empire', as you put it. They are at that stage in their evolutionary process—that perilous tipping point—when they may well end up destroying themselves. They are as likely to do that as not. You would have me defer gratification now for the uncertain prospect of further feasts to come? I will not."

"But the human race has such potential. To snuff it out before it can fully flourish…"

"I am almost as old as the universe itself," Galactus declared. "I have seen stars be born, grow old and die. I have seen civilizations rise, wither and fall. Eternities pass by, in my perception, like eye blinks. To one such as I, the survival of a single paltry species squirming away in a lonely galactic backwater is of no consequence. You, Watcher, may be fond of these humans, but I regard them as mere fodder. If they serve any purpose at all in the grand cosmic scheme, it is to sustain me. That, and only that, is their true value."

"I beg you to reconsider."

Galactus made a dismissive gesture. "Cease this pleading. You have tried my patience enough. It is only out of respect for your race that I have been willing to hear you out at all. Be grateful for that. It has been a long time since last I fed. Hunger pangs gnaw at me. My craving is all-encompassing, and I must sate it. There is an end to the matter."

Uatu clearly had more to say, but knew he would be wasting his breath. With a small, dignified bow, he conceded defeat and withdrew a few paces back from Galactus.

The Devourer of Worlds nodded, as though submission had been no more than he expected from Uatu. He moved to a corner of the rooftop, rested one foot on the parapet, and gazed out contemplatively across the city.

"Yes," he said, seemingly to himself. "This will do. This will very much do. I sense abundant life here, energy aplenty. My herald has chosen well. I detect his presence not far from this spot. When he returns to me, I shall be sure to congratulate him. In the meantime..."

That was when Ben Grimm got involved.

o———o

BEN WAS unable to restrain himself any longer. He stepped forward, brushing off an attempt by Reed to waylay him.

"All right, that's enough out of you, buster," he said, peering up at Galactus. "The Watcher's played nice, and it hasn't made any difference. So I'm going to play not so nice. This is your first, last and only warning. Get in your fancy Magic Eightball spacecraft over there and go back to Galactusville, or wherever it is you came from. You ain't welcome here."

Galactus twitched his head, as though bothered by a buzzing bee.

"Yeah, you heard me, Tall, Dark and Gruesome," Ben went on. "Do as I say, or I'm going to introduce you to a very special event that only a lucky few folks ever get to experience."

Galactus scarcely seemed to be paying him any heed. His only response was the merest shrug of the shoulders, an action conveying either contempt or indifference—it was hard to tell which.

"Okay then," Ben said. "Don't say I didn't give you a chance."

He planted his feet and reeled back one fist, turning his torso slightly.

"It's..."

CLOBBERIN' TIME!

IT FELT good to finally utter his battle cry.

Felt great, in fact.

Especially after trying and failing to do so when he fought the Silver Surfer.

Although, as things turned out, it wasn't "clobberin' time" after all. Not really.

Ben gave it everything he'd got. He didn't hold back, because he knew he mustn't. He unleashed every ounce of his cosmic-ray-granted strength.

His fist connected with Galactus's shin, the impact loud as a thunderclap.

It was a blow that would have splintered the trunk of a giant redwood into kindling. It would have shattered the concrete supporting pillar of a freeway overpass. It could conceivably have felled the Washington Monument. It might even have KO'ed the Hulk.

To Galactus?

It did nothing.

It didn't make him flinch.

It didn't budge him the tiniest bit.

It certainly didn't topple him.

All it did, if it achieved anything, was finally get him to turn his attention on Ben.

That huge, helmeted head came round and stared down.

Ben stood there, fist still raised. The look on his face was almost comically distraught.

"You didn't even feel it, did you?" he murmured, aghast. "I pounded you hard as I could, and I may as well have been ticklin' you with a feather duster."

What was worse, his hand now throbbed painfully. Punching Galactus had been like hitting the proverbial immovable object. The only one of them it had hurt was Ben.

He craned his neck to meet Galactus's gaze.

The expression on the face of the Devourer of Worlds was hard to read. Aggravation? Amusement? Puzzlement?

Ben readied himself for what might come next. He understood that he was about to die. Galactus would just hand-wave him out of existence, the way he had the Matter Mobilizer.

Ben thought of Alicia. What he wouldn't give to see her one last time. Hold her close. Tell her how much he loved her and what a difference she had made to his life.

At least I tried, babe, he said to himself. *Tried to save you and everyone on Earth. I gave it my best shot. Not my fault it wasn't enough.*

Galactus raised a hand.

Here it comes, Ben thought.

But what actually came was a strange little missile that streaked out from the doorway in Galactus's ship. It was bulb-shaped, with a trio of stabilizing wings at the rear like the flights on a dart. It dropped down in front of Ben.

And burst open.

Billows of green gas gushed out, enveloping Ben in an instant. The gas invaded his nose, got into his eyes, coated the back of his throat. His eyes stung. His nostrils felt as though they were on fire. He started choking and spluttering.

"Yicccchh!" he croaked. "What is it? What in blazes is happenin'?"

o———o

REED HAD a fairly good notion what was happening.

Galactus had hit Ben with some kind of aerosolized irritant. The way Ben was coughing and staggering, Reed inferred the substance wasn't lethal. Otherwise his friend would have dropped dead on the spot.

It was a repellent. Equivalent to a mosquito spray. Designed to keep pesky little annoyances at bay.

Even as he was making this deduction, Reed sprang into action. He flung himself at Ben, expanding and flattening his whole body until he was more or less a human blanket.

Ben was lying on his side, curled into the fetal position, gagging and frantically rubbing his eyes. The repellent gas lingered over him in an acrid green cloud.

Reed, holding his breath and squeezing his eyes shut so that the gas wouldn't affect him, enfolded himself around Ben. With his friend wrapped safe and snug inside him, he rolled the both of them across the rooftop, out of that nebulous toxic shroud.

When they reached safety, Reed rapidly unfurled. Ben came tumbling out like Cleopatra from a rug. He levered himself up onto all fours, retching, his eyes streaming with tears, while Reed snapped back to normal.

"Ugh," Ben said. "That was disgustin'."

"Ben," said a concerned Sue. "Are you all right?"

"Yeah. Leastways, I will be in a few moments." He spat out gobs of saliva. "Could've been worse, I guess. I mean, I played college football. I've been in locker rooms after the game. You don't dare even breathe when you're in that kind of atmosphere."

Sue laughed bleakly. "Well, if you're making jokes, that's a good sign. I was worried. I thought Galactus had killed you."

"And I thought a good thump would stop him," Ben said bitterly, "or at least make him think twice." He coughed out the last of the gas from his lungs. "Seems we were both wrong."

"You don't realize how lucky you are, Ben," said Reed. "Galactus could easily have annihilated you."

"Yeah, well, he didn't. Probably knew bashful, blue-eyed Benjy is just too popular to kill. Didn't want to upset my legions of fans."

"How *do* we fight him, Reed?" Sue asked.

"There is no way," her husband replied. "Not directly. Ben just proved as much. A frontal assault is only going to get us injured, or worse. But there has to be something," he added, "*something* we can do to stop him."

"Yeah, there is," said Johnny. "But you guys had better stand back." He flamed on and took flight.

o——o

"JOHNNY! NO!" Sue cried.

Johnny Storm ignored his sister. He hurtled headlong through the air towards the blue-and-magenta-clad giant.

Ben had done his best against Galactus. Ben, however, did not have the flame powers of the Human Torch.

Specifically, he did not have the Human Torch's nova burst.

Johnny's baseline flame temperature was around eight hundred degrees Fahrenheit. He knew this because Reed had measured it on numerous occasions. Reed seemed to like nothing better than gauging his teammates' abilities and noting down the results, compiling spreadsheets about each of them. He tested Ben's strength with monotonous regularity, constructing all sorts of bench-press machines and electromagnetically weighted barbells for him to use, in order to find out just how many tons the Thing could lift. It was one of his many scientific obsessions.

Similarly, by employing various sensor-laden machines, Reed had established Johnny's uppermost flame temperature: a little shy of 1,000,000°F. Johnny could achieve and sustain such a level of heat for only a few seconds, and it left him depleted afterwards and needing time to recover.

This sudden, intense flare was what Johnny had dubbed his nova burst.

And maybe, just maybe, if he directed all of it at Galactus now in a single focused beam, it might take him out. At the very least it might make the big guy realize the true level of the opposition he was facing and convince him to change his mind and leave Earth alone.

In his heart of hearts, Johnny knew this was a forlorn hope. But while there existed the remotest chance he could repel Galactus, he was damn well going to take it.

The Devourer of Worlds watched him approach, showing little other than a vague, distant curiosity. Perhaps he was wondering what this human firefly had in mind. Perhaps he was briefly entranced by the flicker of Johnny's flame, just as anyone's gaze can be drawn and held by the sight of a bonfire or a crackling hearth.

Halting to hover above Galactus's head, Johnny focused on raising his flame to its highest intensity. His body's glow went from lambent orange to fierce white, bright as burning magnesium, too bright for the ordinary human eye to bear. He became a shimmer of sheer incandescence.

Then, bringing both his hands together in front of him, he loosed off every last scrap of thermal energy he possessed. It streaked down at Galactus, and for several moments the godlike being was enveloped in a shell of searing white fire.

Johnny poured it on, feeling the heat leave him, transferring itself to Galactus. Even as his own glow faded, the brilliance that sheathed Galactus increased.

Surely, Johnny thought, it was going to be enough. *Surely it was going to bring Galactus to his knees, if not flatten him altogether. Nothing could withstand temperatures like that and endure.*

At last, he couldn't keep it up anymore. The flame drained from him and he couldn't stay aloft. With the few final flickering dregs of his power, Johnny descended to the rooftop. He collapsed to a kneeling position, arms hanging, feeling as limp and exhausted as if he'd just run several marathons in a row. If anyone had asked him to flame on again at that moment, he wouldn't have been able to. He couldn't even have managed to conjure up a spark.

He peered up to see what had become of Galactus.

The answer was: nothing.

Galactus just stood there. The rooftop around his feet was blackened and bubbling, but on him there wasn't even a scorch mark. His clothing was neither singed nor smoldering. Nowhere on his body was there the least sign of charring. He gave no indication that moments earlier he had been subjected to a level of heat that could have reduced solid tungsten to molten slag.

All he did was study Johnny, then slowly shake his head from side to side in a way that was both pitying and mildly incredulous.

Next moment, he turned around and looked at Uatu.

"Watcher," he said, "what are these puny little creatures doing? Can they really believe they will achieve anything by attacking me?"

"You will recall," Uatu said, "how I described the human race as intrepid, and how I told you that they do not lack courage, not least the ones with extraordinary gifts. You are seeing such qualities exemplified now. These four will continue to defy you. They will, if I am not much mistaken, resist you to their dying breath."

Galactus gave something that sounded like a sigh. "How tiresome. Please instruct them, on my behalf, to abandon their efforts. They are accomplishing naught other than wasting their time."

"Tell us that yourself, you arrogant creep!" Ben shouted. "You *can* talk directly to us, you know. We mayn't be all high-and-mighty intergalactic beings like you or the Watcher, but that don't mean we're worth diddly-squat."

The Devourer of Worlds either wasn't listening or chose to ignore the taunt.

"Can't you hear me?" Ben persisted. "Maybe that big, dorky hat of yours is on too tight."

"Ben," said Sue, "flinging insults at him isn't going to help."

"I don't know. It's definitely makin' *me* feel better."

"Sue's right," said Reed. "We're of no consequence whatsoever to Galactus. We're like gnats to him."

"I thought ants," Johnny said, staggering over to join his three teammates. Sue put an arm round her brother's shoulders to steady and comfort him.

"Ants, gnats, what's the difference?" said Ben. "He's treatin' us like we're barely even here. It's humiliating, is what it is. 'Specially so after me and Matchstick both hit him with all we've got. Now I really do know what chopped liver feels like."

"We should withdraw," Reed said. "Regroup. We need a new strategy. There has to be some way of preventing Galactus from consuming Earth. We just have to work out what it is."

"I agree," said Sue. "Perhaps we can call in reinforcements. I'm thinking in particular of the Avengers."

"Hah!" Ben snorted. "The Avengers ain't such a force to be reckoned with these days, not like they was. All the big guns have quit. Now it's just Captain America and those three ex-villains he recruited—the archer guy with the trick arrows and that brother-and-sister pair, the one who runs fast and the one who waves her hands and makes weird things happen. Not a patch on the likes of Iron Man, Giant-Man and Thor."

"I will consult them," Reed said. "At the very least, Captain America is never short of sound tactical advice. But I fear that raw power—even as great as, say, Thor's—still wouldn't be enough. We need something else. I just don't know what it is."

Uatu came over to speak with the four of them. Galactus, meanwhile, headed for his ship and disappeared inside. His movements were purposeful, as if there was work to be done and no time like the present to start doing it.

"You are correct, Dr. Richards," Uatu said. "Galactus will be busy for the next hour or two, making preparations, so for the time being your best option is retreat. I intend to depart, too, and return home."

"You mean you're abandonin' us?" Ben said.

"No. I merely wish to investigate certain possibilities, which I can best do amid the equipment housed in my residence on the moon."

"Sure sounds to me like you're abandonin' us," Ben grumbled.

"Take it how you will, Mr. Grimm," Uatu said. "Rest assured, I am not giving up on the human race. You have my solemn word on that. But for now, farewell."

Uatu closed his eyes. The air around him seemed to pucker and flex in on itself, and then, where he had once been standing, suddenly there was no one. He had teleported back to his base in the moon's Blue Area.

THE FANTASTIC Four trudged off to the elevator, which carried them down to their headquarters.

As they descended, Sue Richards eyed her husband concernedly. She had never seen him look as fatigued as he did now, nor as downcast. Both Johnny and Ben looked fairly dejected themselves—not surprising, given how easily Galactus had fended off their strongest attacks. Reed, however, seemed utterly defeated.

Sue knew he prided himself on being able to come up with a solution to any problem. It was one of his most appealing traits, as well as, at certain times, one of his most aggravating. The fact that he was currently at a loss how to deal with Galactus was, she could tell, eating away at him inside, causing him to doubt his own skills and resourcefulness. He styled himself Mister Fantastic not so much because of his uncanny powers of physical malleability, but because of his remarkable, one-of-a-kind intellect. His brain was, figuratively speaking, perhaps the most elastic part of him. It stretched the boundaries of what was scientifically possible. It could adapt readily to any situation and formulate an appropriate response. Even after failure it always bounced back, like a rubber ball.

Right now, though, Reed was plainly stumped and all out of options. It was not a position he liked to be in.

"Let's all go clean ourselves up," Sue said, "get some food inside us, get our strength back. Then we can come back to this afresh. Reed, dear, I really think a shave is in order. You're starting to look downright scruffy."

"Hmm?" said Reed. "A shave? Yes, Sue. Fine."

"And by the time you're done doing that," Ben said, "you'll have figured out a dozen ways of gettin' rid of Galactus. I know you, Stretch. It's only a matter of time."

"Seconded," said Johnny. "Ben's not always right. In fact, he's usually wrong. But this time he's bang on the money."

Sue understood that both her brother and Ben had complete faith in Reed. They weren't just pinning their hopes on him fixing things. Nor were they seeking reassurance from him. They were simply convinced he would, in due course, come up with a workable plan, which they would then, unquestioningly, help him implement.

"You *will* figure something out, right, Reed?" Ben said.

Reed did not reply.

"I mean it. You got this, buddy. Don't you?"

Again, Reed did not reply.

There was silence in the elevator for the rest of the way down.

THE SILVER Surfer was puzzled.

Defiance.

It was not entirely unexpected.

Few worlds, in his experience, surrendered meekly to their fate when confronted by the coming of Galactus. The prospect of imminent extinction galvanized their inhabitants into action.

If possible, they fled. Civilizations that had mastered space travel deserted their planets in flotillas of starships and took their chances out in the wilds of the cosmos.

If they could not flee, they offered whatever resistance they could. In the past the Surfer had been pelted with flint-tipped spears by a tribe of saurian hominids belonging to a race who had only lately discovered the use of tools. He had also been bombarded with particle beams, EMP bombs and sonic cannons by various ultra-advanced societies. Neither type of assault, the primitive or the sophisticated, was any more successful than the other.

Sometimes, when he arrived on peaceable worlds, people simply congregated at their places of worship and prayed to their deities for deliverance. Sacrifices were made, offerings given—for all the good it did.

On one occasion, the population of a planet which had reached roughly the same stage of development as Earth elected to commit mass suicide. In a fit of collective despair, they detonated every thermonuclear warhead they owned. The thinking seemed to be that if they could not have their planet anymore, neither could Galactus. They thought that by poisoning it with radiation, the Devourer of Worlds would not find it palatable—failing to appreciate that radiation was just another form of energy and therefore still assimilable by him.

Such resigned acceptance was rare though. Defiance was far commoner.

The kind of defiance demonstrated towards the Silver Surfer by the humans on top of the Baxter Building, however, was unusual. The foursome had shown neither fear nor hesitation. They seemed well aware that the Surfer was too powerful for them and they posed no real threat to him. Nevertheless, they had boldly, unflinchingly, thrown themselves into the fray.

The same had been true when Galactus himself arrived, shortly after the Invisible Woman had sent the Surfer flying away from the skyscraper. The Surfer had slowed to a halt in midair somewhere over the part of the city called Tribeca, reunited with his board, and then watched from afar as the Fantastic Four challenged his master and were duly repulsed by him. He found himself admiring the passion and selflessness they showed.

It reminded him of…

Of…

Something.

Something in his past.

Something that was cloudy in his recollection, a memory he could glimpse but only as if through thick fog.

A man, standing up for his world.

Making an offer.

Stalwartly sacrificing himself.

The harder he tried to grasp the specifics of the memory, the farther away it slipped from him.

What had also left a distinct impression on the Surfer was the way Reed and Susan Richards had tried to reason with him. Their arguments had been well put, if fruitless, but something Mrs. Richards said in particular had stuck with him.

Do you not have feelings? Don't you feel guilt over the countless deaths you have been complicit in?

The Surfer had replied to the effect that his only role in life was to serve his master.

You do have other urges, Susan Richards had then said.

The Surfer had told her those were irrelevant.

But why had he even said that? He wasn't sure any such urges existed in him at all. He seldom thought of anything except finding the next planet for Galactus to feast upon. He was single-minded in that pursuit, and had little time, or desire, for inner contemplation or reflection. You might as well ask an arrow in flight if it had any goal but hitting its target.

They were intriguing nonetheless, this so-called Fantastic Four. In all his many centuries as Galactus's herald, the Surfer hadn't encountered anyone quite like them. Although his interaction with them had been brief, it had made an impression. It had left him filled with a certain curiosity—a sense of doubt, even.

That was why he hadn't returned to the Baxter Building immediately, to join Galactus there as he knew he ought. He had decided to hold back instead and leave his master to take care of things by himself. Galactus did not need his herald by his side for succor or aid; all the same, it had become customary for the Surfer to accompany him while he prepared to consume a planet. It was a pattern they had fallen into over the millennia: the Surfer standing in attendance as Galactus assembled the components of his Elemental Converter—the awesome piece of apparatus that transmuted matter into pure energy, which he could then store and imbibe at his leisure.

The Silver Surfer had the nagging feeling that what he was doing right now—keeping his distance from Galactus—might be deemed disloyal. Galactus knew exactly where the Surfer was; nothing escaped his master's nigh-omniscient awareness. He might well be wondering why his herald was staying away.

The Surfer himself could not quite explain his reasons. All he knew was that he wanted room to think, to ponder on the strange, perplexing emotions that had been aroused within him.

He began to ride his surfboard slowly across New York on a vaguely northward heading, drifting above the grid pattern of streets and blocks, gazing down.

The city pulsed with life. Everywhere, busy people scurried and idle people dawdled. Traffic ebbed and flowed along the roadways. Now and then the shrill siren of an emergency vehicle punched the air. Far above it all, jetliners roared with fuselages full of hopeful and anxious passengers.

The Surfer saw the yard of an elementary school, thronged with children at play, shrieking joyfully.

He saw lovers strolling hand in hand through the greenery of a park.

He saw an altercation between a newsstand vendor and one of his customers, which almost came to blows until a passing police officer intervened and calmed things down.

He saw hordes of people at their desks in offices, some industrious, others bored.

He saw luxurious penthouse apartments with solariums and lap pools, and down-at-heel districts where the residents could only dream of such prosperity.

He saw a cathedral whose architectural splendor seemed intended to suggest a greater, less material glory.

New York counted itself among the foremost cities on Earth, and the Surfer could understand why its denizens felt that claim was justified. It was frantic and densely packed, soaring and energetic. It sprawled, mapping itself onto the existing contours of the landscape. It hemmed in the rivers, burrowed below the ground, and leapt high into the sky, asserting its dominance in every direction. It was dirty, rowdy and loud, but somehow seemed to make those qualities virtues.

It was, in short, a perfect metaphor for those who had built it. It was the human race embodied in glass, concrete and stone.

As he continued to glide over the metropolis, the Silver Surfer's eye was drawn to something perched on a rooftop in the neighborhood known as SoHo.

It was a flying vehicle, open-topped, rounded at both ends, straight along the sides.

What caught his attention was the stylized number 4 emblem on the front of the aircraft. In color and shape it matched exactly the badge which every member of the Fantastic Four, apart from the Thing, wore on their chest.

He flew a little closer, noting that the aircraft comprised four sections, each of which could detach from the others and be piloted independently.

He discerned the hand of Reed Richards in its construction. The engineering was that little bit cleverer, that little bit more innovative, than anything another human could have devised.

The Surfer felt compelled to probe further. He descended to the rooftop, alighting next to the aircraft and setting his board to one side.

Why was the vehicle parked here, and not at the Fantastic Four's headquarters a mile uptown? Was this building some additional center of operations for the team? He didn't see how it could be. To all appearances, it was just a conventional four-story apartment building, home to thirty or so civilians. That could, of course, be mere camouflage—outward ordinariness to disguise the building's true nature—but the Surfer's senses did not detect any sophisticated machinery lurking within its walls, only telephones, televisions, kitchen appliances and so forth. Nor were any of the occupants super-powered.

The Silver Surfer frowned. He could only assume someone who lived here was associated with the Fantastic Four. It was the likeliest explanation for the aircraft's presence. Perhaps the team had ancillary members that could be called on when needed.

"Who's there?"

The voice came from behind him.

The Surfer turned to see a woman emerging from a door that led to the roof from below. She was slim and very beautiful, with a heart-shaped face and pale blue eyes. Her hair was cut short in a style that suggested a desire for unfussiness and practicality.

"I heard footsteps above my ceiling," she said, turning her head from side to side in a quizzical fashion. "I know there's someone up here."

The Surfer swiftly discerned that the woman was sightless. Her eyes, although they appeared to look, did not *see*. Some impairment of her retinas was to blame, judging by the severe scarring he could discern on them.

"I thought it might be my boyfriend," she continued, "but I know his breathing. You're not him. Whoever you are, I recommend you don't touch the Fantasti-Car. You'll set off an alarm, and also trigger a stasis field that'll hold you in place until the car's owners arrive. And believe me, you wouldn't want to be around when they get here. Especially not if it's Ben. He's very attached to that Fantasti-Car, even though he says it looks like a bathtub and flies like one too."

"Ben," said the Surfer.

"Yes," the woman said. "Ben. As in Ben Grimm, of the Fantastic Four. Who happens to be the boyfriend I mentioned."

"I know him."

"Do you indeed? Then you'll know that he's the big, lumpy guy with the super-strength and the short fuse. So maybe you should leave, while you still can."

"I have fought with him," the Surfer said. "Just lately."

The woman shrank back slightly, apprehensive now. "You're one of the FF's enemies? Well, in that case, you wouldn't be here if you didn't know who *I* am. But if you've come to kidnap me or menace me or anything like that, I'd advise against it. That would make Ben *really* mad."

She had one hand on the frame of the doorway and looked poised to bolt.

The Surfer said, "I have no intention of kidnapping or menacing you. I came merely because this aircraft belongs to the Fantastic Four, whom I have met very recently."

The woman's brow creased. "Who *are* you? Your voice—it's unusual. I can't place your accent. Come to think of it, you don't sound like a super villain. Believe me, I know how they talk. I know it all too well."

"They call me the Silver Surfer."

"Okay," she said. "Well, Mr. Silver Surfer, they call *me* Alicia Masters. And if you've been in a fight with my Ben, I can only assume he won and you've retired to lick your wounds."

"No," said the Surfer. "That isn't what happened. The truth is, he is not my enemy, nor am I his. We have clashed, but the hostility was entirely on his part, not mine."

"Was it all a misunderstanding, then?" Alicia Masters asked. "Because, with super beings, that's quite often how it works. Fight first, ask questions later. Ben especially. He can be... belligerent."

"I would not call it a misunderstanding. I had a duty to fulfill, and so did your Ben, and those duties were not compatible."

Alicia Masters said nothing for a moment. Then, drawing in a breath, as though filling herself with resolve, she took a step forward.

"Silver Surfer," she said. "I have no idea who you are and where you're from. But I have an instinct about people, and it's rarely ever wrong. Do you know what I hear when you speak? Loneliness.

Disquiet. Uncertainty. You're a troubled soul. I'd like… I'd like to touch your face, if I may."

"Touch my…?"

"It's how I get to know strangers. I'm blind—in case you haven't already worked that out. Sighted people learn a lot about others just by looking at them. I don't have that faculty, so I use my hands instead. I'd like to run my fingertips over your face. It'll help give me a clearer impression of the sort of person you are. Of course, if you object, I won't. Some people are uncomfortable about it, and I respect that."

The Surfer gave it some thought. "I do not object," he said finally.

"Thank you," said Alicia Masters, and she walked towards him, hand outstretched.

o———o

ALICIA HAD not known what to expect.

Since embarking on a relationship with Ben Grimm, she had moved in circles where abnormality and bizarreness were par for the course. These things had become everyday to her. The art world had its share of eccentrics, outsiders and oddballs, but it was nothing compared with the world of super heroes. Artists couldn't shrink to the size of an insect, or swing across Manhattan on strands of webbing, or whip up ice ladders out of thin air, or bend steel bars with their bare hands.

When it came to super-powered people, Alicia had thought she was immune to surprise.

The Silver Surfer, however, was startling.

His skin was smooth and slippery, like polished metal. Yet, unlike metal but like skin, it was soft and pliant. It also made her fingertips tingle, as though she was receiving a constant, tiny electric shock.

He was entirely hairless, lacking even eyebrows. He had no ears either.

Once she had absorbed these facts, Alicia concentrated on his facial features. The Surfer had a small but dignified nose, a pensive set of lips and a prominent, forthright brow. Cheekbones, jawline, chin—everything suggested conventionally handsome looks, but distilled down to a simple, almost preternatural perfection.

All in all, his face exuded dignity, nobility and a certain inexpressible, deep-seated sadness.

She withdrew her hands.

"I hope that didn't feel too intrusive," she said.

"No," the Surfer replied in those sonorous, otherworldly tones of his. "It is strange. I have not been touched like that by anyone in a long, long time. I—I had forgotten how it feels."

"Can you tell me more about yourself?" Alicia asked. She was still somewhat unnerved by the Silver Surfer, not knowing exactly what sort of being he was, and whether or not he was lying about why he had come to be on the roof of her apartment building. She was genuinely curious about him, though, and a little fascinated. "I may be wrong, but I have a feeling you are not from this world."

"I am not, Alicia Masters," the Surfer replied. "I am from..." He faltered.

"From where?" she prompted.

"I cannot say."

"You mean you won't?"

"No, I mean I cannot."

"You don't know where you're from?"

"No. I simply cannot remember. I can tell you my vocation. I am the herald of Galactus, he who is known as the Devourer of Worlds. That has been my purpose and my responsibility for as long as I can recall. I travel the spaceways, seeking out planets for Galactus to consume. But as to my erstwhile home..."

Alicia sensed the Surfer shrugging haplessly. She had taught herself to "hear" the gestures that sighted people made, inferring them from the lengths of the silences in which they occurred and the words that preceded them.

"When you say 'planets to consume'," she said, "I take it you mean this Galactus is some kind of powerful extraterrestrial entity."

"You could call him that."

"And you've chosen Earth as his latest port of call."

"Yes."

"Oh." Alicia digested this news. "Then, unless I'm jumping to conclusions, the Fantastic Four have shown both you and him that Earth isn't there for the taking."

"On the contrary. Even as we speak, my master's procedures for consuming your world are well under way. It is only a matter of time before he begins draining Earth of all its energy."

"So then what's become of the FF?" She almost didn't want to know the answer.

"They still live."

"Oh, thank God."

"They appear to have grasped that opposition to Galactus is futile," the Surfer said. "I imagine they are gathered together in private, making the most of their last few hours of life."

"If you think that," Alicia said, "then you don't know the Fantastic Four. You definitely don't know my Ben. He won't give up. He'll keep fighting. They all will, all four of them. And what's more, they'll win."

"Interesting," said the Surfer. "You truly believe that." It was a statement, not a question.

"I don't just believe it, I'm sure of it. You've picked the wrong world, Surfer. We have people who protect us from threats like you and your Galactus. Not just the FF, others as well. They've done it before and they'll do it again. Outer-space bullies like you never stand a chance."

The Surfer uttered a soft laugh. "I am no threat."

"What are you, then, if not?"

"I am simply the herald of Galactus."

"So you've said, but what does that mean? A herald makes proclamations or serves as a sign that something significant is about to happen."

"The arrival of Galactus is surely significant."

"But it's still a euphemism for what you really are," Alicia said, "which is someone who enables genocide."

The Surfer was taken aback. She could tell from the slight catch in his throat and the pause that followed. Perhaps she had spoken a little harshly. But still, nothing she had just said was untrue.

"Genocide?"

"How else would you describe wiping out an entire species? An entire *world*, for that matter?"

"I would describe it as a necessity. If Galactus does not feed, he dies."

"And you don't care what he feeds on—how many billions of sentient creatures have to perish so that he can live?"

"It is not my job to care."

Alicia softened her tone a fraction. "I'm not so sure that's true."

"What makes you say that?"

"When I touched your face earlier, do you know what I felt, Surfer? I felt nobility. I felt regret. I felt a lost soul who has known love and kindness and compassion in the past but has since lost touch with those emotions. Tell me I'm wrong. Tell me that's not you."

"Such things are meaningless to the herald of—"

"The herald of Galactus, yes," Alicia said, overriding him. "But who is he, this herald? Who is he really? You must have had a name before you became the Silver Surfer. You must have been someone else."

"I… I suppose I was."

"But you can't remember who. That's it, isn't it? You can't remember where you're from originally or who you once were. Perhaps it was all so long ago, it's slipped from your mind. But I sense the man you were—the good man, the noble man—is still in there somewhere."

She extended her arm and placed her hand on the Surfer's chest.

"In *here*," she said.

Again, through her palm, she felt that eerily smooth skin of his, which seemed both epidermis and armor, and the buzzing electric sensation it gave off, like a soft crackle of static.

He did not feel human to her.

And yet, at the same time, he felt very human indeed.

"Can I be honest with you, Surfer?" she said, pulling her hand back.

"Have you not been so far?"

"I pity you."

"How so?"

"You're just a tool for your master. You no longer think about the consequences of your actions, if you ever did. You've been Galactus's herald for so long, you have no other identity any more except that. You're a slave."

"Slave?"

"What other name is there for it?" Alicia said. "You do his bidding, unthinkingly, unquestioningly. It doesn't sound as though you receive any reward for it. You've surrendered whoever you used to be in order to be what you are now."

"Is this how you wish to spend the precious few hours that remain to you, Alicia Masters?" the Surfer retorted. "Trying to analyze me. Probing my psyche. Do you hope to provoke some sort of reaction? If so, what reaction and why?"

"I've already told you this isn't the end of the world, Surfer. The Fantastic Four are going to save Earth. It's just what they do. But to answer your question, I'm merely reaching out to the man within you—a man who is sad and in pain and longs for connection with others even if he doesn't realize it. Is there anything wrong with that?"

The Surfer hesitated. "No. I do not think there is."

"Good." Alicia about-turned. "I'm going indoors now, down to my apartment. You're welcome to follow. I can make us tea, and I'm pretty sure I have some cookies in the cupboard, unless Ben has snaffled them all without telling me. We can sit and we can talk. If that isn't what you want, though, okay. You stay up here. No problem. Just remember—please don't touch the Fantasti-Car. The alarm is deafeningly loud."

"You are inviting me to… consume foodstuffs with you?" the Surfer said.

"And chat."

Alicia made for the doorway. She had counted the number of steps she'd taken when walking from it to the Surfer, and she retraced the journey now, counting them again. She reached the doorway with unerring precision.

As she went down the stairs, she asked herself if she was being wise. Wasn't it incredibly reckless of her to invite the Silver Surfer—a complete stranger and, moreover, an alien—into her apartment? Ben would no doubt tell her it was. The Surfer must possess extraordinary powers, given that he had fought Ben and come away unscathed. He surely posed a danger to her.

Somehow, though, she thought not. If she was right about the Surfer, a gentle, sensitive person lay beneath that icy, seemingly unemotional exterior. He wouldn't harm her.

And if she was wrong…

But she couldn't afford to dwell on that. She was taking a dreadful risk here, but she had faith that it would work out all right.

And sometimes, when it mattered, faith was all you needed.

THE SILVER Surfer did not know what to make of this woman.

I pity you, she had said.

Nobody had said anything like that to him—not in living memory, at any rate. Maybe once someone had. Maybe…

An image flashed into his mind.

A beautiful woman. Long, lustrous, raven-dark hair. Piercing, emerald-green eyes.

Gazing up at him with compassion.

With regret.

With love.

This Alicia Masters reminded him of that other woman. Alicia was beautiful too, but there was more to it than that. She was spirited, intelligent, frank with her opinions, unafraid to get to the heart of the matter. The other woman had been the same.

Who was she, this phantom of memory that had just flitted through his brain? Why did her face mean so much to him? What had she been to him, and he to her?

The Surfer put his hand to his chest, where Alicia had placed her own hand just moments earlier.

He could feel something unlocking inside himself. A key turning in his heart. A shrouded truth yearning to be revealed.

But it remained stubbornly elusive still.

Could Alicia help? Could talking with her entice out into the open that which was buried?

There was only one way to find out.

Leaving his surfboard on the roof, he followed her down into the building.

o———o

ALICIA MASTERS'S apartment was in most respects just an average human abode. Not very large, decorated plainly, with a minimum of furnishings and few luxuries.

In other respects, however, it was a wonderland.

No sooner did the Surfer enter than he was drawn towards the biggest room, a well-lit space filled with sculptures. There were statues, busts and figurines in a range of sizes and stances. All were rendered with exquisite skill, fashioned so deftly that their creator appeared to have breathed life into inert clay and stone. In their faces and the way they posed, these artworks portrayed not just the looks of their subjects but the personalities, the beliefs, the very emotions.

The Surfer stood entranced. He turned his gaze from one sculpture to the next, unable to decide which of them impressed him the most. Each had something unique about it, something striking, something that commanded attention.

He finally settled his focus on a representation of his antagonist from a short while earlier: Ben Grimm, known as the Thing.

While it was unmistakably that person, this version betrayed few of the characteristics he had exhibited during the Surfer's brief skirmish with him. There was none of the aggression and braggadocio. Rather, it was a calmer, more wistful Thing depicted here, suggesting that the inner man was a very different proposition from the outward appearance, and that Ben Grimm behaved as he did, not because that was who he was, but because it was expected of someone who looked like him. He conformed to the monstrous image he presented, but it was like an actor playing a part.

"Surfer?" Alicia entered the room, carrying a tray.

"Yes."

"You're looking at my sculpture of Ben, aren't you? I can tell by where your voice is coming from. I finished it just yesterday. What do you think?"

"It is…" The Surfer groped for a suitable adjective. "Extraordinary."

"Thank you."

"Is that how Ben Grimm really is?"

"It's how I see him."

"And you have an instinct about people and you are rarely wrong." He was quoting her own words back at her, but not with irony or sarcasm. Alicia had been stating a fact, clearly, and he wished to acknowledge that. "He is not the blustering, bantering pugilist he pretends to be."

"Oh, he's that," she said. "Sometimes. But he's so much else too. He shows the public what he wants them to see. Deep inside, however, he's as thoughtful and considerate a person as I've ever come across. There's that hard outer shell of his, and then there's the Ben within that he only ever reveals to a few of us, the ones he knows he can trust. I think you're a bit the same, Silver Surfer. I just think that, with you, it's been so very long since you've had anyone to trust, you've forgotten there's another you inside at all. You're all shell."

"Meaning I am hollow?"

"No. Meaning you just have to dig a little deeper to get to yourself."

Alicia moved to a worktable and set the tray down. On it were a teapot, cups, saucers and a plate bearing the circular sweetmeats known as cookies.

"Come sit." She motioned to a chair. "I'm told there are clay spatters everywhere in this room, and I apologize for that. Occupational hazard. They're dry at least, so they won't stain. Not that I think that's an issue for you, Surfer. That hide of yours strikes me as pretty stain-proof."

The Surfer was still somewhat baffled by this whole situation. He understood that Alicia was showing him the hospitality rituals common among humans: when you invited others into your home, it was customary to ply them with food and drink, and they, in turn, were obligated to partake and show due appreciation.

What mystified him was why she should be doing this. She seemed both unsuspicious of him and unconcerned that his master was in the process of destroying her planet. Her actions spoke of either complete naïveté or a trusting nature that far exceeded the normal parameters. Certainly the Surfer detected no ulterior motive here, no sham, no deceit.

Alicia Masters was exactly as sincere and kindly as she appeared to be.

He sat.

She poured tea into the cups. Each time, she first located the cup's position with her free hand, then used that same hand to guide the teapot's spout to it.

She placed one of the cups in front of the Surfer, and lodged a cookie in the saucer with it.

"Chocolate chip," she said. "Ben's favorite. One time, he mistook an oatmeal raisin cookie for a chocolate chip, and you should have heard him. The absolute disgust. He spat it out like somebody was trying to poison him."

"I..." the Surfer began.

"What?"

"I do not eat, Alicia Masters," he said. "Not in the conventional manner. I have no need to. I absorb ambient energy from my surroundings automatically, organically, through my skin.

My body then converts it into the nutrients I require to live, courtesy of the Power Cosmic that infuses me."

"You don't ever get to taste things, then?" Alicia said. "Shame. Because, I tell you, these cookies are delicious."

"No. However, in order to align with your race's notions of politeness, I shall ingest your offerings thus."

He placed a hand over the tea and the cookie, and converted them—cup, saucer and all—into raw energy, which he drew into himself through his palm.

"I felt a wave of heat," Alicia said. "That was you eating?"

"For want of a better description, yes."

She laughed gently. "I appreciate you making the effort, Surfer. Look, I can't go on calling you 'Surfer'."

"Why not? It is my name."

"No, it's a title. And it's not your actual name, is it?"

"No. No, I don't think it is."

"I suppose you can't remember what people used to call you," Alicia said, "the same way you can't remember the place you hail from."

"No. I..."

The Surfer broke off.

A name had just surfaced in his mind, unbidden. It seemed to have risen from the deepest recesses of memory, like lost treasure being hauled up from the ocean bed.

Norrin Radd.

"Surfer?" said Alicia. "You've gone quiet. What's the matter?"

"Norrin Radd," he said, wonderingly.

"What does that mean?"

"It does not mean anything," said the Silver Surfer. "Or perhaps it means everything. Norrin Radd, you see, is *me*."

ON THE communications screen at the Baxter Building, the face of Captain America gazed down.

Johnny Storm, seated alongside Reed, Sue and Ben, mused on the fact that you could not look at this man—the best possible argument for patriotism—and not feel inadequate.

Captain America had stood shoulder to shoulder with Allied troops throughout the Second World War, bringing the fight to Hitler on just about every battlefront, from rousting Bundists at home to opposing Axis forces all across the European theater, and beyond.

Then, after being trapped in suspended animation for decades, frozen in a block of Arctic ice, he had been miraculously revived; and now he carried on the good fight in the present day, as resolute and undaunted as ever, both on his own and as a member of the Avengers. He wasn't the strongest or fastest or most agile super hero out there, but what he lacked in those departments he made up for with sheer grit and determination. Not to mention that disc-shaped shield of his, a dual-purpose defensive and offensive weapon, which he wielded with preternatural skill.

Every time Johnny met him—whether in person or, as now, remotely—he had to fight the impulse to salute. He refrained only because it felt impertinent for a non-military person to do so to a soldier.

"Thank you for calling, Dr. Richards," Captain America said. "I was about to get in touch with you anyway. I wanted to talk about what's happening up on your roof. I'm guessing that's why you've reached out."

In the background, the three other current serving members of the Avengers leaned in over Cap's shoulder. There was Hawkeye, clad in purple and black, with his bow slung across his chest and his arrow-filled quiver on his back. There was the speedster Quicksilver, his green uniform emblazoned with a diagonal lightning bolt, like a sash; and beside him his sister the Scarlet Witch, fine-featured and ethereal in red leotard and face-framing headdress.

"It's all over the TV news," Cap went on. "Footage of a gigantic figure and some sort of spaceship on top of the Baxter Building. Who is he and what's he trying to accomplish?"

Reed explained succinctly about Galactus and his intentions. He was freshly showered and shaved, his hair washed and combed, and he looked a lot tidier and more composed than before, though his eyes were still red-rimmed from lack of sleep.

"Holy cow!" exclaimed Hawkeye when he had finished. "I've heard of bad guys trying to take over the world, but have it for breakfast? So this is the way the world ends—not with a bang, or a whimper, but with a great big *munch*."

"Yakk it up, Robin Hood," said Ben acerbically. "This ain't no laughin' matter. We hit the big G with our best shots, and he brushed us off like we was pikers. We're fresh out of ideas how to tackle him."

"And so you came to us," Hawkeye said. "Who'd've thought it? The FF going begging to a proper super team."

"Hey!" Johnny bristled. "You people aren't so hot. All your heavy hitters have bailed on you, apart from Cap. What have you got now? Two ex-members of the Brotherhood of Evil Mutants, a known terrorist organization, and a carny sideshow trick shooter who used to be a crook and an enemy spy."

"Jonathan Storm!" Sue scolded. "That is uncalled for. Apologize."

"What have I said that isn't true, sis? If it weren't for Cap leading them, nobody'd even begin to take this version of the Avengers seriously. Most of the news outlets don't, that's for darn sure."

Johnny was thinking of the largely negative media coverage that had attended Captain America's announcement of the new Avengers line-up a few weeks earlier. Among the wider public, the jury was still out on "Cap's Kooky Quartet", as they had been dubbed. There was understandable skepticism as to whether three former super villains could truly reform, and the significant power downgrade the team had undergone left their longstanding nickname, Earth's Mightiest Heroes, looking a somewhat hollow boast.

Hawkeye leaned close to the camera, jabbing a callused forefinger at Johnny.

"Now, you listen up, Storm, you little smartmouth," he said, his face contorted in a snarl. "One, I was never a crook. I was wrongly accused of theft, and cleared afterward. Two, I was no damn spy. I got used, is all. And three, I don't take that kind of lip from anyone, least of all a snot-nosed punk who lucked into getting some flame powers. I *worked* to get good at what I do, and if you were here at Avengers Mansion right now, I'd show you what a 'carny sideshow trick shooter' is capable of. Believe me, you'd be hollering for your mommy in no time."

"As for my brother and me," said the Scarlet Witch, chiming in, "we wholeheartedly denounce our time as allies of Magneto."

"We were coerced into working with him," Quicksilver growled, "and left at the first opportunity."

Johnny was about to retort, but Captain America got in before he could.

"Hawkeye, Wanda, Pietro," he said, calm but stern. "Can it, all three of you. And you, Mr. Storm—I appreciate you must be under a great deal of strain, but there's no need to take it out on my colleagues. The Avengers are here to help the FF any way we can, and squabbling amongst ourselves is the least productive use of our time."

Johnny immediately felt chastened and foolish. It was like being told off by your father. Worse: it was like being told off by the entire nation.

"Yes, Cap. Sorry, Cap," he mumbled.

"Think nothing of it, son," Captain America said. "Everyone's allowed to blow off steam once in a while. Dr. Richards, what do you want from us? Name it. Anything."

"Frankly, Captain," said Reed, "I have no idea. Galactus has us stymied. He's just too powerful to confront head-on. I... I don't know what to do."

"I'd like to say I could call up Thor and Iron Man. Technically they're still reserve members of the Avengers, and I very much doubt they'd mind pitching in. They said they'd always drop everything and help out in cases of emergency, and if this Galactus business isn't an emergency, I don't know what is. The only trouble is, we don't know their current whereabouts, either of them. Thor was last seen scrapping with Hercules here in the city, but after that he vanished off the radar. Chances are he's in Asgard. That's usually where he goes when he isn't on what he calls Midgard, and we call Earth."

"And there ain't no phone hotline to the realm of the Asgardian gods," Hawkeye chipped in.

"As for Iron Man," Captain America said, "he too is MIA. Rumor has it that Tony Stark—who, you don't need me to remind you, Iron Man bodyguards for—has been abducted by the Mandarin. That's the chatter in US intelligence circles, at any rate. Meaning Iron Man will have gone to find him, so they're both most likely somewhere in China; and while I've no doubt Shellhead will manage to pull his and his boss's fat out of the fryer, there's no telling when they'll get home. Then there are our two other founder members…"

"Giant-Man and the Wasp are on a leave of absence," the Scarlet Witch said. "As I'm sure you know, they are a couple, but things are shaky between them and they're taking time out to work on their relationship."

Captain America steepled his fingers. "Which leaves just the four of us—the Avengers minus, as young Mr. Storm put it, the 'heavy hitters'. We're at your disposal, of course, Dr. Richards, but…"

"But," said Reed, "with all due respect, Captain, your team as it stands doesn't have the sheer muscle required. And even with the likes of Thor on board, you still wouldn't."

"I don't think I would dispute that. If the Fantastic Four themselves can't seem to put a dent in this Galactus entity, I don't see how we could. What I will tell you is this."

The Living Legend of World War II bent a little closer to the camera. His bright blue eyes shone with conviction.

"I do not doubt for one second that you four are equal to the task. I understand that at the moment the situation looks hopeless. There's a godlike being who's threatening to bleed this planet dry, like some sort of cosmic vampire, and nothing you've done so far has persuaded him to back off. But I've been in hopeless situations before, and one thing I've learned: the human spirit will prevail."

His words fell on Johnny's ears like the pealing of church bells. It wasn't just what Captain America was saying, it was the passionate intensity with which he was saying it. This was a man famed for never backing down, never giving up, no matter the odds against him, no matter how slim the prospect of success.

"There is always a way," Captain America continued, "a way to bring down even the fearsomest of foes. The tyrants who seem invincible, the oppressors who think the world is theirs to do with as they please—in the end, they always fall. We've proved it countless times in the past, and today you four are going to prove it again. We Avengers aren't just relying on you, we're rooting for you. The whole planet would be, too, if people were fully aware what's going on. Earth's future hinges on the Fantastic Four achieving victory this day, and in my view, we couldn't be in safer hands."

With that, Captain America cut the connection.

The Fantastic Four sat there, quietly stunned.

At last Ben broke the silence. "Boy, if I had hairs on the back of my neck, they'd be standin' up right now."

"Agreed," Sue said. "I have chills."

"Me too," said Johnny, "and that's not something a Human Torch says often."

Even Reed looked impressed. "No getting around it, that was a stirring speech."

"Stirring?" said Ben. "I want to head up to the roof this second and march on Galactus while singing 'The Star-Spangled Banner'. And I ain't even kiddin'."

"I would query the wisdom of such a course of action."

This comment came from a fifth party.

The Fantastic Four, as one, turned.

Behind them, having appeared as if out of thin air, stood Uatu the Watcher.

o———o

"OH, SO you're back, huh?" said Ben. "How was the moon? Did you get bored up there or somethin'? Decide what's happening down here is a lot more entertaining?"

His caustic humor was lost on Uatu, who merely blinked at him, then said, "I have not been idle during my brief lunar sojourn. I have spent the time scouring the Watcher computer archives, delving deep into our extensive records."

"Am I to take it that you've found something in them?" Reed said. "Something that might help us in our hour of need?"

"It is possible I have. I cannot guarantee that it will be advantageous. The promise it holds out may well prove false."

"But anything is better than nothing," said Sue.

"Indeed, Mrs. Richards," said Uatu. "What I am referring to is a certain artifact of almost immeasurable power, which may be capable of deterring Galactus. The act of retrieving this item, however, lies so far outside my remit as a Watcher that I cannot even consider the idea. One of you must do it."

"Which one?" said Ben.

"Any of us would be willing," said Sue.

Uatu turned towards Johnny and fixed him with a somber stare.

"You."

Johnny pointed at his own chest. "Me?"

"The artifact is known as the Ultimate Nullifier," Uatu said, "and you—and only you, Mr. Storm—stand a chance of retrieving it."

THE SILVER Surfer seemed, to Alicia, both delighted and disconcerted. She could sense him shifting in his seat, tipping his head from side to side as though hearing strains of distant music. She could almost *feel* him rubbing his brow.

"Norrin Radd," she prompted. "That's your real name?"

"That is I," he replied. "Or *was* I. And it's not all I remember. More is coming back to me. I recall a world. My homeworld. It was known as… as Zenn-La."

"Zenn-La," Alicia echoed. "What a lovely name."

"It was a paradise, Alicia Masters. To some, at least."

"Please, just call me Alicia. And in return, may I call you Norrin?"

"You may," the Surfer said, "Alicia."

"Tell me about this paradise of yours. About Zenn-La."

But there was no answer from the Silver Surfer. He appeared to have lapsed into reverie.

Alicia waited patiently. She was very aware how peculiar this all was: sitting in her studio, conversing with an alien being—an enigmatic creature who, half an hour ago, had been a complete stranger to her. Even by the standards of someone who socialized with the Fantastic Four, it was an extraordinary situation.

And yet there was something pleasingly mundane about it too. The two of them were talking and sharing tea and cookies, just as Alicia might with a human acquaintance.

Her thoughts strayed to how she and the Surfer would look to an outside observer, and from there, as was a habit with her, she started to form the image of a sculpture in her mind—the pair of them face to face across a table, as a kind of study in contrasts. Herself depicted in the tradition of Rodin: figurative, with a certain solid heft, posed as though in motion, slightly contorted. The Surfer depicted in the style of Elisabeth Frink: monumental, not so representational, his anatomy simplified but still expressive. One world meeting another. Their postures mirroring each other's, to accentuate both their differences and their similarities.

At last the Surfer spoke again. "I have recalled another name. Shalla-Bal."

"What is that? Another world?"

"No. Shalla-Bal was… She was significant to me."

"I'd like to hear about her."

The Surfer seemed to be making his mind up about something. "Alicia, why are you showing such interest in me?"

"Simple. I'm interested in people. I *like* people. And you're a person."

"I am not human."

"Does it matter?"

"I have led Galactus to your planet. I have ushered in your world's demise. In the past, when carrying out this duty of mine elsewhere, I have been met with hostility, even hatred."

"I've already explained, this isn't the end of Earth. The Fantastic Four, remember?"

"Even so."

"Surfer—Norrin—I was raised by my stepfather," Alicia said, "a very bad man. Thanks to that, I've learned not just how to forgive but how to see the best in anyone. I'm also quite convinced that there isn't an evil bone in your body and that I couldn't hate you if I tried. So, go on. Zenn-La. Shalla-Bal. I want to know all about them."

There was a pause, and then the Silver Surfer said, "Very well."

A LONG TIME AGO…

...ON A planet far, far away.

Zenn-La.

A marvel of the universe.

Zenn-La.

A glinting gem of a world that seemed to have achieved perfection.

Zenn-La.

Where war, crime and illness were just dimly remembered stories.

Where all challenges had been conquered, all injustices overcome, all ambitions achieved.

Where people lived nigh-on endless lives devoted solely to the pursuit of pleasure.

Where machines and computers catered to their every need, freeing them to indulge their whims.

Zenn-La, a name that many might—and did—consider synonymous with heaven.

All except one man.

Norrin Radd.

NORRIN RADD, alone among Zenn-Lavians, was discontented.

Others were happy to drift along in a state of constant idleness, questioning nothing, accepting everything, treating the extraordinary comfort and ease of their existences as simply their due.

Not Norrin Radd.

Norrin could not ride the conveyor-belt walkways through Zenn-La's teeming, majestic cities without wondering when people had become too lazy to move their legs.

He could not attend one of the parties that always seemed to be going on somewhere and not wish he was anywhere else, away from these laughing, jabbering fools.

He could not ride the monorail cars that wound through the wildlife parks and fail to think how the docile captive animals below weren't much different from the people staring down at them.

He could not see schoolchildren sitting in their rows, hooked up to instant-learning hypno-cubes, without asking himself whether an education so easily acquired was worth having.

He could not view the proceedings of the Zenn-Lavian parliament, where politicians debated for hours on end with the utmost solemnity about complete trivia, and not feel despair at the pointlessness of it.

As often as possible, Norrin would take himself off to some remote, uninhabited wilderness spot, in order to get away from all the endless, mindless prattle, the sybaritic wallowing in luxury, the soul-sapping mechanization. There, by himself, he would ruminate on the meaninglessness of life on Zenn-La. He firmly believed that people were supposed to strive, to struggle, to yearn. They were not supposed to have everything handed to them on a plate. It robbed them of their drive to improve.

He would dictate thoughts like these into his speech journal, recording his dissatisfaction—although who would ever read his musings, or care about them, he did not know.

"Those to whom no distant horizons beckon," he stated on one occasion, "for whom no tests and trials remain, though they have inherited a universe, they possess only empty sand."

And on another occasion, he said, "We may have achieved utopia, but it was gained for us by those who came before. *We* have not earned it. Therefore it is not truly ours."

And on yet another: "My people have lost the spirit of high adventure, the thrill of discovery, the longing to inquire further. I, however, refuse to suffer such a fate. I will not chase the fleeting phantom of hedonism. I will not fritter away a centuries-long lifetime in decadence and self-gratification. But how? How may I escape the tyranny of a golden age and become the free, whole man I know I am meant to be?"

One of his frequent haunts was the Museum of Antiquity. Here were stored the few surviving scraps of Zenn-La's imperfect past. He was drawn time after time towards the Weapon Supreme, a relic of the era of war that had riven the planet several millennia ago. It was still functioning, kept operational simply to prove how unnecessary it now was; the Zenn-Lavians *could* fire it if they wanted to, and the fact that they never did only went to show their total lack of bellicosity.

At the museum, too, there were immersive-reality dioramas where you could relive parts of history as though you were actually present. You could watch your savage, fur-clad forebears, from pre-civilized times, slaying the huge marauding beasts that preyed upon them. You could bear witness to battles from the ten-thousand-year-long age of wars, when Zenn-Lavian fought Zenn-Lavian to the death over such petty bones of contention as territory and resources. You could see the period of enlightenment that followed, born from a desire to renounce conflict and embrace peace and wisdom.

Thereafter came the great expansion, when pioneering astronauts answered the siren call of outer space and traveled far and wide through the galaxies, searching for wonders. Fearlessly they probed the unknown, planting the flag of Zenn-La on countless worlds.

And then it seemed that the Zenn-Lavian race had gone too far, seen too much, found more than it ever wished to; and no longer did people care about the distant stars and the universe's other lifeforms. They withdrew to their mother world, never to venture forth again. They grew insular and inward-looking.

Or that was Norrin's opinion, at any rate. They gave up on all they could have accomplished, all that potential, to concentrate purely on personal enjoyment.

Norrin seldom left the Museum of Antiquity without feeling justified in his sense of disgruntlement. While others went there to remind themselves how fortunate they were to live when and where they did, he went to have his innermost doubts validated.

o———o

THERE WAS no one Norrin could share these feelings with.

No one, that is, apart from Shalla-Bal.

Anyone else with whom he broached the subject either turned a deaf ear or called him ridiculous. "Why complain?" he was told. "Why find problems where there are none? What is so wrong with being happy?"

Only Shalla-Bal tolerated his grumblings, and then grudgingly.

She and Norrin had met as children, and over the years, as they matured into adulthood, love had blossomed between them. At first Norrin had found it difficult to express his attraction to Shalla-Bal. His intense, brooding introversion made him distant and reticent. She, however, intuited the depth of their bond better than he did, and gradually broke down his defenses until at last he was able to admit he loved her. She in turn declared that she had never *not* loved him.

Since then, they had been as close as any couple could be, although now and then Norrin's dark moods did put a strain on their relationship. Shalla-Bal repeatedly insisted that he should stop obsessing on his unhappiness. Everything he could ever want or possibly need was right here on Zenn-La.

"It is right here, indeed, in me," she would say, pressing his hand to her heart. "In the love we share. Why can you not accept that, Norrin? Is it so difficult? I know that the rest of Zenn-La seems hollow and empty to you, but this—what we have between us—is solid and true."

Her words would soothe his troubled breast, at least for a time. Her beauty and her compassion, her kindness and her kisses—these should be enough for anyone. More than enough.

Yet still, inevitably, the gnawing ache would return. The shadows would darken in Norrin's soul. The hunger—for endeavor, for fulfilment, for *more*—would grip him, and nothing could truly assuage it, not even Shalla-Bal's reasoned arguments and soft caresses.

Then came the day, the fateful day, when everything changed.

ZENN-LA'S DEEP-SPACE scopes registered the sudden approach of a planet-sized starship at the outermost periphery of their range. It was on course for Zenn-La itself, and the scopes detected unimaginable levels of power contained within it. What the starship presaged, what designs its occupants had on Zenn-La, remained unclear, but the very fact of its arrival was cause for concern.

Parliament was hastily convened, but the politicians dithered and quarreled among themselves. Never in living memory had they been confronted with a situation like this, and they had no idea how to respond.

In the end they agreed to leave the decision-making to Zenn-La's computers. The computers, after all, ran everything, controlled everything. Zenn-Lavians had long ago surrendered mastery of the minutiae of day-to-day living to them. The computers would know what to do.

The computers made their calculations and were definitive in their conclusion.

Attack.

And so the Weapon Supreme was deployed. The curators at the Museum of Antiquity oversaw the preparations, making sure the device was in full working order, as they had done for generations—the difference being that now, for the first time in eons, the thing was actually going to be fired.

The Weapon Supreme was wheeled out into the open. Its enormous barrel was trained skyward. A firing solution was entered.

All of Zenn-La watched, either at first hand or on their telescreens. Watched, and waited, and held their breath. Each person felt a trepidation such as they had not known before. This event was unprecedented. Never had so drastic a step been taken.

The Weapon Supreme used the planet's molten core for its power source, and it had been designed to be the ultimate deterrent, unleashing a huge, focused pulse of antimatter mighty enough to shatter a moon. Its creation had, in fact, helped bring Zenn-La's era of warfare to an end and usher in the ensuing eternal peacetime. When you had a single weapon easily capable of destroying the whole world, the risk of continued conflict, and possible self-annihilation, became just too great.

The land trembled as the Weapon Supreme was fired. Buildings were rocked. Mountains cracked. Seas surged. A vast, iridescently shimmering beam shot up out of the atmosphere and struck the approaching starship.

Its aim was dead on target. The starship was lost from view

amid a brilliant, coruscating explosion that, for a time, outshone the sun in the Zenn-Lavian sky. Surely it had been destroyed.

Although it had come at a cost, this outcome was nonetheless greeted with joy by the population. Whatever threat the menacingly vast starship may have presented, it had been neutralized. Zenn-La was damaged but saved. Already the machines were beginning to make repairs, shoring up broken buildings, restoring power wherever there had been an outage, and healing the injured. In no time, things would be back to normal. Zenn-Lavians could return to their lives of blissful cossetedness.

So it seemed, for just a few heady minutes…

Until it became apparent that the starship had survived the assault.

And not just survived: it was intact. It had shrugged off the full force of the Weapon Supreme as though the Zenn-Lavians had hit it with nothing more powerful than a flyswatter.

As the starship loomed ever larger in near space, terror seized the populace. Terror like none they had known before. They turned to the computers for advice, but the computers could offer little of any use. That was perhaps the most terrifying thing of all: these electronic brains which people had relied on for so long were suddenly impotent. They began spitting out gibberish answers, as though succumbing to a kind of madness.

One man, and perhaps one man alone, saw the worldwide crisis as an opportunity.

Norrin Radd.

NORRIN RADD knew that Zenn-La was sorely endangered, even if he didn't know the exact nature of the peril. He also knew that someone had to do something about it, and reckoned that that someone was Norrin Radd.

He hurried to Shalla-Bal, to inform her of his intentions. Her residence was strewn with debris—window shards, broken ornaments, pieces of cracked ceiling tile—as a result of the firing of the Weapon Supreme. Domestic robots were making inroads into cleaning it all up.

"If the starship contains an invading army, as seems likely," he said to her, "that gives me someone I can parley with. I am going to fly out in a spacecraft and do just that."

"Why, Norrin?" Shalla-Bal said. "Whoever is in that ship means us ill. Otherwise our computers would not have counseled attacking it. Whether the occupants mean to subjugate us or destroy us, either way Zenn-La, as we know it, is doomed. Stay with me. If the end is coming, let us meet it together, in each other's embrace."

"No!" He held her by both arms. "I will not surrender meekly. I refuse to. Don't you understand, Shalla-Bal? This is what I have been searching for my whole life. A true test of my mettle. A chance to prove that I have fighting spirit, even if everyone else has lost theirs."

"But if you were beside me, both of us proclaiming our love even as catastrophe descends, would that not be defiance enough?"

"Shalla-Bal, I do love you, and that is why I cannot be by your side now," Norrin said. "To save you—and every Zenn-Lavian, but you above all—I would try anything, dare anything, face any hazard. I would risk my life for you, and if I were to lose it in the name of protecting you, I would think that a price worth paying."

"Is that so, Norrin? Or is it that you seek glory and are merely claiming to do so in my name, in an attempt to justify the deed?"

"Shalla-Bal, I—"

"Go, Norrin." She pushed him away. Tears glistened in her emerald-brilliant eyes. "Go and chase your destiny, vainglorious as it is. Nothing I can say is going to stop you. Just know that you have broken my heart. Think on that as you depart on this futile mission of yours."

Norrin's own heart was breaking as he left Shalla-Bal in the wreckage of her home. He was wounded by her accusations and refused to admit they might have some truth in them. He consoled himself with the thought that if he was successful and managed to avert the coming disaster, he would return a hero. Shalla-Bal would acknowledge that he had been right all along, as would all Zenn-Lavians. He would have shown everyone, by example, how vital it was to be bold, to be willing to risk everything. He would have shone a bright light on the passivity of their lives, and this might rouse them out of their apathy and inspire them to become again the venturesome race they had once been.

He commandeered a small, personal-use spacecraft, one designed for taking joyrides into low orbit. He took off and was soon escaping Zenn-La's gravity well and hurtling through the void towards the starship.

Never had he beheld so colossal a construct. It was like a loop of metal twisted in on itself, both simple and elaborate, stately in a way, but intimidating too. Even as he approached, he noted that its progress towards Zenn-La had slowed, and by the time he reached it, it had come to a complete standstill. He didn't know whether this was pure coincidence, or if the starship's occupants had detected the presence of his craft and recognized him to be an ambassador from the nearby planet.

He had his answer a few moments later when a hatch opened in the starship's hull. Clearly this was an invitation to come aboard.

Soon Norrin was treading warily through immense, gleaming halls, hearing the susurration of unseen machinery all around him and the echo of his own footfalls. He walked for hours, it seemed, encountering no one. The proportions of the starship's interior—from doorways to staircases—suggested it was built for giants, beings easily three times his height. But where were they?

After a while, he began to wonder whether the ship was uncrewed. Perhaps it was entirely automated, journeying through space on some kind of cruise control. Perhaps those traveling inside it were long dead, and the starship was simply carrying on without them, mindlessly following a preprogrammed flight plan.

Alternatively, the occupants might all be held in suspended animation somewhere amid this world-sized labyrinth, perhaps refugees from some fallen civilization. They were waiting for a habitable planet to hove into view; and once one did, such as Zenn-La, they would be awoken and swoop in to colonize it.

Norrin imagined these and many other scenarios to explain the apparent absence of life aboard the ship.

That was until he at last came across a living being.

o———o

THE MAN was a giant, just as Norrin had surmised.

He was, moreover, no mere man.

He stood, proud and imposing, in a cathedral-like chamber filled with light—so much light, Norrin could scarcely look at it. It hurt his eyes.

Squinting against the dazzle, Norrin perceived that the giant was bathing in the light. No, more than that. He was drawing it into himself, suffusing himself with it. The light was pure energy, and it sizzled and frothed around the giant like sea foam, before vanishing into his body.

It was an awesome sight, and Norrin felt it was one that mortals were not meant to behold.

Gradually, the light faded. The giant drew a deep, satisfied sigh. Then he turned and gazed down upon the quailing Norrin. A few last flickers of dissipating energy rippled up and down his blue-and-magenta garb. His eyes, through the narrow slits in his high-crowned helmet, were dark and baleful.

"I know who you are, Norrin Radd," he said, "and I know why you have come here."

"H-How?" Norrin stammered.

"I am Galactus. All is known to me."

"Galactus."

The word dredged up a dim recollection in Norrin's brain. Once, in the Museum of Antiquity, he had stumbled across a reference to an entity by that name. It was contained in a report made by one of Zenn-La's most intrepid astronauts, Daquan Caddo, who had voyaged farther and visited more corners of the cosmos than his peers. Caddo had heard rumors of a godlike being, Galactus, who roved the universe seeking worlds to devour. He dismissed the idea, thinking it to be nothing more than interstellar folklore, or some sort of baseless traveler's tale—the sort of scary story that could be shared over a drinking table, to bring a pleasurable little shudder to listeners.

But Galactus, it turned out, was real.

And Norrin was looking right at him.

Once he had recovered his wits, Norrin forced himself to address this mighty figure. He had come this far. How could he not go through with his plan?

"Hear me out, Galactus," he said. "You have doubtless come to consume Zenn-La. I say to you that there are other worlds you might choose, ones less developed, uninhabited ones even—ones whose destruction would not represent such a loss."

"I have already monitored your planet," Galactus answered. "Your race has stagnated. It no longer advances or innovates. Can you truly argue that it is more deserving of survival than any other? On the contrary, Zenn-La is past its prime and, for that reason alone, merits culling. But also, it is rich in energy, and I have depleted my last reserves. It is that which you just witnessed—Galactus using up the very last of his stored sustenance. I must replenish my supplies, and your world will serve admirably in that regard."

"But what of the people there?" Norrin protested.

What of my beloved Shalla-Bal? he nearly added.

"It is regrettable that my feeding must often be accompanied by the annihilation of sentients," Galactus replied, "but I have long since ceased to lament that fact. My continued existence trumps that of others. Now, this discussion is closed. I must begin the process of converting the matter of your planet into energy."

"Wait!" Norrin cried. A desperate idea had formed in his mind. "I have an offer to make to you."

Galactus peered at him in mild perplexity. "An offer? What could one as lowly as you possibly have to give to one such as Galactus?"

"My loyalty." Norrin could hardly believe the words he was speaking. "Take me as... as your herald. Send me out into the universe to find planets for you to consume. Let me probe the spaceways, scouting for worlds, saving you the inconvenience of doing so yourself."

Galactus said nothing, which Norrin took to indicate that he was considering the proposition.

"And in return," he went on, "you are to leave Zenn-La alone. That is my price. My undying servitude, in exchange for sparing the planet of my birth. What do you say, Galactus?"

"Think, Norrin Radd," the giant figure said. "You would be giving up your world, your people, all you have ever known, for all time. Once you have made this sacrifice, there is no going back. You will always and ever after be my emissary. Is that truly what you desire?"

Norrin weighed it up, but in the end it was really no choice at all. For almost as long as he could recall, he had yearned for more than just the dull, contented trudge of life on Zenn-La. He would, in truth, miss nothing about his homeworld, save for Shalla-Bal.

He hoped she would understand.

"I accept," he said.

"Then we have a bargain," said Galactus. "And so, prepare

yourself." He extended a hand over Norrin, who did his best to stand tall and not cringe. "You are about to be transformed. Remade. Reborn. I cannot promise that it will be painless."

o———o

IT WAS not.

It was moments—or perhaps an eternity—of sheer agony.

Norrin was bathed in searing light and heat. Hurricane-like forces whirled around him, tearing at him, flensing, flaying. He could feel his body being rent asunder, his very molecules being dismantled and then assembled anew.

So great was the pain that he longed to lose consciousness; but somehow, through it all, the essence of Norrin Radd remained intact and he felt every second of his metamorphosis. The starburst explosion of each cell as it was ripped apart and reconfigured. The inversion and eversion of flesh. The snapping and putting-back-together of bone. The all-over twisting and bending of his form as it was molded like clay in the potter's hand.

He was *becoming*.

He was shrugging off the fragile, mortal trappings of Norrin Radd and being forged into something sleeker, more durable, almost unbreakable.

And when it was all over, he was on his knees, and vapor was purling off him, and there was power within him—crackling, effervescing, pulsating—such power! He was charged with it, brimming with it, to the point where he thought he hardly could contain it all. Power so exceptional and unparalleled that it even had a name: the Power Cosmic.

"Arise," intoned Galactus, and Norrin Radd did as bidden, getting shakily to his feet like a newborn foal. He peered around himself with eyes that could see in frequencies he had never realized existed, eyes that could delve into microscopic detail, eyes that could perceive the perpetual jostling interplay of subatomic forces.

He looked at his arms, which were now coated in a flexible metallic substance.

He looked at his hands, which he knew now could unleash bursts of phenomenal power.

He saw the reflection of his own face in the mirror-like surface of his palms, and recognized little of Norrin Radd in it. It bore just the vaguest resemblance to his old self, as though his features had been sanded and smoothed.

"Your body," Galactus said, "has been encased in a silvery membrane of my own creation. It is a carapace that will shield you from heat, from cold, and from lack of available oxygen. From this moment forth, neither the frigid emptiness of space, nor the all-consuming radioactive inferno of the hottest sun, can cause you harm."

Norrin did not doubt that any of this was true.

"Furthermore," said Galactus, "to transport you through the unending, trackless cosmos, I give you the perfect vehicle."

From out of nothing he conjured a long, flat board that appeared to be made of the same metallic material sheathing Norrin's body.

"An indestructible flying surfboard," Galactus said. "Yours to control with but a thought. Responsive to your slightest whim or directive."

The board hovered in front of Norrin. He stepped onto it and immediately felt connected with it, he a part of it and it a part of him. They were bonded at some deep, intrinsic level, linked even when physically separated.

"No longer are you Norrin Radd," Galactus declared. "That life is lost to you. Now and forevermore, you are my herald. Now and forevermore, you are..."

THE SILVER SURFER

FOR NORRIN Radd, it was indisputable.

Already, everything he had ever known about himself was beginning to slip away. His youth and upbringing on Zenn-La, his family, his growing feelings of disaffection and isolation, his love for Shalla-Bal—even now, these seemed far-off, like land on the horizon viewed from the stern of a ship, receding slowly into the haze of distance. In time, he sensed they would vanish altogether.

He activated his surfboard. It sprang to life at his mental command, and together he and it raced through Galactus's starship, in search of an exit. He soared out into the pure vacuum of space, his board carrying him at speeds no conventional spacecraft could ever match.

For a time there was nothing in his heart but exultation as he tested the surfboard's capabilities and found them all but limitless. That which he imagined the board could do, it did. It seemed an extension of not just his body but his very soul.

At length, the thrill subsided. A sober thought struck him, and he veered off in the direction of Zenn-La. Before he embarked upon his new life as Galactus's herald, there was someone he must first say farewell to.

o———o

SHALLA-BAL RECOGNIZED him almost immediately.

"Norrin?" she said, her voice quavering somewhat. "It *is* you, isn't it? What has happened to you? You reached the starship. You must have. But what did they do to you there? What have you become?"

"The Norrin Radd you knew, Shalla-Bal," he replied, "is no more. From this day forward, there is only the Silver Surfer."

"You speak with Norrin's voice, yet you sound so distant, so detached."

"I am here to tell you that Zenn-La is safe. I have struck a bargain, and your world will live."

"But it is your world too, surely."

"No longer," said the Surfer. "My side of the bargain is that I must leave. I now am beholden to Galactus. He is my master. Wherever he goes, so must I. His will shall I serve, his bidding shall I do, henceforth and ever after."

"Galactus?"

"He who came to destroy Zenn-La, and he who, through my intercession, has agreed to abstain from doing so."

Shalla-Bal understood. "At the price of *you*. Oh, Norrin! It is too high a cost."

"No cost is too high," the Surfer said, "for the life of my beloved."

She touched his silvery skin. "You have done this for me? Allowed yourself to be transformed thus, for me?"

"For all Zenn-La, but yes, mostly for you, Shalla-Bal. I can depart with my head held high, safe in the knowledge that thanks to me, you still live."

Her face darkened. "No! You shouldn't have!" She pounded him angrily on the chest. "I would rather we had perished together than this. Did you not think about me? Did it not occur to you how I might feel, having to carry on with my life, alone, while you are forever elsewhere? Knowing we can never be together again?"

"My actions were selfless."

"Or selfish," she countered. "This is what you've wanted all along, isn't it? Escape from Zenn-La. Freedom from what you see as our world's stifling constrictions. You say you have done it in my name, but that is only an excuse."

"Not so, Shalla-Bal."

She spun away from him. "I—I can't bear to look at you anymore." Her tone was as bitter as could be. "Leave then, Norrin. Go off on this grand adventure of yours. Forget about me. I know you will."

"Shalla-Bal, this acrimony is unjustif—"

"Did you not hear me?" she snapped. "I said go!"

She kept her back turned to him. The Silver Surfer looked at her heaving shoulders, her swaying hair, and heard her sobs; and he knew that nothing he could say would console her. He had hoped she might understand his decision, perhaps even praise it. He had not been prepared for this outpouring of resentment. He did not blame her for it, however. She was right, he hadn't once taken her side of things into account.

He realized, in that moment, that he was not the only one who had made a profound sacrifice here. The difference was, Shalla-Bal hadn't asked to or been consulted. He had forced it on her.

He alighted on his board and glided slowly out of her residence.

Outside, he took off for the skies.

As he went, he heard Shalla-Bal talking to herself. She could not have known that his ears would pick up the sound of her voice at a distance when no normal person might.

"Norrin," she said, "you fool. You had everything—everything a man could possibly wish for—and you cast it aside. And yet… I still love you. I will always love you."

"I will always love you too, Shalla-Bal," the Surfer whispered as he soared into the upper atmosphere, and a single tear trickled down his silvery cheek.

THERE WAS silence in Alicia's studio when the Silver Surfer finished his account of how he came to be.

Eventually Alicia said, "That has to be one of the most tragic things I've ever heard."

"Every word of it is true," the Surfer said.

"I don't doubt it. You poor man." She groped for his hand and laid hers lightly on it. "Please tell me that you have seen Shalla-Bal since then. That the two of you have reconciled."

"I have not. We have not. From that day to this, I have done nothing other than roam the cosmos, seeking out planets for Galactus. At first, I made sure to lead him to worlds where life did not abound in great profusion. Then, when those failed to satisfy him, I led him to primordial worlds where the oceans swarmed with algae and other unicellular organisms, and where the land was covered in nothing but forests and fungi—and thence to worlds where only the lowliest, most basic creatures swam or crawled or slithered or flew. For a time, these sufficed. Galactus was fed, and my conscience was salved. For, in those early days, there was still a part of me that was Norrin Radd, and that part had no wish to see intelligent beings perish. However..."

He paused.

"As the centuries passed," he went on, "Galactus began complaining that his hunger was never truly alleviated. He craved the special, higher levels of energy that could only be derived from more complex lifeforms."

"It was like you were keeping him on a restricted diet," Alicia said.

"You could say that. By then, my previous life had become so remote to me that I had all but forgotten I was ever Norrin Radd. So it seemed of no consequence to start finding planets which bore the kind of life my master desired. The Silver Surfer had no difficulty doing that, even if Norrin Radd would have. The Silver Surfer lacked the necessary empathy."

"As a wise man once said, 'We are what we pretend to be, so we must be careful about what we pretend to be.' Norrin Radd was the Surfer for so long, and did the job so well, so diligently, that in the end there was no longer any Norrin Radd. Until now, at least." She withdrew her hand. "Now, you've rediscovered who you are."

"Thanks to you, Alicia," the Surfer said.

"Oh, I don't think I did anything."

"But you did," he insisted, "if only because you reminded me of Shalla-Bal. Had I not met you, these memories of mine would have stayed repressed. You, simply by being you, and by possessing all the qualities I loved in Shalla-Bal, brought them flooding back. Once more, I know who I am. And now I can see how wrong I have been. How appallingly misguided."

"In what sense?"

"In the sense, obviously, that I am guilty of condemning countless billions to death!" the Surfer said, heat entering his voice. "I am as responsible for that as Galactus is. If not for me, all those worlds, those civilizations, would still exist."

"I think you're being too hard on yourself."

"I am not being nearly hard enough."

"You cannot help it that you lost sight of your humanity,

Norrin," Alicia said. "Galactus more or less took it from you when he made you into the Silver Surfer. You clung on to it for as long as you could. But time is a thief. It steals the goodness from us, if we're not careful. You've been out there in the universe for centuries…"

"Millennia," he interjected.

"A phenomenally long time. Out there, on your own, surfing, searching. I doubt you've spoken with anyone during that period apart from your master."

"Rarely. This is the longest conversation I have had since leaving Zenn-La. Only with Shalla-Bal could I talk as freely, and as intimately, as I am with you."

"There you go. All that solitude, that lack of interaction and companionship—little wonder your personality became eroded to a nub. You mustn't condemn yourself. You were in Galactus's thrall. You were his implement, the knife he used to commit murder. And the knife isn't accountable for what it does; the one who wields it is."

"You use the past tense when referring to my actions," the Surfer said, "as if you believe I am not that person anymore."

"I believe," Alicia said, "that Norrin Radd has returned. He was never truly gone, only dormant, and now, whereas before the Silver Surfer was him, he is the Silver Surfer. He is in control again."

The Surfer was quiet for a long, long time.

Then he said, "There must be restitution." The words were terse and underscored with determination. "Reparations must be made."

Alicia heard him push the chair back and stand up.

"What are you going to do, Norrin?" she asked.

"What is long overdue," came the reply.

She felt his hand on her cheek—warm, firm, vibrant with latent power.

"Thank you, Alicia," the Surfer said. "I fear we shall not meet again, but I want you to know that you, with your gentleness, your curiosity, your courage, have given me back something I had thought long lost."

"And what is that?"

"Hope," he said.

She heard him walk out of the studio. She followed him as he went up the stairs to the roof.

"To me, my board," she heard him say, followed by a *whisk* in the air, which she took to be the sound of his surfboard racing to his side.

"Norrin," she called out. "Norrin!"

But there was only that *whisk* again, a little louder this time, but swiftly dwindling.

The Silver Surfer had gone.

He hadn't said where he was headed.

Alicia, however, thought she had a pretty clear idea where it was.

"Good luck," she said softly, hoping—no, *knowing*—that the Surfer would hear her.

JOHNNY STORM had always thought he was ready for anything. Little could faze him.

Sure, he'd been to some strange places in his time—other worlds, even other dimensions. And sure, he'd come up against some bizarro bad guys, like Wilhelm Van Vile, an artist who could bring his paintings to life using allegedly magical pigments, and the Plantman, a gardener-turned-criminal who wielded a gadget that could animate all forms of vegetation and make them do his bidding.

Johnny had learned to take these things in his stride. They'd become his normal.

Nothing, though, could have prepared him for the assignment Uatu the Watcher was about to send him on.

"So let me get this straight," he said. "You're going to teleport me into outer space."

"Yes," said Uatu.

"To Galactus's starship, which is way out at the edge of the solar system."

"Yes," said Uatu.

"And I'm going to search the ship, which you say is the size of a planet, for an itty-bitty item no bigger than a handgun."

"Yes," said Uatu.

"And then, when I've found it, this Ultimate Nullifier thingy, you'll teleport me back here."

"Yes," said Uatu.

"Okay," said Johnny. "I just need a few moments to wrap my head around all this."

"We do not have a few moments, Johnny Storm," Uatu said. "Time is very much of the essence. In order to aid you in your quest, I am giving you this to wear."

He proffered Johnny a device like an oversized wristwatch. It had a small screen instead of a clockface, and etched into its casing were designs that resembled electronic circuitry diagrams.

"It features a homing signal, attuned to the specific energy signature of the Ultimate Nullifier," he said. "It will guide you to it, somewhat like a compass needle pointing to magnetic north. Once you have retrieved the Nullifier, you need only press the button here on the side. It will alert me and pinpoint your location so that I may teleport you back to Earth."

"Well, that's something, I guess," Johnny said, fitting the device onto his wrist by its flexible strap.

"It is flameproof, of course."

"It'll need to be."

Briefly, Uatu showed him how to switch the homing device on and use it.

"I feel it only fair to warn you that teleportation will not be a pleasant experience," he said. "For one such as me, it is as natural as breathing. For one such as you, with your limited human sensorium, it will be disquieting, perhaps overwhelmingly so."

"All right, I get it. You're a superior being, I'm not, yadda yadda."

"Additionally, Galactus's starship, *Taa II*, will not be without its internal defense mechanisms. Within its confines, you must proceed with caution."

"Anything else?"

"No. That is all."

"Good to hear. I was worried this was going to be difficult."

Uatu squinted at him. "It *will* be difficult. Very."

"I was being sarcastic," Johnny explained.

The other three members of the Fantastic Four had been looking on during this exchange. Now, Sue stepped forward.

"Johnny," she said, "mind you pay attention to what Uatu's just told you. It's going to be dangerous inside Galactus's ship. You keep an eye out, and don't do anything rash."

"Understood, sis."

She enfolded him in a tight hug. "You'd better come back safe and sound, Jonathan Storm," she said in his ear, "or so help me, I'll be mad. And you wouldn't like me when I'm mad."

"I remember from when we were kids," Johnny said. "Only too well. Everyone thinks *I'm* the Storm with the short fuse. They never saw you when you lost it. Like that time you thought I'd been using your toothbrush. Mom and Pop had to haul you off of me."

Sue flushed. "I was sometimes a tad harsh on you, little brother, I know. Rest assured, I loved you then and I love you now."

She broke the embrace and moved away, lowering her head and running the tip of a finger across her eyelashes.

Reed approached him next.

"Best of luck, son," he said, shaking Johnny's hand briskly and firmly. "I know you'll do us proud.

"I sure hope so," Johnny said.

"Uatu has chosen the right candidate for the task. You're a lot smarter and more resourceful than people give you credit for, Johnny."

"Uh, thanks, Reed. I think."

Finally it was Ben's turn.

"Listen, Flamebrain," he said. "You better get back here with that Ultimate Nelligan doodad, pronto. No dawdlin', you hear? 'Cause it sounds like the sooner we get it, the sooner we can use it to zap Galactus, or whatever we're supposed to do with it."

"Don't worry, Ben. I don't plan on hanging around."

"'Course, why Uatu's sending a scrawny little twerp like you on a mission as important as this, I have no idea. Not when there's big, brave piles of rock like me available."

"Could be the job description doesn't say 'musclebound idiot'."

"Hey! That's *Mister* Musclebound Idiot to you."

Ben playfully punched Johnny in the midriff. He used only a tiny fraction of his strength, but even a playful punch from the Thing wasn't much fun for the recipient. Johnny doubled over with an "Oof!"

"What are you trying to do, Ben?" he said hoarsely, wincing. "Cripple me?"

"Nah. Just… Come back in one piece, okay? There ain't no one else who can annoy me like you do, and I don't want to have to start go lookin' for a replacement."

"I love you too, Benjy," Johnny said. He turned to Uatu. "Okay, Watcher. If we're going to do this, let's do it."

"Are you ready, Johnny Storm?"

"Ready as I'll ever be."

"Then brace yourself."

Johnny looked at his three teammates.

The people closest to him.

His family.

"Be seeing you," he said. His mouth felt dry. The words were hard to get out.

Uatu the Watcher raised a hand.

And then Johnny was…

ELSEWHERE

AND NOWHERE.

And everywhere at once.

Pulled in a million different directions, as though he had been plunged into a river with a million different currents.

Wrenched this way and that, up, down, sideways.

Now he was surrounded by pinpricks of light, a swarm of them chasing one another around him like a school of scintillant fish.

Now he was engulfed in absolute, Stygian darkness.

And then there were thousands of Johnny Storms, distorted versions of himself wherever he looked, as though he was trapped in some infinite hall of mirrors at a fairground.

And then he was alone, as alone as anyone had ever been, separated from everything he had ever known, a tiny speck of life amid an unendingly vast nothingness.

His head swam. His head ached. His head felt as though it was no longer part of him.

How long?

How long had he been in this giddying, disorienting state of flux?

Minutes?

Hours?

Days?

A lifetime?

It was like an everlasting rollercoaster ride, and Johnny could not get off.

He prayed for it to end, even as rainbow waves of sound crashed over him and then weird glowing tentacles of light entwined themselves about him.

"Johnny?"

The voice was faint, almost inaudible.

"Johnny?"

He recognized it nonetheless.

"Crystal?" he said, disbelievingly.

All at once, she was standing in front of him. Crystal, of the Inhuman royal family. The girl he had fallen hopelessly, head-over-heels in love with.

"What are you doing here?" he asked.

She gazed at him wisely, knowingly. She didn't seem real—she *couldn't* be real—but Johnny reached out to her anyway.

His hands passed through her body, touching nothing but thin air. This was some intangible spectral Crystal.

"I'm here because you need me to be, Johnny," the intangible spectral Crystal said. "You need something to anchor your mind. You might go insane without that. Just focus on me now. Think about nothing but me—Crystal, your Crystal."

"I am. It's not hard. I think about you all the time, Crys. I miss you so much."

"Hold on to that feeling, Johnny. Let it tether you. Let it remind you who you are, so that you don't lose sight of it."

"I… I want us to be together. You trapped in the Great Refuge, and me outside, unable to reach you, to see you—I can't stand it."

"I know. We'll figure it out, Johnny. But right now, you need to keep your mind on what you're doing. You're nearly there. Just hold on a little longer."

He knew she was right. He concentrated on her face—her sweet, beautiful face—and on the hope that someday soon they would be reunited.

And it worked. It tethered him amid the chaos of the teleportation. It kept the madness around him at bay. He felt calm, as though he were in the eye of a storm, untouched by all the conflicting forces and the bewildering mirages. He clung to the mental image of Crystal, like a life raft.

Then abruptly, the journey—

STOPPED.

Johnny lay sprawled on a hard surface. He felt its solidity beneath him, and he knew he wasn't moving anymore, but all the same it took him several moments to reassure himself that he really had arrived. He still felt as though he was hurtling through… whatever you called the realm that people being teleported hurtled through. His mind had not quite caught up with his body yet. It was like an extreme form of jet lag. Teleport lag, you might call it.

He forced himself to stand up, and instantly regretted it. He was as dizzy as if he had just spent an hour on an out-of-control carousel. He fought the urge to be sick.

Gradually the nausea cleared. On impulse, he looked around for Crystal. He knew she had been just an illusion, a figment his mind had conjured up to protect him in his moment of need. Yet if there was the remotest chance she had been real…

No Crystal.

Only a vast chamber, one so huge, so soaringly spacious, he could barely make out the farthest walls, or the ceiling.

At its center was a raised, throne-like chair, with an array of consoles in front of it, each fitted with screens and a profusion of buttons, dials and readouts. Enormous levers and handles jutted from the consoles, angled towards the chair. You didn't need to be a pilot to realize this was some kind of flight deck—or, to put it in terms a car nut like Johnny understood, the driver's seat. It was built to three times human scale, the right size for Galactus.

This, in other words, could only be the place where the Devourer of Worlds flew his starship from. Which meant—as if there had been any doubt—that Johnny was aboard *Taa II*. The Watcher had got him to where he was supposed to be.

As the last lingering ill-effects of the teleportation faded, Johnny roused himself to action. There was no time to stand around rubbernecking. He had to find the Ultimate Nullifier.

He activated the homing device on his wrist. The tiny screen lit up, showing a set of pulsing concentric circles. He waited. Uatu had said it might take the device a little while to locate the Ultimate Nullifier's energy signature, but once it did, it would—

Ping.

A little white dot appeared in the upper right quadrant of the screen. It flashed lazily, and with each flash the device emitted another—

Ping.

Johnny oriented himself so that the white dot sat directly ahead of him, in the "north" position on the screen.

Ping.

He flamed on, rose from the floor, and flew off across the cavernous chamber in that direction. He exited through an appropriately huge doorway, entering a corridor as tall and broad as one of the tubes of the Lincoln Tunnel. As he raced along this, he noted that the white dot was beginning to flash more frequently and the intermittent *pings* were closer together. He knew that the nearer he got to his objective, the rapider the flashes and *pings* would become.

So far, things were proceeding swimmingly. Maybe this

mission wasn't going to be anything like as hard as the Watcher had predicted.

Famous last words.

o———o

JOHNNY ROUNDED a corner, and all at once a huge metal rod shot out from a wall, lancing across his path. If he hadn't halted in the nick of time, it would have rammed him against the opposite wall, pounding him flat.

The rod retracted, sinking back into a circular recess. Johnny saw that the corridor, as far as the eye could see, was lined with similar recesses, all roughly two feet in diameter. You might think their purpose was purely decorative. That was if you hadn't just been almost squished to death by a cylinder of solid metal embedded within one of them.

These must be some of the internal defense mechanisms the Watcher had warned him about. They were, Johnny reckoned, motion activated. Triggered by the presence of anyone moving along this corridor—except for, presumably, Galactus himself.

According to the homing device, the corridor led towards the Ultimate Nullifier. Possibly he could turn back and try another route, but the detour could cost him precious time. It made sense to carry straight on, assuming he could skirt around the deadly, thrusting rods.

A thought crossed his mind. What would Ben do in a situation like this?

Answer: bulldoze through. If you put an obstacle in his way, he'd just keep plowing on until it wasn't in his way anymore. It might not be subtle, but it was usually effective.

Johnny wasn't Ben, but he could do much the same thing, Human Torch–style.

He took flight again, pouring on both speed and flame.

Rods pistoned one after another from the walls as he zoomed along the corridor. Each time, their solid ends turned to a spray of glowing orange globules as they met Johnny's blazing body. They withdrew, partly melted, in his wake, leaving long spatters of steaming, sizzling metal on the floor.

When the corridor ran out, so did the rods. Johnny landed, extinguished his flame, and caught his breath. The smell of molten metal behind him was acrid and strong.

He was in another chamber, this one somewhat smaller than the last. It was filled with gleaming, throbbing, churning machinery whose purpose he couldn't even begin to fathom. The air seemed to crackle and vibrate with sheer power. Perhaps this was *Taa II*'s engine room. Equally, perhaps it was Galactus's coffee percolator. Reed might be able to figure it out; but there was no way an average joe like Johnny could hope to.

He consulted the homing device and swiveled himself to face the right direction. He had no clear idea how far away the Ultimate Nullifier actually was. He would just have to keep going until he reached it.

He flamed on again and started to fly across the machinery-crammed chamber.

He did not notice as a set of winged robot drones, each no larger than a housecat, crept out from various crevices and crannies. They numbered in their dozens, and had vicious-looking gun barrels slung beneath their fuselages. They rose aloft on whispering turbofans, gathered together in a swarm, and flew in pursuit of the being who had encroached upon their domain.

Their programming was straightforward.

Chase intruder.

Intercept.

Exterminate.

ITEMS OF equipment trooped out from Galactus's shuttle craft one after another in a line, floating along as though carried on the backs of invisible porters. Under his telekinetic guidance they were assembled on the Baxter Building's roof, section slotting into section, module fastening to module, with terrific neatness and precision.

The whole thing was mesmerizing to watch, yet also chilling, if you knew its purpose. For this was Galactus's Elemental Converter being constructed, bit by bit—the apparatus that, when completed, would usher in the end of the world.

News helicopters circled the skyscraper, camera operators filming the blue-and-magenta giant and his incrementally amassing machine and transmitting the footage to TV studios who, in turn, relayed the images to viewers the world over. There was plenty of commentary from reporters and pundits, speculating on who the figure atop the Baxter Building was and what he might be up to. It was generally presumed that something insidious was afoot, and anxious questions were asked. Where were the Fantastic Four? Why were they allowing this to happen on their roof? Was Earth in danger—again?

That day's late edition of the *Daily Bugle* had been rushed to the newsstands and was selling fast. Its front page sported a picture of Galactus taken not long after he had shown up in his shuttle craft, beneath the headline MYSTERIOUS MAN-MOUNTAIN MENACES MANHATTAN. An above-the-fold sidebar added a little editorial context. IS SPIDER-MAN TO BLAME? it asked, rapidly concluding that the answer to the question was, despite any supporting evidence, "very probably".

Crowds of gawkers had gathered at the foot of the Baxter Building and were growing by the minute. People peered upwards, gesticulating, wondering aloud, clamoring. They were anxious and agitated but, so far at least, peaceable. Regardless, the NYPD had set up barricades to hold them back, in case they got it into their heads to storm the skyscraper. Emotions were running at fever pitch, and mob madness could erupt at any moment.

o——o

GALACTUS PAID the news helicopters no more heed than if they had been buzzing flies; as for the milling throng thirty-five stories below, he barely even registered them. He was intent on his task, his somber, dark eyes focused on nothing except the pieces of the Elemental Converter as they came together.

At last it was done. The finished machine was a cylindrical tower standing some forty feet tall, capped with a dome and anchored in position with spider-like legs that gripped the skyscraper's sides. From the apex of the dome a curved stem protruded, with a bulbous, cup-shaped attachment at its tip. This looked like some huge, sinister orchid—or perhaps the hose and nozzle of a vast vacuum cleaner. The attachment's open end faced out across the city, towards the ocean.

Everything was ready. It only remained for Galactus to grasp the Elemental Converter's igniters—a symmetrical pair of sliding contact-switches which, when brought together, would activate the machine. He took hold of the handle on each and drew them towards one another along their grooved rails.

There was, just visible on that monumental face of his, a look of eager anticipation. The glorious moment had arrived. Seconds from now, the Elemental Converter would begin transforming the raw material of this planet into pure energy, which it would then send spaceward to *Taa II* as a microwave beam. There, it would be collected and stockpiled in the starship's storage cells, for Galactus to draw on anytime he needed sustenance.

It was only then that Galactus spared a thought for the little creatures who clustered down on the ground and hovered around the building in their crude, noisy aircraft. According to the now-absent Watcher, these human beings were of significance; their civilization harbored the latent potential for greatness.

Arguably, however, the humans' true purpose in the rich, complex tapestry of the universe was to become nutrition for Galactus. And was that not a worthy role? Should they not be grateful for it?

The igniters met, and Galactus looked up at the Elemental Converter, expecting it to rumble into life.

Nothing happened.

Never, in all the many millennia he had been employing it, had the machine failed him before.

Had he misassembled some crucial part? Doubtful. But one of the components could have burned out or malfunctioned. That wasn't beyond the realms of possibility. Even the best-manufactured machinery could succumb to wear and tear after long and repeated usage.

The Devourer of Worlds stepped back to survey the Elemental Converter from top to bottom.

He swiftly identified the problem.

THE PROBLEM was Ben Grimm, A.K.A. the Thing.

Moments earlier, unseen by Galactus, Ben had clambered up the side of the enormous contraption, digging his thick, powerful fingers into its metal sides for purchase.

At the top, he had begun peeling back its casing to expose the workings within. He'd peered at the high-tech innards briefly, not at all sure what was what. There were snaking clusters of stuff that looked like wires, and tubes that could be ducts, or maybe diodes. Everywhere there were bits of hardware that vaguely resembled things he was familiar with—couplings, fasteners, bearings, circuitry, sensors—but not to the point where he could name their function with any certainty.

Not that it really mattered. Reed had told him just to make a mess. And Ben was only too happy to oblige.

He delved his hands inside the machine and started wrenching, twisting and yanking. Every time he pulled something free, he crushed it to a pancake between his palms or stomped it to smithereens underfoot. A big, gleeful grin split his face all the while.

There were times when he liked nothing better than to be the proverbial spanner in the works. Especially where bad guys were concerned.

He knew he'd succeeded in his goal when Galactus's enormous head reared over the side of the machine.

The alien giant looked affronted, as though he couldn't quite believe what he was seeing.

"You!" he boomed. "Paltry creature! You have the temerity to sabotage Galactus's Elemental Converter?"

"Guilty as charged," Ben said, brandishing a fistful of mangled mechanism.

"You fool. I can repair, in a matter of moments, whatever damage you have caused. You have done nothing save postpone the inevitable."

"Go ahead. Fix the dad-blasted thing. I can keep wreckin' it as fast as you can keep mendin' it."

"Not if I eradicate you first," Galactus rumbled menacingly.

"Yeah? You and whose army?"

So saying, Ben grabbed hold of the stem that jutted from the top of the Elemental Converter and, with one mighty heave, ripped it loose from its mooring.

"Batter up!" he cried, swinging the huge metal tube at Galactus's head.

He caught the Devourer of Worlds by surprise. Galactus clearly hadn't expected this bothersome, lumpen little lifeform to attack him directly. Not again: not after the last time when his assault had been so notably ineffectual.

To be honest, Ben himself hadn't thought it would work. He'd reckoned Galactus would at the very least duck out of the way, if not vaporize the piece of machinery—and possibly the person wielding it too—with a wave of his hand.

Instead, Ben fetched Galactus a serious blow upside of the head. Not only that, but he managed to stagger him. Galactus stumbled back to the edge of the rooftop, his heels against the parapet.

That was when Reed and Sue pitched in.

REED AND Sue had accompanied Ben back up onto the roof, and since then had been awaiting their moment. Reed had predicted that Galactus would react with aggression when he discovered Ben ruining his machine, and that Ben, naturally, would retaliate.

All had gone as foreseen, and Ben had done his part. Now it was time for Mr. and Mrs. Richards to do theirs.

In a flash, Reed rolled himself into a ball, wrapping his limbs tight around his body and tucking his head in so that only the blue of his uniform showed.

At the same time, Sue shaped an invisible forcefield in the form of a coiled spring and positioned it directly behind her now-spherical husband. They had practiced this stratagem several times. Sue called it their Pinball Maneuver.

She released the spring, which propelled the ball-shaped Reed straight at the teetering Galactus. Her aim was true, and Reed struck the giant being right in the navel, his center of gravity. He bounced harmlessly away, while Galactus, already off-balance, was toppled.

The Devourer of Worlds fell off the side of the Baxter Building and plummeted towards the street below.

He descended no more than a few stories before abruptly coming to a halt. Reed snapped himself back to his default form, and hurried over to join Sue at the parapet. They peered down, to see their foe hovering in midair. Galactus looked unfazed but perhaps a little nonplussed.

"I suppose it's a good thing he didn't fall all the way," Sue said. "People down there could have been hurt."

"I didn't doubt for a moment that he'd stop himself before he hit the ground," Reed said. "His power set is, frankly, limitless. There's no way any of us can hope to hurt him. All we can do is what we're doing."

"Delaying tactics. Buying ourselves some time."

"Buying *Johnny* some time," Reed clarified.

Sue nodded. "How long do you reckon it's going to take him to come back with the Ultimate Nullifier?" she said. It was getting on for half an hour since Uatu had teleported her brother away with more or less a snap of his fingers. "Uatu wasn't willing to make a prediction. He said there are all sorts of factors to consider."

"Well, I know even less about it than Uatu, so I'm not even going to speculate," Reed said. "I think the real question is, how long can the three of us hold out against Galactus?"

SUDDEN PAIN speared through Johnny's left shoulder.

He crashed to the floor, his flame sputtering out.

He peered at his shoulder. A neat little hole had been burrowed through the fleshy part at the top. Blood seeped out, front and back. The wound throbbed excruciatingly.

A soft whirring caught his attention. He looked up in horrified dismay as dozens of small flying robots gathered in formation around him. Each had what was obviously some kind of gun attached to its underside. The weapons were trained uniformly on him.

Johnny's mind raced. No ballistic projectile could penetrate his flame; it would melt on contact. That meant these drones were firing something other than bullets, and his money was on lasers.

The first shot had been designed to bring him down. And now that they had him surrounded, the drones could pick him off at their leisure. They were about to dice him into a hundred pieces with a volley of crisscrossing laser fire.

Johnny thought of what his sister might do when confronted with an attack like this. Sue would set up a hemispherical forcefield to protect herself on all sides.

The Human Torch, however, could go one better than the Invisible Woman.

Gritting his teeth against the pain from his shoulder, Johnny enclosed himself in a dome of fire. Then, instantly, he made it expand outwards until it engulfed every single drone.

Charred and inoperative, the drones dropped to the floor with a massed metallic clatter.

Johnny got to his feet and surveyed his handiwork. Most of the drones were defunct, here and there emitting sparks like a last gasp of life. A few, though badly damaged, still worked, in as much as their turbofans continued to spin and they were trying their best to get airborne again.

Johnny went around skewering each of the survivors with a spike of flame, finishing what his fire dome had started.

When all the drones were toast, he cast an eye over his wound again. It still hurt like blazes but the bleeding had stopped. Favoring that arm, he flamed on once more and continued on his way.

The homing device on his wrist was letting out *pings* at ever-decreasing intervals. He couldn't be far from the Ultimate Nullifier now, surely. He must just keep going.

He spared a thought for his three teammates. While he was busy locating the Ultimate Nullifier, Reed, Sue and Ben had the task of keeping Galactus distracted, preventing him from constructing something called an Elemental Converter. Galactus had already begun putting the machine together when Uatu dispatched Johnny across the solar system to *Taa II*. Uatu had said the work of assembling it wouldn't take more than an hour and was already over halfway done.

Johnny estimated he had been aboard *Taa II* for at least thirty minutes. Given that teleportation was instantaneous—and it hadn't felt like that, even though Uatu had assured him it was—then chances were the Elemental Converter was up and running by now. Unless, that was, the rest of the FF had managed to hold up the process.

If they hadn't, then Johnny's journey would be all in vain. Even if he did obtain the Ultimate Nullifier, he wouldn't return to Earth in time.

There might not even be an Earth to return to.

EARTH ENDURED.

For now.

The same couldn't necessarily be said for Ben Grimm and the other two members of the Fantastic Four.

After his brief toppling, Galactus floated regally and effortlessly back up to the summit of the Baxter Building, as though nothing had happened.

No sooner had he set foot on the roof again than Sue projected an invisible forcefield around his head.

Ben could not see the forcefield, of course, but he was familiar with the particular look of concentration that came over Sue's face whenever she exercised her power.

"What are you tryin' to do to him, Suzie?" he inquired.

"Asphyxiate him," she replied. "Make him black out."

Galactus fixed her with a stare that was equal parts surprise and derision.

"You think to deprive me of air?" he said. "You think that Galactus actually needs to *breathe*?"

He waved a hand in front of his face, and Sue let out a groan and reeled backwards. Reed sprang to catch her before she collapsed.

"Sue!" Reed exclaimed, cradling her in arms that he had made puffy and swollen like inflated air cushions. "Are you all right?"

"Y-Yes," she said, clutching her forehead. "Galactus erased my forcefield from existence, like it was nothing. The psychic feedback caught me unawares, that's all. I'll be fine in a moment."

Galactus, not sparing the three humans another glance, gestured towards his shuttle craft. His fingers flicked in a beckoning motion.

From within the vessel, a humanoid robot came clanking out.

"I shall not sully my hands dealing with you irritants any further," Galactus announced. "Rather, I shall leave that to my indomitable android servant, the Punisher."

The Punisher was short and squat, with a flat-topped, froglike head set deep onto its shoulders, seemingly lacking a neck. Its limbs were made from overlapping metal bands, and whereas its hands mimicked those of a human, its feet were starfish-shaped. What passed for its eyes was a pair of thick projecting stalks, glowing at the ends. Most of its body was a deep purple, apart from its extremities, which were dark green.

The two contrasting colors reminded Ben, uncomfortably, of the Hulk. Ol' Greenskin always seemed to be wearing purple pants. Ben hoped that the Punisher wasn't nearly a match for the Hulk in sheer strength, but knowing Galactus, the robot wasn't going to be a pushover.

"All right," Ben said to Reed and Sue. The latter was back on her feet, but with the former still supporting her. "Looks like Galactus is siccin' his watchdog on us, instead of facin' us himself. You better stay back, kiddies. This is my department."

"Careful, Ben," said Reed. "We have no idea how powerful the Punisher is, but we can only assume it's formidable, otherwise Galactus wouldn't have summoned it."

"And that's exactly why it's got to be me tacklin' him first and not you two pantywaists. Me, I'm built for 'formidable'."

Ben lumbered towards the Punisher, which stood its ground,

eyeing him as he approached. Those two lambent discs on the ends of their stalks seemed to be gauging him, assessing his potential strengths and weaknesses. Ben made a point of moving with all the confidence he could muster. Projecting an air of invincibility was important in the run-up to a fight; it could give you a psychological edge over your opponent. Ben didn't know if the trick worked on androids as it could on living creatures, but there was no harm in trying.

All of a sudden, the Punisher burst into motion. It threw itself at Ben, forcing him into a clinch. Next thing he knew, he was being subjected to a relentless flurry of punches. They came thick and fast, the Punisher's fists a blur.

Ben struggled to keep his guard up. It was hard to defend against so many blows arriving in such swift succession one after the other. He could barely see where the next was coming from. He managed to keep his head protected, but his arms and torso took a severe pummeling. The pain began to mount. His ribs ached. His abdomen throbbed. Tiny chips of his rocky, rust-colored hide flew in all directions as the Punisher's onslaught whittled away at it.

Ben knew he couldn't take much more of this. All he needed was an opening, a break in the attack that he could exploit. One good solid hit on this furshlugginer robot, that was all he asked.

Sue gave him that opening. She enfolded Ben in a forcefield. All at once, the Punisher's fists seemed to be landing on thin air, inches from their intended target.

"Good work, Suzie!" Ben cried. "Now gimme a hole I can hit him through."

"It's there, Ben. I've made you a gap big enough for a right cross."

"Say no more."

Ben hauled back his right arm. He knew Sue would have put the hole in her forcefield exactly where it needed to be and exactly the correct size. He trusted her implicitly.

"Punisher, you want to know what time it is?"

He clenched his fist.

"Clobberin' time, naturally."

He whammed the robot straight in the face.

The Punisher staggered backwards, and for one brief, shining moment Ben thought he had done it; he had disrupted the damn thing's workings, and it was going to keel over, unconscious, or whatever you called it when an android got belted so hard it stopped functioning. Short-circuited. Out of service. On the fritz. Something like that.

"Yeah!" he yelled in triumph. "Take *that*, you hunk of rusty bolts! Drop the forcefield, Suzie. This bozo's finished. One and done."

He should have known that nothing was ever that easy. The Punisher just gave a shake of its stumpy head, then renewed its assault on him.

This time, it came at him spinning its body over and over in a rapid-fire somersault. Now Ben was being struck not just by its fists but by its feet too. He sorely regretted telling Sue to dispel her forcefield. The Punisher was indeed living up to its name, and there didn't seem much he could do about it except take the punishment.

That was until Reed got involved.

Reed made his arms and legs as flat as rubber bands and entangled them around the whirling robot, bringing its gyrations to a juddering halt, rather like clogging up a propeller with taffy.

"Ben, I can't hold it indefinitely," he said, as the Punisher strained within his grip. "It's going to slip out of my clutches at any moment."

"'Nuff said, Stretch."

Ben aimed a battery of punches at the android's face. He landed blows that cumulatively would have turned a Mack truck into so much scrapyard junk. He kept hammering away right up until the moment Reed let out an agonized groan and released the Punisher.

"Couldn't... restrain him... any longer," Reed gasped, flopping to the ground. His limbs trailed in all directions like limp noodles.

The Punisher stood stock still. Outwardly, it looked unharmed, not so much as a dent in it. That was surprising, but again Ben wondered—hoped—he had pounded it hard enough to break something vital inside. Maybe it had frozen up. Maybe it just couldn't move anymore.

No such luck.

The Punisher sprang back into action, subjecting Ben to a fresh salvo of punches.

"You darned dumb robot!" Ben said, hunching over and protecting his head. "Normally when I clobber somethin', it stays clobbered. Don't you know that?"

"Ben!" Sue called out. "Quickly. I'm going to put up a forcefield. Take three steps back and you'll be inside it."

"Nah, I can handle this."

"Don't let your pride get the better of you. This isn't the time for valiant last stands. Do as I say."

Ben weighed up the pros and cons. Stay put and get beaten to a pulp by the Punisher, or retreat to the safety of Sue's forcefield? It wasn't really a choice at all.

He lurched backwards from the android, and suddenly the Punisher was battering away at thin air once more, or so it seemed. Sue stood next to him with her hands held up, palms out, fingers splayed. Her brow was furrowed with the effort of maintaining the forcefield.

Reed was inside the forcefield too. He was back to human form again, apart from one leg, which was still extended to three times normal length. He was having to reel it in and mold it with both hands, something he only did when he had overtaxed his stretching powers. The leg must be numb and reluctant to resume its usual shape unaided.

 The Punisher thumped and pounded at Sue's invisible forcefield without let-up, nothing but inscrutable blankness on its face. Its blows made no sound, giving the impression that the android was some kind of demented mime artist.

Meanwhile, behind it, its master had patiently set about repairing the Elemental Converter. In no time, the damage Ben had done would be rectified. Then the process of draining Earth of its energy could begin in earnest.

"Suzie," Ben said, "how long do you think you can keep your forcefield up?"

Sue's face was a mask of determination. Sweat beaded her forehead. "The Punisher is fearsomely strong. It's taking everything I've got just keeping the forcefield intact. I'm not sure I can stand much more of this."

"You have to, Sue," Reed said. "If you can't, we're as good as dead."

"Yes, thank you darling. I'm aware of that."

"You got to let me out," Ben said. "I've got my breath back now. I can take that runt, I swear. I'm the only one of us who can."

"I don't think that's true," said Reed. "I don't think any of us can stop the Punisher."

"What are you saying? We're doomed? 'Cause I ain't buyin' that."

"I'm saying we have to hope Johnny gets back here imminently," Reed said. "And failing that, we have to hope for a miracle."

THE HOMING device on Johnny's wrist was getting very excited. The *pings* were coming thick and fast.

Since the drone attack, Johnny had flown through *Taa II* unhindered. He still wasn't accustomed to the vast proportions of the starship. He felt like a doll exploring a normal-sized house. Was this how Henry Pym felt when he went adventuring as Ant-Man? Mind you, Pym was able to enlarge himself as well as shrink, and so adopt the guise of Giant-Man, meaning he saw it from both perspectives. Sometimes he was David in a world of Goliaths, and sometimes the other way round.

Johnny arrived at another vast, open doorway and came to rest on the floor, flaming off. The homing device screen was flashing red now, blinking as rapidly as a strobe light. He could only infer that the Ultimate Nullifier was close at hand—in all likelihood, right on the other side of this doorway.

Even though Johnny's quest seemed to be at its end, this was the time to be more cautious than ever. If the Ultimate Nullifier was anywhere near as powerful and dangerous as Uatu made it out to be, Galactus wouldn't leave it unprotected, would he? He'd surely have put it in the space-god equivalent of a gun safe and installed some extra layer of protection.

Johnny took a tentative step towards the doorway and peered through. What lay on the other side appeared to be some sort of trophy room. Ranged along its walls were shelves and alcoves, and there were pedestals as well, dotted around the floor. All contained some kind of artifact. He glimpsed weird statues, like specimens of abstract art. Suits of fantastically elaborate armor, some ancient-looking, some futuristic. Swords as fine-spun and complex as any blacksmith might have wrought. Bizarre confections of wood and metal that could only be musical instruments. And a lot else besides.

He took another step, and the doorway was abruptly filled from top to bottom with bands of writhing light. They swirled lazily around one another like a school of translucent, fluorescent eels.

He'd been right. This was doubtless that extra layer of protection.

Backing away, Johnny experimentally lobbed a fireball into the doorway. It collided with one of the bands of light and was snuffed out. He tried again using something more solid—one of his gloves—with the same result. The glove struck a band and vanished with a fizzle.

Johnny now had a pretty shrewd idea what would happen to him if he touched any of the bands. *Poof!* No more Human Torch.

Well, the doorway might be off-limits, but he could surely create an entrance of his own.

He moved a few yards along and unleashed his flame, full force, on an empty section of wall. Pretty soon he had melted a hole wide enough for him to fly through.

Just as he was about to do exactly that, more of those bands of light appeared, snaking across the hole. It seemed Galactus was quite keen nobody should get into this room, by conventional means or otherwise. The bands of light were designed to seal up any aperture, like stitches over a wound.

Johnny wondered whether he could somehow dodge them.

Sometimes gaps appeared between them just large enough to accommodate a flying teenager. The gaps didn't last for more than a second or two, but if he was quick…

He returned to the doorway. The hole he had made was a tight fit. The doorway, a little over thirty feet high and about twenty across, offered a lot more wiggle room.

He studied the motion of the bands, recalling an exercise routine Reed had put him through several times. Reed would turn his body into a spacious maze, flexing himself continuously so that the route from one side to the other never remained consistent. Johnny would flame on and thread the ever-shifting tangle of torso and limbs, contorting his own body to adapt to its twists and turns. Reed, for his part, had to keep from getting singed. If Johnny miscalculated, Reed needed to pull himself out of the way sharpish, or else. The aim was to allow both of them to hone their abilities and also cement trust between them. It worked, mostly, although on one occasion Johnny did accidentally scorch off a chunk of Reed's hair.

Had the exercise given him enough practice to negotiate the lethal bands of light?

There was only one way to be sure.

Johnny flamed on yet again and rose to a hover. He watched the bands intently. There was no pattern to their movement, no regularity, nothing that enabled him to predict when the next gap would appear and time his moment to dart between two of them. They squiggled and shimmied completely at random.

He was just going to have to launch himself forwards and trust his own instincts and reflexes.

Who ever said the life of a Human Torch was easy?

He rose to horizontal, body parallel with the floor. Then he squeezed his legs together and pointed his arms ahead, making himself as narrow as possible, as though executing a swan dive.

With a yell of "Geronimo!" he propelled himself into the doorway.

He was through almost before he realized. He had the vaguest recollection of corkscrewing his body first clockwise then the opposite way, and seeing one of the bands of light brush past his nose with millimeters to spare.

Then he was standing on the other side, looking back at the ever-shifting barrier, scarcely able to believe he had made it through in one piece. Flaming off, he permitted himself a celebratory "Wahoo!" with his hands clasped together above his head like a champion racing driver who'd just whooshed past the checkered flag.

After that, it was straight back to business.

The homing device was signaling like crazy. If it had been a sniffer dog, it would have been straining at the leash. *This way*, it was telling him. *The Ultimate Nullifier is over here!*

Johnny let it steer him to a pedestal near the center of the room. Along the way he passed countless artifacts he would have loved to stop and examine, had he had the time. The place was a museum of oddities and curiosities, every one of them all but incomprehensible to Johnny's eyes. He had a feeling he'd been right in judging this to be a trophy room. His hunch was that Galactus collected these objects from the worlds he devoured. They were mementos, the last remnants of countless lost civilizations. Perhaps he kept them for sentimental reasons, but it seemed likelier they were simply a record of his conquests—a single item from every planet he had consumed, to indicate that he had been there. Like a diary of destruction.

Finally: the Ultimate Nullifier.

The homing device couldn't have made it more obvious that Johnny had reached his goal. The entire screen was solid red, and the *pings* had coalesced into a single shrill whine.

But… could this really be it?

The object sitting on the pedestal in front of him was very small—small enough to fit comfortably in the palm of his hand.

It was slim, metallic, rounded at one end and sporting two projections at the opposite end, one straight, one curved, at right angles to each other. On top was a tiny hinged lever, S-shaped, possibly some sort of trigger.

Maybe the homing device had made a mistake. Whatever this thing was, it didn't look like it was capable of deterring Galactus, as Uatu had claimed. It didn't look like it was capable of deterring a *mouse*. Was it even a weapon? A high-tech cigarette lighter, yes, or a fancy TV remote—it could easily be either of those. But a weapon? No.

Still, the homing device was insistent. And Johnny knew he didn't really have a choice in the matter. He had to get back to his teammates pronto, and he couldn't return empty-handed. Better this than nothing.

He plucked the object off the pedestal. He somehow expected it to exude sheer raw power when he held it, but the Ultimate Nullifier—if that was what it truly was—just sat there in his grasp, inert, light as a feather.

Filled with misgiving, Johnny depressed the button on the side of the homing device which would signal to Uatu that he was ready to come home.

He braced himself for another head-spinning teleportation experience. At least he might see Crystal again, even if it wasn't the genuine her. That was some consolation.

o————o

BUT HE didn't see Crystal.

The teleportation was a long-drawn-out millisecond of kaleidoscopic chaos, as before.

Like any return journey, however, prior acquaintance with the route made it less of a novelty. It was still strange and trippy, but nowhere nearly as much as the last time, and hence Johnny's mind didn't feel the need to invoke an image of the girl he loved in order to steady him.

When it was over—the end arriving both abruptly and yet seemingly long overdue—he collapsed in a nerveless heap. It took him several moments to orient himself. He almost couldn't believe he was back in the familiar surroundings of the Baxter Building. He groped for a nearby armchair, drawing comfort from its solidity, its practicality, its sheer leather-upholstered ordinariness. He felt a sudden, overpowering love for that armchair. It was exactly the size an armchair should be. An armchair for humans, in a room proportioned for humans. A room in which everything was made by humans, for humans to utilize. Johnny almost wept with joy. He had never felt so glad and so grateful to be back home.

"You have it?"

The stern voice of Uatu broke in on his burst of happiness, like rain through a rainbow. The Watcher was right beside him, stooping over, his great bald head bent low.

"Yeah," Johnny said. "Yeah, I've got your Ultimate Nullifier. At least, I hope I have."

He held out his hand to show Uatu the small, underwhelming-looking item. Worry gnawed at him. Could he have accidentally picked up the wrong thing? If so, did that mean he would have to travel all the way back to *Taa II* and try again? Was there even enough time for that?

"Ah," said Uatu. "I see."

Johnny's heart sank. Uatu's tone was neutral, but Johnny took the remark to mean he had messed up. Instead of bringing back the Ultimate Nullifier, he had committed the ultimate blunder.

"Excellent," Uatu then said, and took the little metallic artifact out of Johnny's hand. In his much larger hand, it looked even punier.

"That *is* what you sent me for, right?" Johnny said. "I've done good?"

Uatu gave the merest of nods.

"Phew! That's a relief."

With a heartfelt sigh, Johnny sank back against the side of the armchair. His shoulder was keen to remind him that it had recently been perforated by a laser blast, but the pain was just about bearable.

"You should rest now, Johnny Storm," Uatu said. "You are exhausted. I shall take the Nullifier up to your teammates."

"Yeah, no, I can… I can do it myself."

But there seemed to be no strength left in Johnny's limbs. It was all he could do just to sit upright against the chair and not slump to the floor.

"Okay," he said wanly, "I'll let you go instead. I'll just… just stick around here for a bit. But I'll get up there soon as I can. Wouldn't want to miss the grand finale."

Uatu didn't answer. He had already turned round and was striding out of the room.

Johnny leaned his head back, closed his eyes, and lapsed into a stupor.

Who knew? Two teleportations, with various escapades aboard Galactus's starship sandwiched in between, could really take it out of a guy.

THE PUNISHER had almost broken Sue's forcefield.

Ben could tell just by looking at her.

She was trembling from head to toe. Her legs were shaking, her knees clearly ready to buckle at any moment. Her face was deathly pale. A vein in her forehead pulsed and writhed like a stricken earthworm.

"Suzie," he said, "I'm tellin' you, you got to drop the forcefield. You keep this up much longer, it's going to kill you."

"And if I do drop it," Sue replied, every word a breathless gasp, "the Punisher's liable to kill *us*."

"I won't let that happen," Ben insisted. "That thing's got to have a weak spot. I just ain't found it yet."

"Ben's right, darling," Reed said. "You've never put yourself under such severe strain before. You're at risk of doing yourself serious harm—quite possibly an aneurysm."

"And if I stop now," Sue said, "what then?"

"Then I pick up where I left off," Ben said. "I'm itchin' to have another crack at Robbie the Robot there."

"Very well." She appeared to have made up her mind. "But Ben, Reed, listen," she said, still grimacing with the effort of maintaining her forcefield against the Punisher's tumultuous assault.

"If this is it—if it's really all over—I want you both to know how much I love you. Reed, you're the best husband anyone could wish for, and were we ever to have had children, I have no doubt you'd have been an amazing father. And Ben, you're the best friend I could imagine anyone having. I only wish Johnny were here with us, so I could tell him how much I love him too."

"Ah, stop talkin' like that," Ben shot back brusquely. "I don't hear no fat lady singing, so the show ain't nearly over. More to the point, I still got plenty of fight left in me." But he wished he felt a tenth as confident as he sounded.

"All right." Sue lowered her hands. "Get ready. I'm going to dispel the forcefield in three… two…"

She didn't get to "one".

A bolt of searingly bright light shot down from above.

It passed through the Punisher from side to side, and immediately the android went rigid.

Then its top half slid away at an angle from its lower half. The pugnacious android had been sliced diagonally in the middle, and its head and upper torso fell to the right while the rest of it, from the waist down, toppled to the left. Both sections hit the roof with a loud *clang.*

Exposed circuitry sparked and sizzled. Hydraulic fluid leaked out from truncated pipes and pistons, like clear yellow blood.

The two halves of the Punisher each gave a few spasmodic twitches, as though it was struggling to come back to life.

Then the android lay quite still.

"What in blazes…?" Ben breathed.

"Not what," said Reed. "Who." He pointed upward.

Over the skyline of Manhattan, a familiar figure soared into view.

The Silver Surfer.

"THE SURFER?"

Sue sounded as thunderstruck as Ben felt.

"Sure looks like him," Ben said. "But how come he just zapped Galactus's little tin toy? Ain't they on the same side?"

The Surfer swooped low, gliding to a halt beside the trio of super heroes, his board level with their heads.

Ben clenched his fists. Maybe the Surfer had destroyed the Punisher by mistake. Maybe his bolt of Power Cosmic had actually been intended for the three people the android had been beleaguering, but his aim had been off. If so, there was no way Ben was going to let him fire off a second shot. Not a chance.

"Hear me, Reed Richards and comrades," the Surfer said, "and heed my words." He held his hands out in a placatory manner. "No longer am I your foe. Rather, I stand with you this day against Galactus. I shall endeavor to set right the wrong he is committing."

"You're turning on your master?" said Reed.

"I am—for all the good it may do. I have seen the error of my ways, and now I mean to defy him whom I have served all these millennia."

"But… why?"

The Silver Surfer paused before replying. "Suffice it to say, I have been shown that this world is worth saving, and also that the many worlds to which I led Galactus in the past were likewise of value and ought not to have been destroyed just to slake his hunger. Life is precious and must be safeguarded. It is an ethos I myself once espoused, until eons of solitariness eroded it to nothing."

"What's brought about this change of heart?" Sue asked. She had dropped the forcefield.

"The answer to that," the Surfer said, "lies with one who is not unknown to you three. Her name is Alicia Masters, and she it is who helped me rediscover who I truly am and what I must stand for. She, moreover, demonstrated by her very existence—by her spiritedness, her generosity of heart, not to mention her remarkable artistic talent—that the human race is imbued with inherent greatness."

"Alicia?" Ben said. "You've been with Alicia? *My* Alicia?"

The Surfer nodded. "I have, Benjamin Grimm. By chance I came across her dwelling. One of your team's proprietary vehicles sits on the roof there. She and I fell to talking, and over the course of our conversation, for all that it was relatively brief, I learned much about her and also about myself. You are, if I may say, Mr. Grimm, a fortunate man to have won such a woman's love."

"Don't I know it. But listen here. You weren't puttin' the moves on my gal, were you? 'Cause if you were, then I got three words for you, and they rhyme with 'It's slobberin' time'."

"Ben, calm down," Sue said. "This isn't the time and place for jealousy."

"If it ain't, when is?"

"I'm serious. Put a lid on your insecurities. I mean, do you honestly think Alicia would even consider another man? You *know* she's crazy about you."

"Well, he may be skinny and all silvery, but Chrome Dome here is way better-lookin' than me, that's for sure. This mug of mine ain't good for much except crackin' mirrors."

"And when did looks matter to Alicia, who is, need I remind you, blind?"

"Yeah, okay, there is that," Ben muttered.

"Alicia is the soul of kindness, Mr. Grimm, and a being of rare physical beauty," said the Surfer. "Rest assured, though, my heart belongs to another—a woman from whom I have long since been parted and who, indeed, may be dead after all this time, but whose memory I shall forever cherish. All that, anyway, is of no consequence at this present moment. Galactus, I see, is preparing to activate his Elemental Converter. I must prevent him. Even if it should cost me my life," he added, "which it may very well do."

"How do we know this ain't just some trick?" Ben said.

"Somethin' you and the big purple planet-eater have cooked up together? You pretend to be our pal, only to go and sucker punch us when our guard's down."

"Surely my treatment of the Punisher should have convinced you of my trustworthiness, Ben Grimm. But if you need further proof, I shall supply it. Let my actions hereafter affirm the honesty of my words."

So saying, the Silver Surfer jetted off towards Galactus.

SERVANT DREW to a standstill in front of master.

Galactus gazed somberly down at his herald. In either hand he held one of the pair of igniters. He was scant moments away from starting up the Elemental Converter.

"I have destroyed your Punisher," the Surfer said.

"I am aware," said the Devourer of Worlds. "I trust you have an explanation."

"It hardly seems necessary to give one. You must know, Galactus, as I do, that consuming this planet is wrong."

"I know no such thing. I know only that my hunger must be appeased and that the energies this world harbors will fulfill that function."

"Are billions of lives worth less than your own?"

"You would ask such a question of mighty Galactus? One who was old when the universe was young? One who is supreme among living beings? One whose needs supersede those of all others?"

"This is my plea to you," said the Surfer, "as he who has loyally done your bidding for years beyond number. Leave. Choose another world, an uninhabited one, and take its energies instead. I shall find such a world for you, gladly. But leave Earth alone. Primitive though it is, and full of flaws, it is also wondrous, and its people deserve a chance to prosper and propagate."

"I do not judge the moral worth of the worlds I devour," Galactus argued. "I judge them purely according to the quality of nutrition they can provide."

"You were not always Galactus. Once, you were a man. This much you have told me, in our rare conversations. Can you not remember that man you were? Do you not think he would be appalled at the unfeeling monster you have become?"

Galactus bristled in annoyance. "I am no longer a man, nor am I a monster. Such concepts are utterly meaningless to me. I am Galactus. And, Surfer, my patience has worn thin. If you have chosen to challenge me, after all this time, that is your prerogative. Know, however, that it will avail you naught. Your power is as nothing to mine. I gave it to you, and only a fool would bestow so much power on another that the other could possibly pose a threat."

A hollow barking sound emerged from his throat which could only be taken for laughter, and contemptuous laughter at that.

"I know I am no match for you," the Surfer said stalwartly. "That will not stop me, as it has not stopped these valiant humans. I have tried reasoning with you. Now comes the time for action."

The Surfer unleashed a tremendous torrent of Power Cosmic at his former liege lord. The three members of the Fantastic Four shied away, shielding their eyes against its brilliance. For a time, it seemed as though a miniature sun was blazing directly over the Baxter Building.

The awesome dazzle faded, and where Galactus had been standing, now stood a large, rough-hewn ovoid. Smoke trailed off its surface. Heat radiated from it, tangible even to the three humans who were several yards away.

"Surfer," said Reed, "what have you done?"

"I have contained Galactus."

"So I can see. It appears you've formed a kind of cocoon around him."

"Just so, Dr. Richards. Strange though it may seem to you,

I could not bring myself to cause Galactus injury. Instead, I chose to place him under restraint."

"I understand," said Sue sympathetically. "You still respect him, even though you now oppose him."

"That is exactly it. My heart grieves at the thought of battling one with whom I once shared the universe."

"Well," said Ben, "you mayn't've polished him off, but you've at least stopped him doing what he wanted—and that's more than that overrated chump Uatu managed."

He approached the cocoon.

"Say, what's this thing made of anyway?" he said, reaching out a hand. "Looks pretty strong, but is it strong enough?"

"Ben, I wouldn't touch it if I were you," Reed warned.

Too late. Ben had already laid his hand on the cocoon. He recoiled immediately.

"*Yeoowwch!*" he cried, shaking out his arm. "It's like it was pushin' me away. And I mean really pushin', hard as a piledriver."

"I have created the cocoon to be reactive," the Surfer said. "It actively repels the slightest attempt to breach it, from inside as well as from outside."

"You could've told me."

"I did not feel it needed saying. Besides, your comrade advised against touching it, did he not? And you ignored him."

"Yeah, well, Stretcho knows I don't listen to him when he's pontificatin'. It's always 'Ben, don't', 'Ben, wait', 'Ben, you'll regret it'. Never 'Go ahead, Ben, 'cause I respect you enough to let you make your own decisions'. I mean, someday he's—"

Ben broke off, because just then, with a loud crunching sound, a crack appeared in the cocoon, near its base.

"That wasn't me," he said quickly. "That's definitely nothin' to do with me putting my hand on it."

"Get back, all of you," the Surfer said.

Reed, Sue and Ben retreated across the rooftop, while the

Silver Surfer took to the air.

The cocoon was trembling, chunks of its surface falling away as the crack spread upwards, branching, becoming a multiplicity of fractures. The thing was losing cohesion right in front of their eyes, succumbing to enormous pressures from within. The building shuddered beneath their feet with the forces that were at play.

Slowly, a hand emerged from the crumbling cocoon, magenta-gauntleted. An arm followed, and then the regal, helmet-encased head of Galactus.

Galactus flexed his chest, and the disintegrating cocoon shattered around him, breaking into a thousand pieces. Sue erected a fresh forcefield to protect herself and her teammates from the hail of debris.

When the dust had settled, the Devourer of Worlds was standing much as before, seemingly unperturbed after his temporary confinement. The only evidence that he had been inconvenienced in any way was the glare in his eyes as he looked around for the person who had sought to imprison him.

"Where," he rumbled, "is my herald?"

"Here," the Silver Surfer replied, gliding into view. "But your herald no more. That is now beyond question."

"You have served me in the past," Galactus said, "and you shall serve me in future. I am not vengeful. I give you this one chance to recant your opposition to me, repent your rebellion, and resume your ordained role. Do that, and we shall not speak of this incident again."

"I cannot. You must be driven from this world. You must! No matter what the cost."

Galactus nodded pensively and perhaps a touch ruefully. "Then the die is cast. It sorrows me to have to dispose of you, yet dispose of you I must. Our partnership is at an end, Silver Surfer. Prepare for death."

And with that, cosmic combat was joined.

REED RICHARDS, Sue Richards and Ben Grimm could do little but look on as Galactus and the Silver Surfer battled.

Much the same could be said for the New Yorkers gathered below at the foot of the Baxter Building, and the people watching from the roofs and windows of adjacent skyscrapers, and all the many millions viewing the unfolding events that were being beamed to them, live, on their TV screens, not only in the United States but around the world.

In the Oval Office, the president and his staffers were glued to the news channels. The presidential security team had repeatedly advised their boss to get to the subterranean bunker beneath the White House, where he would be safe. POTUS disagreed. In his judgment, it wouldn't make any difference if he was underground or not. As far as he could tell, either the Fantastic Four and their newfound silver-skinned ally saved the day, or it was the end of everything.

In parliaments, congresses and other national assemblies all across the world, much the same decision was reached. Politicians of all stripes came together in emergency sessions and agreed that the situation should be left to the American super heroes, who were practiced in the art of resolving such global crises. The consensus was to let them get on with it and be grateful they existed.

AMONG THAT community of super heroes, a similar calculation was being made.

The likes of Spider-Man and Daredevil, who tended to deal with street-level enemies, understood that they were surplus to requirements today. The villains they customarily fought, even the super-powered ones, were the type who robbed banks, carried out kidnappings or committed murders, wreaking havoc at a human scale only. Cosmic menaces were above the paygrade of Spidey and the Man Without Fear. Individually, each of them came to the conclusion that the situation at the Baxter Building was best left to the FF to resolve.

In Westchester County, upstate New York, at Xavier's School for Gifted Youngsters, the five mutants who comprised the X-Men were gathered around the TV set in their common room. Their teacher and mentor Professor Charles Xavier was with them, seated as ever in his wheelchair.

The X-Men were debating among themselves whether they should travel to the city to help the Fantastic Four or whether that would only make matters worse. It was Hank McCoy, the erudite, anthropoidal character also known as the Beast, who summed up their dilemma best.

"Should we arrive at the scene," he said, "our presence might well exacerbate the tensions evident among the populace. Doubtless we, as members of the distrusted and shunned species known as *Homo superior*, would be regarded as abettors in whatever nefarious shenanigans are taking place at the Baxter Building, and would be abused and castigated for it, with a violent altercation the likely outcome. Ergo, on balance, it seems that our most prudent course of action is, alas, inaction."

Master of the Mystic Arts, Doctor Strange, was the sworn foe of eldritch, nether-dimensional entities such as Dormammu,

Nightmare and Shuma-Gorath, who coveted Earth for their own and were none of them exactly lightweights when it came to sheer power. He had foiled their plans on several occasions. His magics, however, were ill suited to adversaries like this Galactus.

In his Sanctum Sanctorum in Greenwich Village, Strange floated in midair, cross-legged, before the Orb of Agamotto, and perused the images of the goings-on at the Baxter Building conveyed to him by that magical artifact. The all-seeing Orb was providing a sorcerous equivalent of the newscasts everyone else was transfixed by, one generated by its own scrying powers rather than video cameras.

Strange, bathed in its misty, flickering glow, felt helpless—not a comfortable state of being for a man such as him, who prided himself on confidence and unflappability. He prayed to the wise Vishanti that the Fantastic Four would prevail this day.

In shining Asgard, All-Father Odin beheld the crisis unfurling on Midgard through his own magical means, namely the mighty Odinforce, which granted him a plethora of divine powers, including the ability to observe, remotely, whatever was happening in any of the Nine Realms.

His one good eye—its counterpart sheathed by a jewel-encrusted patch—was narrowed in concern. He understood that his favorite son, Thor, had a rare affection for the people of Earth, and he knew that the thunder god, who was currently lying comatose, near death after doing battle with Odin's treacherous councilor Seidring, would not wish to see the place he considered his adopted home destroyed.

Yet Odin knew, too, that he himself could not lift a finger to assist the mortals. It was not his place to. The Midgardians must fend for themselves; and should they fail, and perish *en masse*, it would be a shame, but it would also be simply what the Norns decreed—and Urd, Verdandi and Skuld, the three sisters of Fate, were not to be gainsaid.

"So mote it be," he murmured to himself, sadly, sanguinely.

One of those Midgardians, Colonel Nick Fury, shared with Odin the lack of an eye; he was also, like the All-Father, unusually long-lived, although not himself immortal.

He, however, was in a less accepting frame of mind than the ruler of the Asgardians. For Fury, the role of bystander grated. He was currently aboard the S.H.I.E.L.D. Helicarrier. The enormous airborne vehicle was stationed just off the coast near Bridgeport, Connecticut, hovering at an altitude of some 20,000 feet. From there, Fury was vigilantly monitoring affairs at the Baxter Building.

A little earlier that day, he had checked in with Captain America at Avengers Mansion, and the upshot of their teleconference was: stand back and leave the Fantastic Four to get on with it. The two World War II veterans—who had fought the Axis powers side by side on several occasions, back when Fury wore a sergeant's stripes—bore an immense respect for each other. On this occasion they had both agreed that sometimes, in a conflict, you just had to have faith in your fellow warriors to hold up their end of things. The FF would come through for everyone.

This hadn't, however, stopped Fury from instructing the Helicarrier flight crew to be ready to race in along Long Island Sound and take up position over Manhattan at any moment, if he thought some heavily armed air support was required. In certain circumstances the cavalry had to ride in even if they weren't called.

As for Captain America and the team he led, they collectively maintained their stance that Reed Richards and company were equal to the task of defeating Galactus. The Avengers, for once, were not the most important assemblage of super heroes on Earth. That honor, today, rested with the Fantastic Four.

REED RICHARDS, it must be said, was not feeling any too important at this particular moment. In fact, he was feeling somewhat redundant.

It was galling for someone as sharp-witted and proactive as him to be demoted to mere spectator.

Then again, the power and fury being unleashed by Galactus and the Silver Surfer was so great, so blisteringly intense, he knew he couldn't compete. None of his team could. As Ben put it, with characteristic demotic candor, "Next to that pair, we ain't nothin' but ninety-seven-pound weaklings."

The Surfer darted around almost faster than the eye could follow. He and his board were a glinting blur against the blueness of the sky.

Galactus, by contrast, scarcely budged. He stood with his feet planted square on the rooftop, turning his head to track his one-time herald's progress and, arm raised, loosing off shimmering bolts of energy from his fingertips.

These the Surfer evaded, threading around them like a lightning-quick needle. Whenever an opportunity arose, he retaliated with energy bolts of his own, firing with one hand or sometimes both.

None of the shots he discharged at Galactus had any apparent effect. The Devourer of Worlds seemed as impervious to them as if the Surfer was squirting him with a water pistol.

In fact, Reed got the distinct impression that neither combatant truly wished to hurt the other. Galactus, for all his talk about "disposing of" the Surfer, was clearly exercising restraint. He could surely have eradicated his erstwhile servant with merely a thought. Instead, he was subjecting him to a barrage of blasts which he must have known the Surfer could run rings around.

Similarly, the Surfer doubtless realized that nothing he did was causing Galactus even to flinch.

To Reed's mind, it looked as though each of them was punishing the other. Their battle was performative—a demonstration of antipathy, rather than a way of settling it. The bond between them had been severed, and both were lashing out as an expression of disgust. The Surfer wanted to prove he had a conscience. Galactus wanted to prove that a conscience was an irrelevant luxury.

Nonetheless, there was something distinctly mythic about their fight. Reed was put in mind of Prometheus defying the Greek gods. Of Frankenstein's monster, repudiating his creator. Of Milton's Lucifer, who preferred to reign in Hell than serve in Heaven. Mythic, and tragic. Epochal too. A kind of Götterdämmerung. Even when just trying to score a point against each other, the two of them were still exerting enough raw power to make the whole of Manhattan quake.

At last, Galactus acknowledged the futility of it all.

"Surfer," he said, "I implore you, one final time: abandon this folly. You know that your place is ever at my side. I can still, even now, find it in me to overlook your imprudence, and forgive. Reaffirm your allegiance to me. Kneel before me and vow to be my herald once more. It is that or die."

"Then it is no choice at all," the Surfer retorted. "I would rather the embrace of sweet oblivion than bear the guilt of one further life lost."

"These humans—these specks of dust—are really worth that much to you?"

"Every life is worth something. To treat other sentient beings as though they are nothing displays not merely overweening arrogance but moral blindness."

"Yet these same humans you so admire slaughter animals for their food," Galactus said, "animals which possess varying degrees of sentience. How is that any different from my own method of obtaining sustenance?"

"I do not pretend that humans are perfect," the Surfer replied. "I point out only that there are alternative sources of nourishment available to you, Galactus, which you choose, by preference, to spurn."

"But you are willing to die for their race."

"I am willing to die for a principle."

"I should have known this day might come." Galactus sounded almost doleful. "From the very first, when importunate Norrin Radd came to me and offered himself as my thrall in exchange for reprieving his homeworld Zenn-La, I should have realized that same selflessness would lead him to turn on me in the end. In hindsight, it was inevitable."

"The flame of altruism in me guttered," the Surfer said, "but it did not die. All it took was the gentle words of a kind, wise woman to fan it back into life."

"Then," said Galactus, "seeing as you care so much for the humans, tend to them now."

With barely a gesture, the godlike giant manifested a set of huge, transparent four-sided pyramids on top of a dozen nearby skyscrapers. To Reed's eyes, the pyramids looked to be made of solid crystal, quartz, possibly even diamond. Each was like an enormous geometrical ice sculpture, crude and rugged.

He performed some swift mental arithmetic. The average New York skyscraper measured around two hundred feet on each side, give or take. Therefore, the base area of each pyramid would be in the region of 40,000 square feet. The pyramids were, he estimated, a hundred feet high at the apex, giving them an overall volume—the equation was height times base area, divided by three—of 1,333,333 cubic feet. He knew that one cubic foot of water weighed sixty-two pounds and that diamond had a weight density approximately three and half times that. Which meant each pyramid weighed, in total, a little shy of 150,000 tons.

It was comforting to a brain like his to perform this kind of calculation, especially at moments of stress.

It was also deeply disturbing, as he could calculate down to the minute when they would all start to crumble and collapse.

Tens of thousands of lives were in imminent, grave danger.

THE SILVER Surfer recognized, in a flash, the quandary Galactus had put him in.

He could continue his battle with his former master, but countless humans in the pyramid-topped buildings would perish. Or he could save those humans, but while he did so, Galactus would be at liberty to activate the Elemental Converter.

Nobody else but him could possibly dispense with those diamond pyramids before the skyscrapers they sat on gave way under their bulk and fell crushingly to the ground.

Yet the Elemental Converter, once it began its work, was both swift and remorseless. In the time it took the Surfer to disintegrate every last pyramid, the machine would already have commuted half of New York State—everything from plants to edifices to people—into raw energy and begun transmitting it up to *Taa II*.

Nor was there any chance of him destroying the Elemental Converter before he dealt with the pyramids. Galactus could shield it from his assault with little difficulty.

Either way, whatever the Surfer did, he was damned. People were going to die.

An agony of indecision gripped him.

It lasted for two or three seconds, right up until he spied Uatu the Watcher appearing on the Baxter Building roof.

It wasn't so much Uatu's arrival that snapped the Surfer out of his wavering.

It was what he was carrying in his hand.

Instantly the Surfer understood that the entire calculus of the conflict with Galactus had changed. Uatu had obtained the one thing that would make the Devourer of Worlds rethink his plans. The question was, how best could it be deployed against Galactus? Who would be willing to wield it?

But that was less of a concern right now. The Surfer had more pressing matters to attend to.

He soared off towards the nearest skyscraper, with its towering, glassy cap. The Power Cosmic surged through him, and with it a feeling of exultation as he eliminated the pyramid, reducing it from diamond to a glittering cloud of particles no bigger than motes of dust, which the wind blew harmlessly away.

He set about doing the same to the other pyramids, racing from one to the next as the skyscrapers beneath them trembled and cracked. Windows shattered as their frames were distended by the pressure from above, showering shards of glass down into the streets. Reinforced concrete fell away in flakes. Stonemasonry was riven with fissures. Steel girders groaned as they bent.

The Surfer concentrated solely on vaporizing the pyramids. He didn't have the leisure to consider anything else.

Still, he kept an eye on what was happening on the Baxter Building roof.

The endgame had begun.

"TAKE THIS," Uatu said.

He leaned down and passed the little metallic object in his hand to Reed.

"This is it?" Reed said, peering at it. "The Ultimate Nullifier?"

"Do not be deceived by its innocuous appearance," said Uatu. "It is the weapon of weapons, and perhaps the only thing in the entire universe that Galactus fears."

Reed hefted the Ultimate Nullifier in his palm. It could not have weighed more than a few ounces. "How does it work?"

"The lever on top is the trigger."

"And if I depress the trigger...?"

"Aim the Nullifier at Galactus, depress the trigger, and you will destroy him in an instant. Eliminate him as surely as if he had never existed. But bear in mind," Uatu added, "you stand a good chance of destroying yourself too. That is the great risk with the Nullifier. Put simply, it operates on the principle of reciprocal-intent feedback, meaning it obliterates its target but also its wielder if their mind is not sufficiently focused."

"Focused," Reed echoed.

"In the wrong hands, the Nullifier could erase a universe. Scour a timeline from beginning to end until nothing remains. If you are to use it and not unleash the direst of consequences, Dr. Richards, your mindset must be right and your will must be strong. I believe you qualify admirably on both counts. Now, hurry. Galactus is ready to initiate the Elemental Converter."

Reed gave the Ultimate Nullifier one last look. A part of him—that restless technical brain of his—yearned to examine the device in detail, take it to pieces, figure out what made it tick. How could such vast potency be contained in something so tiny? Where did it derive its power from? Zero-point energy? Some quantum source? Another universe?

He dismissed these thoughts. Now was not the time.

He took a deep breath. Uatu had presented him with the means of ending Galactus's terrible plan. The catch was, Reed had to be willing to use the Nullifier. As he understood it, he could not simply bluff. He must be prepared to sacrifice himself while also killing the Devourer of Worlds. And he must do it with a stout heart and a steady mind, otherwise he might inadvertently wipe out the universe.

Never had he felt such a burden of responsibility.

And, as he always did when he needed support, Reed turned to his wife.

He didn't say anything. He didn't have to. Sue met his gaze and did not say anything either. But her eyes spoke volumes. They told him that she loved him, she was behind him all the way, and she knew he would do exactly what had to be done.

Ben, beside her, did much the same. He offered Reed an encouraging nod and smacked one fist into the palm of his other hand, as if to say *Go get 'em, pal.*

Reed turned back to face Galactus.

"Galactus!" he yelled.

The Devourer of Worlds did not appear to hear him. His attention was fixed on the Elemental Converter's igniters.

"Galactus!" Reed yelled again, and this time the blue-and-magenta giant noticed. He looked round at the human addressing him. His eyes registered the kind of longsuffering irritation a parent might sometimes direct towards a pestering infant.

Reed extended his arm—the one holding the Nullifier—until it was nearly twenty feet long. His hand halted within a yard of Galactus's face.

From mild annoyance, Galactus's expression turned first to disbelief, then to horror.

In that moment, the image of imperturbable, all-powerful entity was shattered once and for all. Gone was the lofty indifference; gone, the weary disdain. Before, in Reed's presence, Galactus had revealed flashes of regret, ill temper, even petulance—the kind of emotions that were supposedly the province of lesser beings. Now, however, the man that lurked beneath the godlike exterior was fully laid bare.

"The Ultimate Nullifier," he gasped, "in the hands of a human."

"In the hands of a human," Reed said, placing his thumb on the trigger, "who is quite prepared to fire it."

"You… You can have no idea of the power you wield. Your feeble mind cannot begin to comprehend it. Put the Nullifier down. I demand it."

Reed firmly shook his head. "No. Not unless you agree to leave Earth alone and never return."

"I will do no such thing."

"Then you leave me no choice." Reed put a minuscule amount of pressure on the trigger. There was a tiny raised nodule directly beneath it on the body of the device, and he reasoned that the trigger had to make contact with this in order to achieve activation. He reduced the gap between the two to only a couple of millimeters.

"No. No!" Galactus urgently put out a hand, as if to ward off an attack. "Stop."

"Consent to my terms, and I'll do as you ask."

"You realize what might happen if you fire the Nullifier?"

"I do. I have been fully briefed."

"You would be prepared to destroy yourself, and possibly more than just yourself, along with me?"

"I would."

Galactus studied him carefully. "I think you actually mean it."

"There is nothing I wouldn't do," Reed declared, "if it ensured the safety of my world and, perhaps more importantly, my family."

JUST THEN, the elevator door opened and Johnny Storm tottered out. Sue took one look at her brother—bedraggled, hunched over, with dried bloodstains on one shoulder—and hastened to his side.

"Johnny! Are you okay?"

"Been better," he replied weakly. "What've I missed?"

"Nothing much," his sister replied in a droll tone of voice. "Reed is just threatening Galactus with a glorified popgun."

Johnny essayed a bleak smile. "Huh. Is that all? Anything I can do to help?"

"No, I'm afraid not. There's nothing the rest of us can do except watch, and wait, and hope."

GALACTUS'S STANDOFF with Reed continued. The Ultimate Nullifier was poised between them, Reed's hand steady and unwavering. Reed knew that Galactus had to believe he would use it. Reed had to believe this himself.

And he did. He had made the calculation. His own death and Galactus's, versus the deaths of the entire human race. Several billion souls, weighed against just two. It wasn't even a question.

Using the Nullifier on Galactus would make Reed a murderer. But again, that was a price he was able to accept. Logic told him it was a justifiable homicide. If he survived firing the Nullifier, he may well have a few sleepless nights afterwards, fraught with guilt and wondering whether there could have been an alternative way of resolving the matter; but he felt that in the long run he would be able to live with his decision. And if he didn't survive? Well, then he'd have nothing to worry about at all. Posterity would judge whether he had done the right thing, but he would not be around to face the verdict.

Galactus wrenched his gaze away from the Nullifier and towards Uatu.

"Watcher," he growled. "You are responsible for this... this *travesty*. Only you could have directed the humans to find the

Nullifier. Only you possess the knowledge and the wherewithal. I ask you: why?"

"To correct an error of the past," Uatu replied. "To make amends in some small way for an oversight arising through the decision of another of my race."

"Namely?"

"A fellow Watcher, many eons ago, had the opportunity to end your existence, Galactus, almost as soon as it had begun. He chose not to."

"I see. So he abided by his vow of non-interference."

"Indeed. He knew what you might become, and he chose to let it happen."

"Then, by your lights, he did no wrong."

"In retrospect, I believe he *did* do wrong," Uatu said. "I believe it was one of those occasions when the Watcher vow should have been disregarded."

"And this, now, is another," Galactus said. "*You* have disregarded your vow, and have given one of these creatures more power than he has any right to handle."

"I am able to reconcile my actions with the dictates of my conscience. You yourself must now choose whether to forfeit your life, or do as Dr. Richards requests and leave Earth alone."

"But my hunger—"

"Will have to be sated elsewhere."

Galactus looked back at Reed.

Then at the Ultimate Nullifier.

Then at Reed again.

Finally he said, "Very well. I accept your terms, human. Return the Nullifier to me, and I shall trouble your world no more."

"Do I have your word on that?" Reed said.

"You do."

"Uatu, can you confirm that Galactus's word is his bond?"

"I can," said the Watcher. "The promise of Galactus is the

living truth itself. You may rest assured that he will keep it."

Uatu directed a warning look at the Devourer of Worlds, implying that he himself would ensure Galactus did not go back on his pledge. Galactus saw the look and gave a curt nod of assent.

Reed released his thumb from the Nullifier's trigger. Then, with just a smidgeon of reluctance, he turned his hand palm up, offering the device to Galactus.

Galactus picked it up between thumb and forefinger. A bubble of energy manifested around the Nullifier, doubtless at his bidding. It was Galactus's way of placing the device safely out of anyone's grasp except his own.

"You have won the day, Reed Richards," he said solemnly. "Enjoy your victory. As for me, I bear you and your race no malice. Nor you, Watcher. My desires have been thwarted, but your motives in doing so are understandable and perhaps pardonable. There is, however, one whose actions I find it difficult to condone. Where is the Silver Surfer?"

As if responding to the mention of his name, the Surfer swooped onto the rooftop. He had just reduced the last of the diamond pyramids to dust, and vaporized the falling shards of glass and debris.

"Surfer," Galactus said, "you have defied me."

"That I have," said the Surfer, stepping off his board and standing before his one-time master with his head bowed. "And I am ready to accept whatever penalty you deem fit. If you mean to destroy me—if you think that is what I deserve—then all I ask is that you make it quick."

Galactus pondered for a moment. "No," he said. "That is not the sentence I shall pass on you. You shall live."

"I thank you, Galactus."

"However," the Devourer of Worlds went on, "I cannot allow this mutiny of yours to go unpunished. There must be consequences."

All at once, twin beams of light burst forth from Galactus's eyes. They transfixed the Silver Surfer, passing through him from side to side.

They lasted just an instant, but the effect on the Surfer was startling. He staggered and fell to his knees, as though all the strength had suddenly ebbed out of him.

"What...?" he croaked feebly. "What have you done to me?"

"I have taken back much of the Power Cosmic I once imbued you with," Galactus said. "Just a small fraction of it remains to you. Furthermore, I am withdrawing from you the freedom to roam the universe. You love these Earth people so much? Then you may stay with them. Walk among them. Let yourself be subject to their whims, their enmities, their warlike savagery, all their manifold primitive behaviors. Learn whether they were truly worth defending—truly worth losing the universe for."

The Surfer's face was a tragic mask of despair. "Mighty Galactus, do not deprive me of the wonders of the cosmos. There are places I would go. Zenn-La beckons. I long to see my beloved Shalla-Bal again, if she still lives."

"You should have thought of that before you crossed me. Now, you must live with the knowledge that you once had everything, and you gave it up for the sake of a race which may not even be grateful to you."

"I implore you, reconsider."

"The decision is made," Galactus said. "It cannot be revoked."

With that, he turned his back on his former herald and began dismantling the Elemental Converter. The Silver Surfer sank down, his head in his hands, lost in abject misery. The Fantastic Four and Uatu the Watcher looked on. For a time, the only sounds on the roof of the Baxter Building were the clicks and clanks of machinery being disassembled, and the quiet sobs of a man whose dreams had been cruelly crushed.

GALACTUS WAS gone.

The parts of the Elemental Converter had been stowed back in his shuttle craft, along with the bisected remains of the Punisher, and then without another word the Devourer of Worlds had boarded the vessel himself. The craft had taken off, hurtling up into the wild blue yonder. Now, aside from a few scorch marks on the rooftop and some fragments of broken machinery, there was little to show that he had ever been there.

"Well, shoot," Ben said, rubbing a hand back and forth across his scalp. "That was a heck of a day, wasn't it?"

"I'll say," Johnny agreed. "Remind me to tell you guys sometime about Galactus's ship. It was something else!"

"You had a rough time of it there, by the looks of things," Sue said.

"You don't know the half of it, sis. But I'll tell you this. If it hadn't been for you three, I'd never have made it out alive."

"How come, Match-Head?" Ben asked.

"I think the simplest way of putting it is, wherever one of the Fantastic Four goes, the rest go too—and that's true even if they're not actually there."

"Okay, now you're just talkin' in riddles."

"I probably am. But it makes sense to me. Wait a second." Johnny looked up. Something had caught his attention. "Over there. The old Fantasti-Car. You see it? It's coming this way. But we're all here, so who's piloting it?"

Ben shaded his eyes. "It's got to be… Yeah. Alicia."

Sure enough, Alicia Masters was seated in the front section of the Fantasti-Car. The aircraft sighed in for a smooth landing on the helipad where, not much earlier, Uatu's Matter Mobilizer had sat.

"'Licia!" Ben cried in delight. "Nice flyin', babe." He hurried over and plucked her up out of her seat by her waist, as though she weighed nothing—which, to him, she pretty much did.

"You mean nice flying for a blind woman?" Alicia teased.

"Nah, I know what you done. You hit the Return Home function and let the autopilot do the work."

"You left the Fantasti-Car key fob at my apartment. I wanted to come over and see what was going on here. This seemed the simplest way."

"Well, you sure are a sight for sore eyes, little lady. Uh, no offence meant."

"Do you mean the 'little lady' part or the 'sore eyes' part?"

"Umm… both?"

She patted him playfully. "I'm just joshing, Ben. But would you mind putting me down? You're hurting my ribs a bit."

"Sorry," Ben said, doing as asked. "Don't know my own strength sometimes."

"Give me an update," Alicia said. "What's been going on? Is it all over?"

"Yeah, you could say that. There's a lot to fill you in on, but basically, it's done. World saved. Ticker-tape parade time for the FF again. By the way, Reed, Sue and Johnny are all here with us. There's Uatu the Watcher as well. Remember him? I told you about him. Big head. Lives on the moon."

"And you're all okay?"

"Every one of us. Johnny's bruised and battered, and he's makin' a big fuss about how much of a hero he's been, but that's par for the course. Aside from that, nothin' to complain about."

"Thank heaven. And the Silver Surfer? What about him?"

"Oh yeah. The Surfer. Kind of forgot about him. Yeah, he's here too."

Ben looked towards the silvery figure, who was still prostrate on the roof, his surfboard stationed close by.

"He's been through the wars," he said. "Galactus did a big number on him, and he ain't too happy right now."

"Take me to him please," Alicia said.

"Sure. Okay."

Ben guided her over to the Surfer's side.

Alicia laid a hand on the Surfer's shoulder. At her touch, he raised his head.

"Alicia," he said, in a hoarse, lonely voice.

"Norrin," she said. "Talk to me. What's happened to you?"

"I am lost. Galactus has robbed me of all hope. He has exiled me on Earth. Nevermore shall I soar the spaceways. Nevermore is there any possibility that I shall see Shalla-Bal again."

"Don't say that. There must be some way you can be reunited with her."

"This Shalla-Bal, she's your girl, right?" said Johnny. "And you're separated from her? Pal, I know just how you feel. For what it's worth, you have my sympathies."

"Reed?" said Alicia. "You can help, surely. Whatever Galactus has done, you can undo."

"I'll try everything in my power, Surfer," Reed said. "I swear."

"And in the meantime," Sue chimed in, "you're welcome to stay here with us at the Baxter Building. This can be your home. It's the least we can offer after all you've done—all you've given up—for us."

The Silver Surfer got to his feet.

"You are kind, all of you, and generous," he said. "But for the time being, I need to be by myself." He set his jaw determinedly. "If Earth is where I must be from now on, then I must explore it. I must discover all I can about it, so that I can learn to live here as one of its denizens. To me, my board!"

The surfboard sprang into motion, slipping across the roof so that its owner could step onto it.

"Alicia, I bid you farewell," he said. "I shall not forget your companionship, nor how you awoke in me my long-dormant true self. Fantastic Four, likewise I feel privileged to have met you and fought alongside you, albeit briefly. You have shown me the values of friendship and family, and the comforts they bring. For now, however, where soars the Silver Surfer..."

He and his board took off for the skies.

"There he must soar alone!"

o———o

AS THE Fantastic Four watched the Silver Surfer depart, Ben slipped an arm around Alicia's waist.

"What a guy," he said. "I thought *I'd* been given a raw deal in life, but it ain't nothin' compared with the one he's got to contend with."

Alicia rested her head against her lover's shoulder. "That has to be one of the nicest things you've ever said about anyone, darling."

"Hey, I have my moments. I'm not a *complete* jerk."

"I beg to differ," Johnny butted in.

"Yahhh, you zip your lip, Torchy. I'm havin' a private moment here with my gal."

"Lip zipped," Johnny said, moving discreetly away from the couple.

"I got to ask, though," Ben said to Alicia, "what's with all this 'Norrin', 'Alicia' stuff? How come you two are on first-name terms?"

"Don't read anything into it, Ben," Alicia answered. "The Surfer—Norrin—is a noble, sensitive man. I can't help feeling desperately sorry for him, and I'm honored that he trusted me enough to tell me everything about himself, and that I was able to help steer him towards standing against Galactus. But still, there's only one person in this world I ever want to be with, and he is even more noble and sensitive, although he'd never admit it."

"Who *is* that? He sounds like a total sap."

"Only some big, dumb, rocky orange idiot who I happen to be head over heels in love with, that's who."

Ben chuckled.

"I don't know what I did to deserve you, Alicia," he said, hugging her close and kissing the top of her head, "but whatever it is, just make sure I keep doin' it, okay?"

A FEW DAYS LATER...

ON A remote, windswept mountaintop in the Andes, a lonesome figure stood, his surfboard by his side.

He gazed up at the heavens, as close here to the firmament as it was just about possible for someone to stand.

The frigid wind did not bother him, nor the rarefied thinness of the air at this altitude. Freezing cold and a lack of oxygen were not even inconveniences to one such as the Silver Surfer.

His only thought was of what he was about to put himself through.

He had tried it countless times before, on each occasion without success.

But that did not deter him from trying again.

He leapt onto his board and set off vertically, knifing up from the troposphere into the stratosphere. He poured on speed, pushing himself and his board to go fast, faster still, as fast as they possibly could. He shot to the very edge of the mesosphere, some fifty miles above the Earth's surface. By this stage he was traveling quicker than a rocket, quicker than a meteor, a silvery bullet in the shape of a man.

He braced himself.

He hoped.

He prayed.

Perhaps this time…

SLAM!!!

He struck it hard and ricocheted away: the invisible barrier which Galactus had placed around the entire planet. A barrier fashioned so that anything could penetrate it, anything at all — except the Silver Surfer.

The impact caused the Surfer to lose his footing on his board. He and it hurtled earthwards, side by side, at virtually the same speed they had risen. The Surfer had been left stunned, his senses reeling. He plunged, limp, numb, achieving terminal velocity in next to no time. The Andean peaks loomed below, like gigantic, jagged white teeth, eager to impale and rend.

At the very last moment, consciousness returned. The Surfer's mental connection with his board was re-established, and the two of them came together. The board swept him sideways, and gradually, as one, they decelerated, descending in a narrowing spiral, until at last they slowed to a hover, not far above the mountaintops.

The Surfer lay himself down full-length, supine, on his board, with one arm thrown across his face, the other dangling.

"Why, Galactus?" he lamented. "Did my actions honestly warrant such harsh retribution?"

It was several minutes before he had recuperated fully. Then he returned to the mountaintop, where he steeled himself to make yet another attempt on the barrier.

He would not give up.

Never.

Time after time, he would hurl himself at the barrier.

He would blast at it with his Power Cosmic, or at least with the greatly reduced amount of the Power Cosmic that Galactus had left him.

He would approach the barrier from every conceivable angle,

from every corner of the planet, seeking some chink in its makeup, some flaw he could exploit.

He would not cease in his struggle. No matter how long it took, no matter how often he tried and failed, he refused to abandon the effort.

One day—he didn't know when, but one day—he would break through. It would surely happen.

"Time is long and fate is fickle," he said to himself, "but my destiny still lies before me. And where it beckons—there shall soar the Silver Surfer!"

o———o

AT AROUND the same time the Surfer uttered these words, a similar event was taking place amid another of Earth's great mountain ranges.

Gorgon of the Inhuman royal family was doing his best to break through a different but no less unyielding barrier—in this instance, the dome-shaped one made of negative-polarity sound which his cousin Maximus had erected around the Great Refuge.

He pounded at it with his formidable cloven hooves, stamping, thumping, hammering with all his might, to no avail.

Elsewhere in the Great Refuge, another of Gorgon's cousins, Karnak, stood in profound contemplation of another section of the barrier. He had been staring at it for close to six hours, probing it with his mind, brow furrowed in concentration, seeking weakness.

All at once, he raised a hand and struck forward with a swift, fierce chopping motion.

This same hand could shatter a block of solid marble, finding a point of vulnerability and setting up a catastrophic chain reaction with a single, deadly-accurate blow.

On Maximus's barrier, however, it was as ineffective as a wafting feather.

Not far away, deep in the basement of Black Bolt's palace, there was a prison cell—a well-furnished space, equipped with amenities and comforts aplenty, as befit a royal personage, but a prison cell nonetheless. Windowless. Locked. Guarded.

Here was kept the barrier's creator, Black Bolt's wayward, would-be-usurper brother.

And from here, at frequent intervals, emanated laughter.

Cold, cackling laughter.

The kind of spine-chilling laughter that could only come from a deranged mind.

Maximus was well aware of his relatives' efforts to free the Inhumans from the captivity he had imposed on them. If nothing else, the thunder of Gorgon's hooves resounded far and wide, sending tremors across the entire city, and there was no mistaking the source of the noise or the intent behind it. But Maximus knew, too, the sort of people his family were. The sort who relentlessly pursued a goal, however futile. The sort who never abandoned hope.

The buffoons!

A visitor came.

Another of his many cousins.

Crystal.

She was permitted into his presence, unchallenged by the guards who stood sentinel over him, simply because she was royalty too. Lineage granted her access.

She peered at him through the bars of the cell, exhibiting both revulsion and a piteous hopefulness.

Maximus had heard her coming and recognized those light, tentative footsteps. He lay on his bed and ignored her for a while, feigning sleep and doing it badly, on purpose.

At last, ostentatiously opening his eyes, he said, "Ah, fair Crystal. To what do I owe this honor? Have you come to gloat, perchance?"

"No," Crystal said, "I have come to implore. Tell us how to lift the barrier, Maximus. Tell us how we may escape."

"So that you can see that paramour of yours once more? That pathetic human boy—what's his name again? Johnny Tempest?"

"Storm. Johnny Storm. Yes, so that I can see him again."

"And, were I to grant you your wish, what do I get in return? What can you, little Crystal, offer me?"

Crystal sighed. "Nothing. Black Bolt alone can pardon you for your crimes and free you from confinement. All I could ever give you is my undying gratitude."

"Gratitude? *Pfah!*" Maximus spat scornfully. "That's of no use to me."

"Is there anything I can say that will convince you to change your mind? Do you not see how my heart is broken?"

"All I see," Maximus said, "is a lovesick little girl, whose pain and inner turmoil are deliciously sweet to me."

"You wretch!" Crystal cried heatedly. "May you stay in this cell forever. May you rot here!"

She turned away, tears flowing down her cheeks.

And Maximus, once again, laughed.

Laughed in delirious, insane glee.

o———o

JUST THEN, half a world away, Johnny Storm was finishing packing his suitcase. He was all set.

"Metro College here I come," he said, to no one, because he was all alone in his room.

All alone in the Fantastic Four's headquarters, as a matter of fact. Reed and Sue were up in the Catskills, on a well-earned and much-needed vacation, while Ben was taking Alicia for a jaunt on his Sky-Cycle, all the way out to the Hamptons for a seaside picnic. Each was with the love of their life, and Johnny was pleased for them but also envious.

He had chosen this moment to depart for college because

he didn't want everyone making a big song and dance about it. He'd told the other members of the Fantastic Four about getting accepted for a place at Metro just a couple of days earlier. From Reed and Sue there had been qualified approval and congratulations; from Ben, some remark about how educational standards must have lowered drastically and just about anybody could become an undergrad these days.

Johnny had insisted to his teammates that this didn't mean the end of the FF. He would simply be away from home, that was all, but they could call on him anytime. Night or day, if there was an emergency, he'd come running.

Now, he closed the suitcase lid and snapped the catches shut. His shoulder was still stiff and sore, but the wound was healing well. The doctor had said it would be as good as new in no time.

Good as new.

New *was* good.

Johnny glanced around his room one last time. A taxi was waiting outside the lobby of the Baxter Building to take him to Metro.

This was it. A new beginning. A chance to start afresh.

He thought of Crystal.

He hoped she was thinking of him.

The future beckoned, and Johnny Storm, suitcase in hand, headed downstairs to embrace it.

ABOUT THE AUTHOR

JAMES LOVEGROVE is the *New York Times* bestselling author of *The Age of Odin*. He has been short-listed for many awards including the Arthur C. Clarke Award, the John W. Campbell Memorial Award, and the Scribe Award. He won the Seiun Award for Best Foreign Language Short Story in 2011, and the Dragon Award in 2020 for *Firefly: The Ghost Machine*. He has written many acclaimed Sherlock Holmes novels, including *Sherlock Holmes and the Christmas Demon*. As well as writing books, he reviews fiction for the *Financial Times*. He lives in Eastbourne in the UK. @jameslovegrove7

MARVEL

A NOVEL OF THE MARVEL UNIVERSE

DOCTOR STRANGE

DIMENSION WAR

ADAPTED FROM THE CLASSIC STORIES
BY STAN LEE AND STEVE DITKO

JAMES LOVEGROVE

MARVEL

A NOVEL OF THE MARVEL UNIVERSE

SECRET INVASION

ADAPTED FROM THE GRAPHIC NOVEL BY
BRIAN MICHAEL BENDIS & LEINIL FRANCIS YU

PAUL CORNELL